TWIST OF FATE
Book One

Fate Hates

Copyright © 2017 by Tina Saxon

ISBN Digital: 978-0-9987762-0-0
ISBN Print: 978-0-9987762-1-7

Edited by: Max Dobson @ The Polished Pen
Proofreading by: Elaine York @ Allusion Graphics
Cover design by: Damonza
Formatting by: Damonza

www.tinasaxon.com

TWIST OF FATE
Book One

TINA SAXON

Chapter One

I'M FINISHED. DONE! I take a deep breath in, blow out slowly, and look around. Campus life. Students are scattered everywhere; some run to make it to their class on time while others relax in the grass, studying for their next exam. And then there are those who need to get a room as I spot two bodies making out under *my* tree. The tree I've spent hours studying under. I laugh, shaking my head. I'm going to miss this. This part of my life is over. I mindlessly walk across campus, relieved after finishing all my exams.

Oomph! I'm knocked over by a five-foot-two pixie.

"Addie!" Sydney screams. "We did it!" We both tumble to the ground. For being so little, I don't know where the hell she hides all that power. I am not a small person—well, next to her I'm not. Sydney is tiny. She has always reminded me of Tinkerbell. With her short blond hair styled in a pixie cut and huge, sparkling ice blue eyes, I swear she's going to start flying one day, sprinkling fairy dust everywhere.

We lie in the grass, looking up at the blank blue canvas just waiting to be painted. It's May in Texas so the heat from the sun is already blistering, but everything is so green from the April rains.

"I can't believe we're done with college," I say, grabbing her hand.

Sydney is my best friend. We've been inseparable since we

were ten. I had just lost my mom and went to live with my aunt; Sydney lived next door. I love her like a sister. We both have strong personalities, but we couldn't be any more different. She studied music and teaching, while I studied criminology and forensics. She believes in fairytales, while I think life is too cruel for such things. But she is the yin to my yang. I don't know what I would have done without her.

She looks over at me, pouting. "I don't want to grow up. Growing up means you leave." I squeeze her hand tighter. The time is coming, but I try not to think about it. Last summer I did an internship with the NYPD's Forensics Department, and I fell in love with New York City, its overwhelming but exciting atmosphere, constant state of movement, horns from cabs racing to their destination, the never-ending nightlife... *I loved it all.* They offered me a job once I graduated. A dream job and one that I couldn't pass up.

I roll over on my side. "Syd, we'll still see each other," I say. "And we'll talk everyday. Anyway, you have *Dean* now," I tease. Syd and Dean met last year at some art festival. He's probably glad I'm leaving; she's always made it clear to any guy she's ever dated that I'm part of the package. Our friendship has always come first.

Until now.

My chest hurts just thinking about leaving her.

"I'd give him up to keep you any day." She smiles as her eyes fill with tears.

"*Don't.* Don't you dare cry and make me feel worse than I already do." My eyes start to well with tears, too. We both sit up and embrace each other.

"I'm sorry, Addie," she says, wiping away her tears. "You know I'm excited for you. I'm just going to miss you like crazy." She sighs.

My phone vibrates in my back pocket. Pulling the phone out, I see it's a text from my aunt wondering how my finals went. I glance at the time.

"Oh, shit!" I jump to my feet. "Syd, I'm late. You know I love you and this summer we'll have lots of time before I leave, but right now I have to run." I blow her a kiss before I turn and speed walk toward my car.

"Wait!" she screams, running after me. "There's an end-of-year party tonight at Dean's. Please say you'll come." With her short legs, she's almost at a run trying to keep up with me.

"I need to get to work. You're slowing me down." I laugh, looking at her.

"Addison, stop! I'm not letting you go until you tell me that you'll go with me tonight." She grabs me, stopping me.

"Okay." I sigh. "I'll meet you at the apartment after my dinner with Howard at eight." She lets out an excited scream and jumps into my arms, wrapping her legs around me. I have to drop my purse to grab onto her, steadying us so we don't end up on the ground again.

* * *

"Good afternoon, Addison." Howard greets me with a warm smile. Howard is a courthouse security guard. In the three years I've been working part-time at Austin's District Court, Howard has become part of my family. I adore him. He's an attractive older man with a fun personality and a heart of gold. When he was in his forties, his wife died. He never remarried or had kids. I never understood why women weren't beating down his door, but he always tells me that his heart was buried with his wife. I don't believe that; he has one of the biggest hearts I've seen.

"Hi, Howie." I smirk, getting ready to go through security.

He looks around. "*Shh*, you know I don't like to be called that at work." Howard likes everyone to think he's a badass, but I know he loves it when I call him 'Howie'.

I offer a bemused smile and head through the metal detector. When I get to the other side, I call out, "See you at dinner?" We're celebrating the end of my finals.

"You bet! Meet you down here at six." I wave my hand in confirmation as I walk to the elevators. "Oh, FYI, Jack was down here looking for you a little while ago," he hollers before I enter the elevator. I look his way and roll my eyes, hearing his laugh as the doors close.

Jack. *My lovely boss.* A middle-aged man who thinks he's God's gift to women. In reality he's pompous, short, round, balding, and suffers from little man syndrome. Never been married. No surprise there. He makes crude comments at the most inopportune time. How he stays the Court Administrator baffles me. I've been his assistant for three years. He's really not that bad now that I'm used to his personality. I just ignore him most of the time. Surprisingly, he's very intelligent but has absolutely zero common sense.

He's already yelling for me as soon as I enter my office. "Addison, nice of you to join me today." His voice drips with sarcasm. I roll my eyes again and take a deep breath before walking into his office.

"Jack, you know I had finals today," I say, leaning in his office doorway, crossing my arms.

"I know. I'm just kidding." Typical Jack response. He's *always* kidding. "Congrats on finishing. I can't wait for you to be full time."

I just shake my head. He's very aware that is not going to happen since I've already given my official notice and only have one more month.

"Jack…" I sigh "…you already kno—"

"I know, I know," he resigns. "You can't fault me for trying. I mean, how can you leave me for New York?"

Very easily.

Ignoring his question, I ask, "Is there something you need me to do? I heard you were looking for me earlier."

"Oh, yeah." He points to a stack of court dockets. "I need these delivered to the correct courtrooms. Apparently, the only thing going for one of the interns is her looks. She delivered these all to the wrong courtrooms," he says, not even looking up from his computer. I used to have a comeback when he made asshole comments, but I've found it's easier just to ignore them. And sometimes I agree with him, *like this time*. I grab the dockets and quickly walk out of his office.

It irritates the hell out of me when the interns get these dockets mixed up. It's not rocket science. And it happens more often than I'd like.

I hand the last misplaced docket to the judge and he shakes his head, then gives me a lopsided smile. I shrug. I know they hate it more than I do. As I'm walking down the hallway, I hear someone yell.

"Add Cat!"

Only one person calls me that. I turn around with a smile as Frankie struts toward me. At least this time he doesn't have handcuffs on. Frankie has been arrested for many things, so he's at the courthouse *a lot*. He seems to know how to get anything illegal from drugs and guns to prostitutes. I wonder who he has in his back pocket since he never seems to go to jail for very long... if at all.

"Frankie, what the hell did you do this time? I told you that you can't go streaking down the road." I cross my arms and twist my lips trying to stop myself from laughing out loud.

"Haha, my little Add Cat. You know I'd only get naked for you." He wags his eyebrows and winks.

"Whatever!" My voice comes out higher than I expect. My cheeks redden and burn. Clearing my throat, I say, "Really, what are you doing here? I thought you agreed to stay on the up and up?"

"I'm here meeting my probation officer. Chill out, girl, I ain't done nothing wrong. I'm trying to prove I'm worthy to my Add Cat." He gives me his lady-killer smile.

My eyes widen. "Would you stop!"

"Woman, you know how to break a man's heart." He puts a hand on his chest. Well, shit. He can't be serious... *can he*? We've been friends a few years and he's never shown any interest in me, which I'm okay with because bad guys usually aren't my thing.

Now if he were a good guy, he'd definitely be my type. He's over six feet tall with lots of muscle. He has naturally tanned skin with the lightest green eyes I've ever seen. I usually don't care for guys with shaved heads, but on Frankie *it's hot.* He is definitely good looking, but very much a bad boy.

"Gotcha!" Frankie throws his hands out, laughing. "Girl, I love ya, but I'm pretty sure you can kick my ass being a third-degree black belt. I don't need no woman to protect me. It'll take away from my street cred!"

Relieved, I laugh, too. Sometimes Frankie comes to the gym to take classes. He's watched me spar a few times then comments that he pities the guy who ever messes with me.

CHAPTER TWO

IT'S ALMOST SIX o'clock when I'm freshening up in the rest-room before I leave for dinner. With a grumbling stomach, I leave the bathroom and hear yelling. *What the hell?* Usually the place is quiet after five; people scramble out of here like ants marching. Of course the commotion is coming from the hall that I need to go through to get back to my office.

I don't like confrontation so I lean up against the wall, wait-ing, hoping they figure their shit out soon so I don't have to inter-rupt. If this goes on for much longer, I could go downstairs and come up on the other side and hopefully miss them. My spine stiffens when someone yells, "Put the gun down."

Wait, I know that voice.

Then another. "You don't know what the hell you're doing!"

Holy shit! That's Frankie. I take off my shoes so my heels don't echo. I glance down the empty hallways, hoping there is some-thing or someone who can help. Dammit, I don't see anything but marble walls and floor. The other man is yelling back at Frankie. I catch something about Frankie ratting him out. The two men go back and forth. The other guy's voice is getting more and more agitated. Frankie is getting uneasy.

I start pacing. Frankie's in trouble, and I can't stand here and do nothing. My heart picks up speed as I walk slowly down the hall. I stop at the corner, taking a few quiet breaths, before peeking around it. The other guy has his back to me, waving around a gun. He stands about six feet away from me, so I size him up. He's not quite as tall as Frankie, medium build. What the hell should I do? I've taken down guys at the gym much bigger than him so I might be able to get the gun away from him. Security has to be on their way up. If I heard all the yelling, I'm sure someone else has, too.

BANG!

I jump at the sound and Frankie screams. Peeking around the corner again, I can see he shot him in the leg.

"Aww, man, I fucking missed. I meant to shoot you in the head," the guy with the gun says sarcastically. "This time I won't miss."

Not thinking, I drop my shoes and run toward the guy. I have the advantage of him not seeing me coming. I grab the arm holding the gun and twist until I hear it pop. The gun falls out of his hand as I throw him over my shoulder, body slamming him to the ground.

"Fucking bitch! You broke my arm!" he screams as he jumps back up. *Damn, he's quick.* He's coming toward me so I kick his knee, sending him to the ground again screaming. I quickly glance at Frankie to see if he's doing okay as I reach for the gun. I don't even see the guy before he yanks me up and throws me against the wall like a rag doll.

I scream as my head slams against the marble floor. My vision blurs as I fight to gain consciousness. Trying to focus, I narrow my eyes. I see the asshole pick up the gun and point it at me. Frankie yells something. It sounds like I'm in a tunnel. My head hurts as I try to sit up. Warm liquid runs down my face and I can only assume it's blood. My surroundings begin to fade when I hear two gun shots then everything goes black.

* * *

When I wake I'm lying on a stretcher being lifted into an ambulance. I struggle to focus and look around. "Addison, please lie still. You hit your head pretty hard. You were..." The voice keeps talking, but I can't will myself to stay awake.

The next time I wake I'm in a bed. I move my hand and feel something attached to my arm. Familiar voices fill the room.

"Doctor, when the hell is she going to wake up?" Sydney says. *Wow,* she just cussed. She must be really upset.

"Shh... Sydney, it's okay." My aunt's voice is filled with concern. "Doctor, can you tell us anything? She's been out for hours."

Hours? Last thing I remember was hitting my head. Well, that makes sense since my head is killing me. I open my eyes to the bright lights in the room then quickly squeeze them shut.

"Can someone please turn out the lights?" I whisper.

"Addie!" Sydney scream as she grabs my hand.

"*Shh.* Head hurts," I whisper as I squeeze her hand. The brightness behind my eyelids goes away, so I slowly open my eyes again. There are just a few dimmed lights on now.

My aunt walks to my other side, grabbing my hand, too. "Addie, boy am I glad to see those beautiful blue eyes," she whispers as she leans over and kisses my forehead.

"You know, if you didn't want to go to Dean's party, you didn't have to go get yourself shot," Syd says jokingly. I look over to my best friend, my brows furrowing with confusion.

"What the hell are you talking about? I wasn't shot." I lift my arms inspecting them and then start patting my chest. When I lift the covers I notice I have about ten stitches on my leg. What the hell? I look at her with huge eyes. "The fucker shot me?" I scream out in pain after sitting up too quickly.

Fuck! I press my hand to my head.

The doctor walks over and tells Sydney to wait over in the chair. I smile, knowing how persistent she can be and how much they must have had to deal with her since she got here.

"Hi, Addison. I'm Dr. Parker. I'm going to check all your vitals. Can you tell me your full name?" he says as he shines a light in my eyes. I answer all his questions while he looks me over. "Okay, you're doing great so far. Can you tell me what you remember last?"

"I remember the asshole who wouldn't go down throw me against the wall," I say. "That's about it. Oh, wait. I remember Frankie trying to talk to him." The memory reminds me about Frankie. "Oh, my gosh, is Frankie okay?" I look at everyone in the room for an answer. The machine I'm hooked up to starts beeping faster.

"Relax, Addison," the doctor says. "Frankie is doing fine. You don't remember getting shot?"

I try to refocus my thoughts. "Um... I think I remember hearing two gunshots but nothing after that," I reply.

"Well, luckily for you the *asshole*," he says, using my sentiment, "wasn't a good shot and the bullet grazed your leg. You'll have a little scar but that's it. Now, your head... that's a different story. You took a pretty bad hit. You have a concussion and had to get a few stitches on your forehead. We're going to keep you here for the night to monitor you." He puts my chart under his arm and walks out. Before leaving the room, he turns to address Sydney. "She needs her rest. Try not to get her agitated, excited, or upset." I giggle as she salutes the doctor. He just shakes his head as he walks out.

She immediately runs and lies down by my side, snuggling up to me. My aunt, still at my side and holding my hand, stands up from the chair placed by my bed. "Sweetie, you had us scared to death. I'm so happy you're okay." She leans over and kisses my forehead again. "I'm going to go out and tell everyone that you're awake and doing alright, but you need your rest. They can come back tomorrow. I'll be here first thing in the morning." She squeezes my hand once more before letting go and walking out.

"Who is here?" I whisper to Syd.

"Um... Ted, who, by the way, is pissed at you for your hero antics." We both giggle, knowing how Uncle Ted can get. "Howard, who is also pissed at you. My mom. Oh, and Jack, who

I think is only here to make sure you don't sue." She quietly chuckles, which makes me smile.

"Have you heard what happened?" I ask, yawning.

"Addie, go to sleep, we'll talk in the morning. Also, the police need your statement, so they'll be back also," she says.

It doesn't take me long to fall asleep. Nurses come into my room to take my vitals and wake me numerous times during the night. Didn't they say I needed rest?

This is definitely not rest.

Morning comes too quickly. My head doesn't hurt as bad, but now my leg aches. I'm sitting up, getting ready to attempt to walk to the bathroom when Syd comes into the room holding my favorite drink: iced chai tea latte. "Have I told you lately how much I love you?" I say, grabbing a quick sip of my drink.

She laughs, taking the drink from me and helping me get out of bed. Thankfully, the nurses unhooked all the wires from me early this morning. "I brought you some comfy clothes to change into. And some bathroom stuff so you can clean up." She brings the bag to the bathroom and shuts the door behind her.

Feeling somewhat like a normal person, I walk back to my bed. Syd brings me my drink and some banana bread. Now I'm feeling much better. Two police officers are my first visitors, which I'm sure isn't a coincidence. I tell them everything that I remember, and they help fill in the blanks.

"The reason he wouldn't go down is because he was on meth." *Well, that makes sense.* I totally underestimated the dude. "After he threw you against the wall, we were told he picked up the gun and took a shot at you but was immediately shot by security. He was pronounced dead on the scene." That explains why I heard two gunshots.

The other cop speaks, "We normally would tell you how much we discourage vigilante tactics, but I'm positive you're going to hear it from our lieutenant." He smirks. *Smartass.* There were definitely times having a lieutenant as my uncle came in handy, but probably not today. I have a feeling Uncle Ted is waiting outside my room right now, ready to pounce once the officers leave.

"He would have killed Frankie if I didn't do anything." I throw my hands in the air, feeling the need to defend myself. "He's alive. I'm alive. The bad guy is dead." I hear Sydney laugh from her corner. I direct my glare at her so she'll be quiet. She laughs harder.

My suspicions about Ted are confirmed when he comes in immediately after the cops leave.

"Hi," I say sweetly, smiling.

"Addie," he firmly states. "What in the world were you thinking?"

"I know you heard me when you were *listening* to my statement with the police. If I hadn't done anything, Frankie would've been killed." I know what I did was stupid, but those words will never come out of my mouth. He walks over and pulls me into a tight embrace. Guilt flows through my body; I feel bad about worrying everyone. "I'm sorry, Ted," I whisper into his chest.

"Addison, I'm not surprised by what you did, but you scared the shit out of all of us," he says as he squeezes me tighter. "Can I change your mind about going into law enforcement?" he chuckles.

"A little too late for that," I giggle.

Aunt Amy walks into the room, smiling. I guess she was eavesdropping, as well. *Nosy people.* She joins our hug. "I love you guys," I say, squeezing them both.

The doctor walks in, breaking up our emotional reunion. They ask the doctor when I'll be released and he replies that it will be later this afternoon. With this news they get ready to leave and tell me to call them when I get home. Sydney is still sitting in the corner, staring at the doctor.

"You still haven't left, huh?"

My eyes widen at Dr. Parker's audacity to talk to my friend like that. I'm about to tell him off when Sydney smiles wide.

She scrunches her nose. "You know you're going to miss me when I leave." She winks.

Winks? She's flirting with him?

What the hell did I miss while I was unconscious. I'm looking between the two, back and forth. Something is definitely going on with them. I tilt my head, looking at Sydney with my eyebrows raised.

He shakes his head but doesn't say anything in response. Dr. Parker steps over to me and takes my vitals. Shining a light in my eyes again, he asks how I'm feeling.

"Much better. A little tired though. Busy morning," I say sarcastically.

"I guess that's what happens when you try and play Superwoman," he jokes, placing his stethoscope over my heart.

"I don't need another lecture, Doc." I sigh.

"Oh, I haven't even begun." I hear Syd bark out from her corner. The doctor lets out a loud laugh. I ignore her because there is nothing I can say that will stop the ensuing scolding from Sydney. She's patiently waiting for her turn, which surprises me more than anything.

"Everything looks good, Addison, but you need to take it easy for twenty-four hours. If you feel dizzy, nauseous, or have vision problems, I need to see you back immediately. Also, you'll need to go to your primary care physician to get your stitches out in ten days. I'll leave your discharge papers with the nurse; she'll come in and get you signed out. Do you have any questions for me?" he asks.

Yes, what is up with you and Syd?

Probably not the right time. Instead I shake my head. As he's leaving the room, Howard taps on the door. Syd tells me that she'll be back, and she follows the doctor out.

I stand up as Howard comes toward me. "*Howie*, I'm sorry I missed our dinner last night," I say, right before he embraces me in a tight hug.

"Addison, when I rounded the corner and saw you lying on the ground trying to get up and then I saw him shoot you, my heart stopped." His voice trembles. I squeeze my eyes shut as I sigh.

Suddenly, I remember what the cop had said about security shooting the guy. I lean back, looking up at Howard. "It was you?" I whisper.

"It took everything I had in me not to keep shooting the son of a bitch to make sure he was dead. Fortunately, all it took was one shot," he says.

"Thank you," I say, wrapping my arms around his waist.

"Addison, you're like the daughter I never had," he murmurs. "And I think Ted and I both agree that you need a new career choice." He chuckles.

"You, too?" I say, playfully hitting his arm. "It's not like I'm going to be in the middle of bad stuff. I'll be working in forensics. I'll be going in *after* the bad stuff happens."

"You'll still be part of that world," he quickly replies. I sigh, knowing arguing is a moot point. "Anyway, I was so relieved to see it was only a graze. My only job now is to find out how the hell he got through security with a gun... because when I find out how, there is going to be hell to pay," he warns. A shiver runs down my spine, fearing for the person who messed up. *Or helped the asshole.*

Two hours later I'm being discharged. The nurse just left, giving me my discharge papers and getting a wheelchair to bring me out. As I'm packing all my stuff up, the door opens. Frankie is being wheeled in by a cute nurse.

"Thanks, baby cakes. You can come back and get me in a few minutes." He flashes a huge smile and winks. She walks out. I just shake my head, using a hand to cover my mouth and stifle my laugh.

"Frankie," I say with a huge smile, "I'm so glad to see you're okay."

"Add Cat, what the fuck do you think you were doing?" His smile fades and his face turns hard. "You could have easily been killed by that strung-out prick." I can see the muscles in his arm flex as he balls his hands into fists. He's kind of scary when he's mad.

"How about a '*Thanks for saving my life, Addison*.' Or are you too worried about your *street cred?*" I air-quote his words he used yesterday with sarcasm dripping from my voice. I'm a little pissed with his ungrateful attitude.

"Woman! You know I don't give a rat's ass about my street cred. I was fucking worried about you!" he barks as he wheels his wheelchair close to where I sit on the bed. "I saw the whole thing and there wasn't a damn thing I could do about it." He grabs my hands. "I owe you my life. You ever need anything, call me." He kisses my knuckles before releasing my hands. He turns his chair around, wheeling himself toward the door. "Anything, Add Cat," he says one last time, looking over his shoulder. The nurse magically appears to wheel him out.

I fall back into the bed, blowing out a long breath. One more lecture to go, and I don't look forward to it. At all.

Syd's waiting in her car as I'm wheeled outside. I thank the nurse as I push myself out of the wheelchair and into the car. We don't even make it out of the parking lot before Sydney starts.

"If you *ever* pull some shit like that again, I'll kill you myself."

CHAPTER THREE

IT'S BEEN TWO months since the shooting. I officially graduated college and quit my job at the end of last month. It was bittersweet leaving. I loved working there. I'll even miss Jack. It was a little awkward after the shooting. I had to convince Jack that I wasn't going to sue. They did take care of my medical expenses since it officially happened during work hours. Then, of course, news spread like wildfire about what I had done, so people were calling me a hero. I tried to downplay it as much as possible. I *hated* the attention. Howard and I never talked about it. We've gone to dinner a couple times, and that was one topic we both silently agreed to never discuss.

Sydney has forgiven me. *Finally*. I just have to keep reminding her that if I had never been shot, she wouldn't have met Dr. Parker. Of course she hates when I say that. She doesn't want to think that was the *only* reason she met Jeff. I finally got some of the story out of her. She and Dean had been having problems—mainly, he didn't like being number two in her life. When he was offered a job in another state after graduation, he decided to take it. They broke up right before she heard about me getting shot. It was amicable. She told me she liked Dean but there were never any fireworks. So she wasn't too sad about it. Then she met Jeff Parker. The version I heard was she was being pushy, trying to get information about me, and he was being an asshole doctor. One thing led to another and now they're dating. And really, nothing's changed. One minute they're fighting, the next minute they're having make-up sex. Sounds a little screwed up to me, but whatever, I don't have to deal with him.

With one more month before I start my new life in New York City, I'm taking a quick trip to Chicago. As I'm packing, Syd comes in and lies on my bed.

"I like your hair," she says.

I glance in the mirror at my new, brunette color. It always catches me off guard when I look at myself. I look like a carbon copy of my mom with my dark hair.

"Are you sure I can't go with you?" she whines as she sticks her bottom lip out.

Even though there are so many positive things in my life right now, there's always a part of me that wonders who killed my mom. I've planned this trip since I was eighteen years old, but I promised Sydney that I'd wait till after I graduated college to go. I feel I can't fully move on with my life and let go of the past until I see for myself who Travis Stein is.

"You know I have to do this alone, Syd," I say as I put my clothes in my bag.

"You don't *have* to," she says stubbornly.

"Sydney." I stall for a moment. "I just want to see who he is. I need to close this chapter in my life, and I need to do it alone. I'll call you everyday, tell you everything." I sit on the bed next to her.

"Fine." She rolls her eyes. "But if you get into trouble again, Addie, I swear I will never forgive you," she threatens as she sits up and pulls me into a hug.

"I promise. I'm not going looking for trouble." I try to reassure her.

She laughs out loud. "Addie, that's not the problem." We pull apart, and she playfully hits my arm. "Trouble has no problem finding *you*."

"I'm only going to be gone for a few days. You won't even miss me." Hopping off the bed, I zip up my bag and glance around the room making sure I got everything. "Anyway, now you'll have the whole apartment to have your make-up sex," I say waggling my eyebrows.

"Addie, there aren't a lot of places left that we haven't *already* had sex in this apartment." My eyes go wide. *What the hell! If she had sex on the kitchen table, where I eat, I'm going to kill her.*

"I don't even want to know." I snicker, shaking my head as I walk out of my room. I immediately see the kitchen table and whip around. Sydney sees where I was looking and dies laughing. Oh. My. God. I'm going to kill her. "Gross!"

"*What?*! He was hungry." She shrugs.

"Oh, my God, stop!" I cover my ears with both hands. Now she's bent over in hysterics; tears from laughing so hard roll down her face. "I'm leaving, nympho. Stay out of my room," I say, picking up my bag. She jumps up, trying to stop from laughing.

I'm not a prude. I've just never had a relationship where sex has been *that* great. I don't think it's the guy's fault. I think it's me. I need to feel in control with everything I do, even sex. It's hard for me to let go.

We hug one last time. Syd twists her lips as she narrows her eyes. "I mean it. Stay out of trouble."

"Well, I mean it. Stay out of my room." We both laugh.

I throw my suitcase in my rented Honda Civic. Taking a deep breath, I pull out of the driveway and put my car in drive. I took Frankie up on his offer of helping me out. He made me a fake license for my trip. I don't know what to expect when or if I meet Travis, but I don't want to have anything identifying who I really am.

The cops told me that they never found my mother's killer.

Even when I had the license plate of the killer. With a small amount of investigating, I found the name of the person who owned the car. Travis Stein. He currently lives in Chicago. And doing a little Google research, I found out a little about him. He's a powerful businessman; many say there is a lot of criminal activity within his empire, but nobody has ever been able to prove anything. He always has a group of bodyguards with him in all his pictures. But what did he have to do with my mom? Was it a random murder? Was it a hit and they killed the wrong person? I need to find out who Travis Stein is.

It is a long seventeen-hour drive, so I plan on stopping halfway. While driving, I think back to the day that changed my life.

Thirteen years ago

"Mom! What are you cooking? It smells delicious?" I let my nose lead me to the kitchen where a delicious, chocolate smell wafts in the air.

"I'm trying out a new brownie recipe. I think you're going to love it"

"Um… yeah! I love anything chocolate." I get up on the barstool.

"Well, since you're *supposed* to be home sick from school today, I thought I'd bake you something special to help you feel better." She comes over and kisses the top of my head, giving me a quick hug.

"Hey, I really didn't feel good this morning!"

"Okay, dear. So it doesn't have anything to do with the fact that Mike is hanging out with Maddie now and not you?" she asks.

"What! How do you know that? And no, that's not it." Rolling my eyes, I sigh.

"Hello, I'm on the PTA. I know a lot of moms. And the one thing moms do is talk about all the gossip going on with their kids. I guess we gossip about gossip." She giggles. "I was up at the school yesterday afternoon and was talking to Amber's mom and got all the details. I'm sorry, baby. It's your first heartbreak. That's why I didn't question the whole sick thing." She looks at me with adoring eyes.

I love her more than anything. She is my world. My father passed away in a car accident when I was one. They weren't married yet when I was born. They were planning their wedding when the accident happened, which is why my last name is different than my moms. I have always wondered what he was like. They met while my mom was on vacation in Mexico. She said it was love at first sight. It was like a fairytale, only with a tragic ending. But I was the light that kept her going.

She's gone on the occasional date, but that's it. I'm her world, too. She is my best friend. I look just like her, except for our eyes and the slight difference in hair color. My hair is a dark blonde, while hers is just a little darker, more like a light brown. Her eyes are brown and mine are a turquoise blue, similar to the Mexico waters she and my father swam in, or so I've been told. Other than that, I'm her 'mini me.'

"So, do you want to talk about it?" she asks.

She takes out the brownies that look as good as they smell. I might enjoy my broken-heart status if she is going to feed me chocolate. I was more irritated than hurt about the Mike thing. I was mad at my supposedly best friend, Maddie, for talking to Mike. My mom places a brownie in front of me and I take one bite and forget all about Mike and Maddie. I guess this is what you do to get over dumb boyfriends and friends… chocolate. Yum.

My mom starts to clean up the plates and the mess she made baking the brownies when we hear a noise at the front door. The mailman's probably dropping something off. My mom is addicted to Amazon. We both move to the living room to check it out. She tells me to stay back, so I step behind the door.

"Hi, can I help you?" my mom asks as she opens the front door. There's a small window where I'm standing, but I can't see the man. I don't hear him say anything.

BANG!

I cover my ears, watching my mom fall backward. She's lying lifeless on the floor beside the door, a bullet right between her eyes.

NO!

NO!

NO!

I am trying my hardest not to scream, covering my mouth to stifle any sounds. I have to keep quiet. *I don't want to die*, but I want to help my mom. I'm silent, pleading with God. Please let her be alive. I watch the man walk away through the window. He turns around and looks back. I see his face before he gets into the car. It's a black sedan with tinted windows. I look at the license plate from the window.

I have to remember it.

I have to remember it.

I have to remember it.

He drives off and I run to my mom.

I scream over and over. She's not moving. I hear sirens in the distance.

"Mom, please stay with me! Help is on the way! Please don't leave me!" I am crying hysterically, holding my mom. There is no way I am going to let her go.

* * *

My mom is dead. I don't have anyone. The whole last two weeks are a blur. I don't want to talk to anyone. My grandma and grandpa came to help with my mom's funeral and stay with me. I stay in my room. I don't want to see anyone. My life is over. The first couple days there were cops coming and going. I told them what happened over and over. It's like they don't believe me. I gave them the license plate number of the car. It is a permanent image in my head that I can't forget. The next couple days there was a lady who wanted to talk to me. She told me that she could help me. Help me understand and cope with the loss of my mother. I definitely don't want to talk to her. They can't make me talk.

A couple times when the police returned, I would listen to see if they had found the man. Instead I'd hear them talk about a safety deposit box and a will. Then I shut my door quietly and return to curl up on my bed. I have nightmares every night and wake up screaming for my mom. My grandparents don't know how to help me. They have also lost their daughter. At least they don't have the whole murder etched in their mind like a constant movie playing over and over. I want this whole thing to go away, to wake up and *this* have been a horrible nightmare. Unfortunately for me, this nightmare is my life.

Today the lady who wants me to talk came over again. I still don't want to talk. I don't want to do anything. Why won't everyone leave me alone?

"Addison, I know you don't want to talk to me right now, but you will need to talk to someone soon," she said, looking at me with soft eyes. The woman is really trying to help me, but I still don't want to talk. "Do you know an Amy Mason?" she asks.

I nod my head. Amy was my aunt on my dad's side. I haven't seen her in years. Why is she asking me that?

"Your mom has a will that named Amy as your legal guardian if something was to happen to her," she explains. "She is on her way here right now. I want you to know what is going to happen. I don't know any of her plans other than she is coming here. I'm going to give Amy some names of doctors in Dallas who I know can help you."

What? Why would she give her names of doctors in Dallas? I don't understand. Why did my mom want me to go with Aunt Amy instead of my grandparents? I mean, I know they are old, but I haven't seen Amy in years. I don't know her that well. The only thing we share is our last name. I have so many questions, but I don't want to talk to this lady. She has no idea what I'm going through.

"Why?" That's all I could muster.

"Addison, I wish I had more answers for you. I can't imagine the tragedy that you have had to live through, but I want you to know that if you ever need anything, you can call me. I'll leave my card on your dresser." She turns around and gently places her contact information on my dresser then leaves the room.

After a couple hours I hear voices in the living room again. It's probably another person bringing us food. Why is everyone bringing us food? It's so weird. I don't care as long as they don't want to talk to me. This time there is a knock on my door.

"Addison," a sweet voice I've heard before but can't place calls my name. "Addison, can I please come in? It's Amy."

No, you cannot come in. No, you cannot take me away. No, I don't want to talk. If I wanted to talk, that is exactly what I'd say, but instead I stay quiet. The door slowly opens. Well, so much for leaving me alone. Amy walks in and sits on my bed, quietly watching me. She has tears in her eyes.

"Hi, sweetie," she whispers. She brushes my hair with her hand and doesn't say another word. We sit there, both crying, for what feels like hours. I finally collapse in her arms. Her warm body holds me, stroking my hair.

"*Shh...* sweet girl. It'll be alright," she whispers in my ear.

I end up falling asleep in her arms as she rocks me back and forth. I can't explain it, but she makes everything feel like it's going to be okay. She doesn't expect me to talk. She comforts me. Like my mom would've done.

The next morning I wake up from a dreamless night—the first time since my mom died. Amy isn't in my room. My stomach growls and I know I need to get something to eat. I walk out to the kitchen and find Amy and my grandparents at the kitchen table. They are in deep discussion and don't notice me walk in. I wonder if I can slip in, grab something, and get back to my room without anyone seeing me. I try my hardest to walk softly, but then I hear, "I'm taking her back to Dallas in a couple days. I've already talked to the school in my city to enroll her."

I freeze. Reality sets in.

"What did you say?" I scream. "I can't leave my friends, my house, my school." *My mom.* I know she's gone, but this is our home. I can't leave.

"Sweetie," Amy says, standing up.

"No!" I cry out. "Why are you here? Why did my mom leave me to you? I'm sure I can stay here with one of my friends!" I try to reason. I mean, I'm sure someone would take me in. I have a ton of friends, all who will hate seeing me leave.

Amy continues walking toward me and grabs me in her arms, holding me tightly again. "Addison, I don't know why your mom wanted you to be with me, but I would love to take you home with me. You've always been so special to me and the only niece that I have," she explains. She brushes her fingers through my hair again. I don't have enough energy to fight with her. My life died two weeks ago anyway. Who cares where I go? My dad left me. My mom left me. Nobody wants me but my aunt.

Two days later we're packed and driving to Dallas, Texas. I am about to begin my new life.

* * *

"Hi, my name's Sydney," the girl who lives across the street from my aunt says to me as we're unpacking my bags from the car.

I stare at her. I don't want friends so I walk into the house. Every day Sydney comes to the door asking if I am home. She's a very persistent girl, but I'm not ready for friends.

After a couple weeks of hearing her at the door, I finally give in. After that we become inseparable.

7 Years ago

I'm so excited! I just turned sixteen and I am getting my driver's license. My aunt is trying to find my birth certificate so I can go and take my test. She called me earlier and told me she got it out of the safe deposit box that my mom had, which then was given to Amy. I still have no idea what's in it. Whenever I ask her, she says important documents... I guess things like my birth certificate. My cell phone rings and I see it's Amy.

"Hi, Amy! Are you almost home?" I ask, anxiously. Not that we are going today to get my license, I just want to know I have everything ready to go.

"Hey, sweetie, I'm almost home. Don't make plans tonight. We need to talk," she says. Her tone worries me. She should be happier knowing she isn't going to have to drive me around everywhere now.

"What's wrong, Amy?" I ask nervously.

"Nothing. Just no plans tonight. I'll explain everything later. Love you." With that, she hangs up.

Hmm... I wonder what that could be about. Then I have a thought: maybe she is getting me a car! She's trying to trick me. I bet that's it. It has to be. I dance around the house. Okay, I need to act excited when she tells me so she doesn't know that I figured it out. I practice my surprise face in the mirror.

Amy walks in the door about a half hour later. I can't contain my excitement so I run and give her a huge hug.

"What was that for?" she laughs.

"Oh, nothing. For being the best aunt ever," I reply with the biggest smile on my face.

"Wow. Thanks. I think you're the best niece, also. And

remember I love you very much." Her reply is definitely not as enthusiastic as I expect.

She walks to the couch and sits down. "Come have a seat with me, Addison."

My original thought of her giving me a car is starting to vanish. Her voice is very serious. I walk over and take a seat right next to her. She grabs my hands and holds them in hers. Looking at me, she says, "We need to talk."

At that point my excitement dies because I am positive I'm not getting a car. In fact, it sounds like I'm not going to like what our *talk* is going to be about. I stare at her, waiting for her to say something. Anything. After what seems like forever, she begins.

"I knew this day would come. You've come so far since your mother's death. You've learned to move on with your life. But there are so many things that you don't know. Things about your mom. Your dad. *Me.* Please understand that everything that we did, we did it for your safety. And I hope that you will one day see it that way."

I can't speak. I'm afraid of what's about to be dropped in my lap. My world crumbled once, I don't know if I can live through it again. Amy continues to hold my hands.

"I love you like a daughter. You have brightened my world and taught me so much along the way. I have dreaded this from the first day I brought you back with me, but it's time you know the truth." She sighs. "Addison... I'm not your aunt. Your mom was my best friend from the time we were five all the way up to when we were roommates in college."

Wait. What? How could that be? I have her last name. If she's not my dad's sister, why do I have her last name?

"I can see the wheels turning in that analytical head of yours. Yes, you have my last name. Before I explain that, let's start from the beginning. Your mom and dad did meet in Mexico and had a whirlwind affair. Your mom loved your dad very much, just as your dad loved your mom very much. But… your dad was a very dangerous man. Once your mom found out she was pregnant, she left him. She didn't want to raise a child in his world. She told him that *she* didn't want to live that way, so he let her go. When she had you, she was afraid he would someday find out about you. So we did a closed adoption and I adopted you so no one would ever know your mom had a child. I was never going to raise you, but it was a way to keep you safe. You would have my name on your birth certificate. She had power of attorney, so she was considered your guardian. Of course, she had planned on having this conversation with you herself when you were old enough."

I couldn't move. My whole life had been a lie up till this point. There is no fairytale, just made up stories.

"Your mom told me about your dad but never gave me his name or any information about him. I thought it was better that way. She told me that if anything ever happened to her, that I should take you and raise you. I promised her I would. But I prayed everyday that wouldn't happen. That I wouldn't need to keep that promise. At first, your mom was very strict about where you went, what you did. But as the years went on, she relaxed. Enjoyed her life with you. Then I received the phone call. The one that I hoped I'd never receive. My best friend had been murdered, and I needed to come pick you up." Crying now, Amy still holds my hands tightly.

I don't know what to say. I'm in shock. I didn't think anything in my life would shock me again. Boy, was I wrong. How many times can someone's heart be shattered before it can't be mended again?

I get up to walk out of the house with Amy following. "Please, let me go. I need time to process this," I beg.

"Addison. Sweetie, I'll let you go but please come home tonight. Just remember that I love you with everything I am. You have been through more in your young age of sixteen than most people have ever had to endure their entire life. You will get through this like I know you can. You are the strongest person I know."

I walk out the door without a backward glance and call Sydney.

"Hey, girl!" answers Sydney.

Silence.

"Addie? Are you there?"

My voice catches with my sobs.

"I'm on my way." Sydney knows I need her. If anyone could get me through this fucked up mess, it's her.

Chapter Four

Present Day

TEARS ROLL DOWN my face as I think back to that day. Devastated doesn't even come close to how I felt. I couldn't believe everyone had lied to me. Trust was ripped from me and tossed out that day. It had been years before I was able to trust anyone. Except for Syd. She never lied to me, even if I didn't want to hear what she had to say. I remember that night when she came and picked me up. We drove out to the country and lay on the hood of her car, looking up to the stars. She listened without ever talking, let me cry, shout, and then cry some more. We ended up pulling some blankets out of her car and fell asleep under those very stars. Sydney wrapped me in her arms and held me.

When we woke up the next morning, Sydney decided it was her time to talk and my time to listen.

"Addie, I love you. You came into my life and I never understood pain until I met you. We were so young when we met. I learned there are horrible things that happen to good people, way more than the Boogieman or monsters under my bed. I can't imagine seeing the things that you have seen. But I also see the love for you in Amy's eyes. She is always there for you. She is the most patient person I have ever met. Sometimes I wish my mom was like her." She giggled as she wiped away her tears. "I love her for loving you so much. She provided a way for you to regain your strength and become who you are today."

I knew what she was saying was all true, but I didn't know if I could ever trust Amy again.

Sydney continued. "What you just learned sucks! I hate this for you, but after knowing how your mother was killed and if whoever the heck did it knew about you, I don't want to imagine what would have happened. I'm being a little selfish here, but if it means that you're here today because of some secrets, then I can't say I'm upset with Amy."

We talked for a long time. Eventually I went home. Amy and I both ended up going to therapy to work out everything that had happened. I think I've spent half my life in therapy. It took time, but in the end, I know that the secrets kept from me were necessary.

I'd become mad at the world for my life and at my mom who fell in love with the wrong man—the same man who was ultimately the reason her life had been taken. I was mad at Amy for hiding secrets. The anger wouldn't go away. Amy felt I needed a release for that anger so she signed me up for Tae Kwon Do. She thought I would also feel a little better being able to defend myself, knowing that deep down I feared someday my father might find out about me.

I immediately fell in love with Tae Kwon Do. I loved the control, the movement, the power. Sparring was the best part. I loved knowing that I had strength within me. Within two years, I had received my first black belt. I continued throughout college, going all the way to my third-degree black belt. In high school I decided I wanted to study criminology. I don't know if it was a result of watching my mom being murdered or that her case was unsolved, but I was always extremely observant after that. I would drive Amy crazy. A man would walk by who we would both look at and I'd always ask her to describe him. We would make it a game. She would call me Detective Addison. I was intrigued by details and surroundings.

With my newfound interest in law enforcement, Amy thought it might be a good idea to teach me how to shoot a gun. She always had a gun stashed in her nightstand; we lived in Texas so it wasn't an uncommon thing. People here love their guns.

The first time Amy took me to the shooting range, I was hesitant. It felt wrong holding a gun. They held so much power: the power of life and death. I'd been up close and personal with that power. I didn't know if I could do it. My hands were shaking so hard, I didn't hit the target after going through the first magazine. A man standing next to us took interest in my shooting, probably wondering why the hell I was holding a gun. Turns out he was a police officer. Officer Ted Smith. He was extremely kind and helped calm my nerves. He showed me how to stand and hold the gun. When I hit the target the first time, I jumped up and down. Then Officer Ted Smith had to teach me how to put my gun down and not point it at anything other than the target, especially when I was so excited.

With help from Ted, I eventually became very comfortable with a gun. I was also a great shot, so much so that I entered action-shoot competitions. I went to the championships and won first place in my age group. I was a better shot than Ted. He always acted like he was jealous, but I knew deep down he was proud of me. Ted and Amy started dating not long after our first meeting. They hit it off right away. Amy told him about everything, but he never pitied me or felt sorry for me. He was always pushing me to do better. He became part of my life, part of my adopted family.

Right before I graduated high school, Amy and Ted got married. I couldn't have picked two better people to be together. Two puzzle pieces lost in this world until one day they found each other and fit perfectly. No cracks or bends, two pieces that became whole that day. I loved Ted like the father who I never had. I was happy to leave Amy in Ted's capable arms. It made me feel better about going away to college and leaving her behind. As much as we had been through those last eight years, our bond was stronger than ever. I chuckle, thinking that I didn't leave her behind for very long. She begged Ted to move closer to me. Loving that they live an hour away now instead of three, I'm not sure how I'm going to manage being a couple thousand miles away from her when I move to New York.

* * *

My thoughts keep me occupied during my drive, so I end up driving longer than I expected. When I drive past a sign for a hotel, I blow out a long breath, finally ready to relax. I pull off the exit and locate the hotel. I park out front and looking at my map, I'm in a town called Mt. Vernon just a little east of St. Louis. I shut off the rental car and grab my overnight bag. After checking in, I get up to my room and immediately head for the shower; I need to wash away the memories. My memories have emotionally drained me, but I'm starving. A quick search on Google tells me there's a great Italian restaurant right down the road from the here. *Yum.*

It is a beautiful night outside. Warm but with a breeze to make it not miserable since it is the end of July. The restaurant is beautifully decorated inside. It's reminiscent of Italy. Well, it's what I think Italy looks like seeing as I have never been there. Hopefully someday I'll be able to go; it's my number one place to visit on my bucket list.

"Party of one, please," I tell the hostess as I walk in, slowly inhaling the mouthwatering scents.

She sits me at a table by the front window. It's perfect. I can people-watch while I eat. People stride along on both sides of the street. Mt. Vernon is a small town and its main street boasts brick roads and small shops. Twinkling lights run on both sides of the street. It's very peaceful and quaint.

"A beautiful woman like yourself shouldn't be dining alone," a sexy male voice greets me, pulling me away from the sights outside as he hands me a menu.

"Well, thank you," I say, looking up and blushing. Standing before me is a *very* attractive waiter: six feet, tanned skin, built in the right places, big, chocolate brown eyes, and a beautiful smile.

"What can I get you to drink, beautiful?" His Italian accent sends a little thrill throughout my body. *I think I'd like to have a drink of you.*

I shake my head at my very inappropriate thoughts. "I'll take a glass of red wine." I smile up at him.

A few moments later my waiter takes a seat in the vacant chair across from me. "My name is Marco. Would you like company for dinner?" he asks.

Confused, I look around the restaurant. "Aren't you supposed to be working?"

"I own this place and I think I need a break." He shrugs. "Especially when a beautiful woman decides to come into my restaurant and sit by herself." His handsome face and perfect smile are hard to resist.

"I'm only here for the night. Just passing through town. But if you'd like to join me for dinner, then please..." I signal to the chair he already occupies. He seems innocent enough, maybe a little flirtatious, but nothing I can't handle.

"What would you like me to feed you?" he playfully asks.

"I love all Italian. How about you surprise me." I smile and raise my eyebrows.

"Mmm... you know I'm Italian," he replies with the huge, sexy grin. I laugh, shaking my head. When I don't respond, he continues. "Okay, I'll surprise you." Marco calls over to another waiter and tells him our order in Italian.

"So, tell me, do you have a name?" He tilts his head.

"I seem to like 'beautiful.'" I smirk.

"Mysterious. I like that. Where are you going?"

"Up north." Since this trip is more of an undercover mission, I don't feel the need to divulge any information to this stranger. No matter how sexy he is, we need to keep this simple.

"Well, beautiful, who is traveling up north, I think my shitty day has turned into one lucky night." Marco leans back in his chair, looking relaxed and smiles.

Talking with Marco is easy. His eyes sparkle when he talks. He's a nice guy. Dinner is amazing, the best Italian food that I've ever had. The wine unwinds me from my long, emotional drive and it turns out to be a great evening. Unfortunately, it needs to come to an end. I stand to go use the restroom and sway a little; the wine affects me more than I thought it would. As I come out of the restroom, Marco is leaning against the wall with his arms folded, waiting for me. My eyes peruse his body and my pulse quickens. With a slow, smug smile, he grabs my hand.

"Let me walk you to where you're staying. It's late and I wouldn't want anyone to take advantage of you." He winks as he flashes a sexy grin. Why do men automatically think a female needs protection? I laugh at my thoughts.

"Are you laughing at me?" He sticks his lower lip out. His lips are perfectly shaped. Images play in my head at what he could do with those lips and mouth. Yep. *Definitely a little too much wine.*

"Marco, you can walk me to my hotel but that's it. Even your little sexy grin won't get you a pass to my room," I playfully respond, putting a hand on his chest.

"Hmm… how about something else that is sexy and not so little?" Oh, my God. I burst, laughing.

"That was a horrible pickup line, Marco." I try hard to contain my giggling. "No, even your big, sexy thing isn't going to get a hall pass."

He shrugs. "Well, I thought I would try, beautiful. Still, I will walk you to your hotel. No expectations. I had a fun night with you, my beautiful, mysterious friend. I hope you find what you are looking for." He intertwines our fingers and we walk out of the restaurant.

When we get to my hotel, I seriously wonder if I should change my mind. This handsome man, who has complimented me all night long and has had my body wound up all night, is standing right in front of me. I fight with myself, but my brain wins the battle. I stare up into his big, brown eyes.

"Thank you for eating with me, Marco. I'm glad I walked into your restaurant." I smirk as I lean up and brush my lips to his, giving him a soft kiss. Time seems to stand still with our lips touching, enjoying the few seconds that our bodies share together. I break our kiss and smile up at him. He gives me his sexy grin one more time and winks.

"Ciao, Marco." I turn and walk into the hotel.

"Ciao, beautiful," I hear him call out.

CHAPTER FIVE

THE REST OF the drive goes quickly. Following the directions on my phone, I drive by where Travis Stein supposedly lives. It looks like a compound and has a fence all around it. *Hmm...* how I should go about this? Do I go ring the doorbell? *Hey, did you kill my mom?* Shit... I should have thought this through more. I'll recognize the guy who killed my mom. That memory never fades away. I hate that the memories of my mom aren't as clear as her murderer's face. I know it wasn't Travis himself but maybe it was one of his men. How do I get a good look at his men?

I park the car a couple of blocks away and stuff my actual driver's license and gun under my seat. I don't plan on going on the property. I just want to look around. In case someone does ask who I am, I'll have my fake license on me. I put the key to my car in a hide-a-key case that slips under my bumper. I don't want to have anything on me that will link me to my real identity.

As I round the corner to the house, I walk along the fenced yard. It's huge and beautifully manicured. The fence is black metal with bushes lining it on the property side. I try to look around the bushes as I walk by, trying to see if I recognize anyone. I let out a quiet growl. It's hard to see anything with these damn bushes, and I don't want to stop on the sidewalk and stare through them. That would be a little too obvious. Maybe if I jump the fence I can hide in one of the bushes and take a better look. I look to see if anyone is around or driving by. The coast is clear so I jump the fence.

Dammit! I've walked too far away from the house. Moving from bush to bush; I get closer to the house. Movement at the front of the house catches my eye, so I stop and duck behind a bush. God, I hope they don't release any dogs. That would be my luck. My heart is pounding.

This is stupid. Go back!

Thoughts of Sydney warning me to stay away from trouble fill my head. Sorry, Syd, I can't stop now. Taking a deep breath, I look again and don't see anything, so I continue edging closer. As I'm in between bushes, two arms wrap around me, holding something over my mouth.

Don't breathe, Addison!

I know it's probably chloroform and need to act quickly. I bring my arm up and elbow the guy as hard as I can. I grab two of his fingers and bend them backward. I hear them crack.

"BITCH," he screams. But he releases me. I take off running as fast as I can, gasping for a deep breath of fresh air. I turn around quickly to see if he's following me before I try and jump the fence again. As I turn back around, another guy grabs me and throws me down on the ground. The second guy catches up and there is no way I'm going to be able to fight them off. The rag is put back over my mouth. I fight it as long as I can.

SYD IS GOING TO KILL ME!

"She's a fucking feisty one."

That's the last thing I hear.

* * *

I wake up in a bed with my hands over my head, handcuffed to a headboard. Panic registers in my brain as I shake the cuffs. Holy shit! I have the worst headache. It's difficult to focus my eyes as I'm still a little groggy from whatever they drugged me with. I quickly take notice that I'm still wearing clothes. *Thank God*. I move my body around, making sure nothing feels *damaged*. Other than my head feeling like it's about to bust open, I'm okay. Once my eyes focus, I look around. It's a beautiful room. Dark wood dressers, walls painted gray, but empty, with white trim everywhere, hardwood floors. I'm lying on a white, fluffy, down comforter. It's definitely better than waking up on the ground in a cellar, not that I know what that feels like, but I can imagine. I lean against the headboard, wondering how the hell I plan to get out of this. The door opens and in walks Travis Stein and two other men. I can feel my heart beat faster. The two beef-heads stand side by side against the wall while Travis moves a chair to the end of the bed and stares at me. I tilt my head to the side. I feel like I'm looking into my own eyes. His eyes are the same color as mine, except they are cold. His gaze sends a shiver down my spine. The pictures online can't show the emotion behind his eyes; in person he is much more intimidating and fierce. His jaw is tense as he stares me. I sit up tall, trying to hide the fear in mine.

I glance over at Tweedledee and Tweedledum standing off to the side. I check both of them off the list of being my mom's killer since they look to be around my age. I notice one of them is wearing a splint on his two fingers. "Hope I didn't break your trigger finger," I spit out, releasing a little anger. *Asshole.*

"Don't worry, bitch, I'm ambidextrous," he hisses.

"Oh, big word for you." I'd clap if my hands weren't tied up.

"BITCH, I oughta break your fucking fingers! All of them!" He starts toward me.

"Joe, back up," Travis commands. He immediately retracts to his place against the wall. I smirk and wink at him.

"Are you done?" Travis's condescending voice asks, and I whip my head back to him to see who he is talking to. It seems that question is for me. I stare at him.

"Do you know who I am?" I shake my head no, claiming

ignorance. "My name is Travis Stein. And you were trespassing on my property."

"Nice to meet you?" It was more of a question. I'm definitely skipping the pleasantries of meeting someone when I'm hand-cuffed to a bed.

"Who are you?" he asks as he tilts his head.

"Look. I'm not sure why I'm here. I was looking for my dog. He ran away from a friend's house that I happen to be staying at. I thought I saw him in your yard. I was trying to get him. Then your thugs attacked me. This could have been easily avoided if those assholes would have asked me what I was doing. Now you have kidnapped me and are holding me against my will." I make a show of my handcuffed hands. Just in case he hadn't noticed what his guys have done to me.

"I'll ask you again. Who are you?" he commands with a chill in his voice.

"Renee Pearson," I respond boldly, sitting up straighter. I'm sure he has my fake driver's license. Travis continues to stare at me. He's clenching his jaw together. I know it's my mother's name, actually her middle name, but it's not an uncommon name. In hindsight, I probably shouldn't have used my mom's name if I thought Travis had any involvement with my mom's murder. But it happened thirteen years ago. Well, note to self: undercover work is not my calling.

Travis and I stare at each other. If this dude thinks I'm going to say anything while he has me handcuffed to a bed, he's going to find out how stubborn I can be.

"JETT." I jump as he barks out some guy's name. Well, I'm assuming it's a guy's name. It could be some torture device, but I'm kind of hoping it's a name. Our eye contact never wavers though.

The door opens and a man walks in.

I quickly glance to the door. *Holy. Shit.*

I don't think I've ever seen a more beautiful man in my life.

He's around six foot two and pure muscle. He's wearing a black T-shirt that fits his wide chest like a glove. The muscles on his arms bulge, making the sleeves fit tightly around his arms. Moving down, his dark jeans fit like they were made for him and only him. I've read books where they refer to a guy as an Adonis and I never got it, but there isn't another word for this perfect male specimen. His jawline is perfectly chiseled, his lips are full, and he has huge, emerald green eyes. His hair is dark brown, almost black and short but long enough to run your fingers through. After my perusal of his body, I look back up to his eyes. He cocks an eyebrow with amusement in his eyes. I blush from embarrassment and look away.

I take that back. Maybe he is the torture device. This might not be so bad. Heat creeps across my body at the thought of that man touching me. *Oh, my God!* What is wrong with me?

Travis gets up from his chair and moves to where Jett stands. I take these seconds to shake my inappropriate thoughts away. They talk quietly and then Travis and his two thugs leave the room. Jett sits on the same chair, directly in front of the bed. He tilts his head, sitting back, arms crossed, legs spread apart. His assessing eyes are fixed on me.

It feels like he's looking into my soul for answers. And holy shit, I'm afraid he's going to find them. They are so intense I have to look away. I take another peek, but he hasn't moved an inch. If his jaw wasn't clenching, I would have thought his face was made of stone.

I can't have this beautiful man sit here and stare at me all day. My body is on the verge of overheating under his scrutinizing stare. The silence consumes me.

"So… any way you can take these off me?" I ask, fidgeting with the handcuffs.

"Nope," he responds with a smirk.

"I'm harmless," I whine. "Look at me, I'm like half of you. My hands are going numb." I try to sound needy. Trying the damsel in distress.

"I am looking at you. I was also looking at you on the security monitor when you took Joe down. You're not as harmless as you say." He brings his full lips into a half smile. A small dimple appears. His voice is all man, deep and rich, which sends vibrations straight down to my sex. I cross my legs to slow the building ache. What the hell is wrong with my body? It's never reacted this way to *anyone*.

What a waste of a beautiful creature to not have that body on display. "I think you picked the wrong occupation." The words are out of my mouth before I can stop them.

He chuckles to himself while raising an eyebrow. "Oh, really? And what occupation do you think I should be in?"

A model, a hot fireman in one of those calendars, anything where that face and body can be shared by all women. I don't reply, though. He shakes his head slightly with a knowing smile. That one dimple turns into two and that smile sends warm waves to my inner core. I squeeze my thighs together, shifting positions. *Shit.*

I look around to avoid his stare. Two windows, three doors. "It ain't gonna happen," he says, watching me. See? Those fucking eyes can read what I'm thinking.

"What's not going to happen? You guys releasing me? You know people are going to be looking for me when I don't return from my walk!" I bark out. If only that were true.

He ignores my questions but responds, "You have beautiful eyes."

I stared at him dumbfounded. My brows furrow.

"Really? Now is NOT the time for pickup lines." I roll my eyes. Even though this is the worst timing, my body doesn't seem to agree.

"So, your name is Renee." It was a statement more than a question. "Why are you really here, Renee?" I wish he'd send in Tweedledee and Tweedledum; at least I could keep my uncontrollable libido in control. His looks and voice are very distracting.

"I don't know why you people aren't listening to me. I was looking for my dog. I'm assuming you don't have him, so can I please go?" I sigh. "Is this something y'all do normally? Kidnap women?"

"Nope… to both your questions."

CHAPTER SIX

JETT

WHY THE FUCK am I in here babysitting this girl? This is not my job. Don't get me wrong, she's gorgeous. Sinfully gorgeous. I could stare at her all day and wish she was under me all night. Seeing her squirm, knowing that I'm making her blush is killing me. I'm having to constantly think about my grandma to avoid getting a fucking hard-on. But she shouldn't be here. I shouldn't be in here with her. Although, when I think of the alternatives, Joe and Bill, it pisses me off. There is no way they are getting anywhere near her. I may think about doing dirty things to her, but hey, *I'm a good guy*. Those dipshits, on the other hand, might try to take advantage of our guest.

We saw her on the security footage way before she jumped the fence. It surprised all of us when she actually did it. Travis has many enemies in all shapes and sizes, so we don't mess around when someone trespasses. But damn, I got a little hard when she took down Joe. When they brought her in, I couldn't help but notice she had the most beautiful body I've ever seen. But nothing could have surprised me more than when I walked into the room and met those eyes. They were familiar. Travis's eyes are the same color. Although Travis's eyes don't do much for me, hers are hard to look away from. It's like they hypnotize me.

Travis wants me to see if I can use my *charm* to get her to talk. Charm, my ass. He means my looks. And fuck if I care if it'll make her talk to get her out of here faster. I'm not really sure what is going on, but when Travis saw the name of the girl, he flipped out. He told me that wasn't her name. So here I am, staring into her Caribbean blue eyes, trying my fucking hardest *not to get hard*.

"If you tell us who you really are and why you're really here, we'll let you go on your merry way." She doesn't seem afraid. Which is a huge mistake. She should be. You don't mess with Travis Stein.

"I've told you my story. Numerous times, in fact. I'm sorry you don't believe me, but that's all I've got," she says as she rolls her eyes. I know one thing for sure; she's from the south. Her sweet, southern drawl is sexy, too.

Okay, this isn't working. How the hell does Travis expect me to get her to talk? She seems to be sticking with her story. It's not a totally unbelievable story, but I can tell she's lying; her pupils slightly dilate every time she tells it. I need to establish a friendly connection with her. I push off the chair. Maybe if I sit on the bed it will help instead of sitting right in front of her trying to intimidate her, which is working oh so well, I sarcastically think.

"If you're not planning on taking my handcuffs off, you better stay the fuck back. My legs aren't tied down." I stop walking and stare at her. Did she threaten me? Fuck, why does that excite me? Not that she could actually pin me down, but I'm sure she'd try. I debate continuing my initial thought because I'd be lying if I didn't want to see what she could do.

"Oh, sweetheart, that sounds like a challenge." I smirk.

"Fuck you," she mumbles.

Fuck yes, please.

"Baby, you'd like that, wouldn't you?" I tease.

"Um... a little too presumptuous? I hate to break it to you, but not all women like the egotistical, narcissistic assholes." She snickers and lifts an eyebrow.

"I've yet to meet one who can resist," I say as I walk back to the chair. I sit down and lift my hands behind my head. Tilting my head, I flash her a knowing smile as she glances at my flexed arms and chest.

The door opens behind me and Travis walks in. "Jett, can you wait outside?"

Well, fuck. I'm rather enjoying myself. Knowing I don't have a choice, I get up and wink at Renee before leaving. I hear her say "asshole" right before I leave. I let out a booming laugh as I close the door. I wonder if I have time to take a cold shower.

Chapter Seven

THAT MAN IS frustrating. He's a man-whore who thinks he can have whatever the hell he wants. I could see the desire in his lust-filled eyes. Well, I don't think so, buddy. Now if only my body would stop reacting to him. I mean I'm a freaking prisoner and my body seems to think *now* is a good time for a hook-up. I close my eyes and release a heavy sigh. I open them meeting Travis's eyes.

Travis once again sits in the chair directly in front of me. "I know your name is not Renee. You will not leave this place until you tell me who you really are," he says in a cold voice.

I stare at him. Even if I had not read about him, I can tell by talking to him that he is a very dangerous man. He seems certain that my name isn't Renee. I'm not sure why, though. Will he believe me if I tell him my real name? For some reason I can't say it out loud. Intuition is telling me to shut up and keep quiet.

"*Fine*. We'll play this game your way. Unfortunately, you will lose." And with that he gets up and walks out.

Jett walks back in with the other two thugs behind him. They both have guns in their hands. I shake my head and laugh while I rattle my cuffs. It's not like I can do anything. Jett walks up to the bed with a smirk. He also has a gun, but his is holstered. I stare at him questioning what he's going to do, readying myself for a fight, if need be.

"I'm going to unlock the handcuffs so you can go to the bathroom. Don't fucking try anything or they are going to shoot you," he warns. I'm sure the asshole with the broken fingers would love a reason to shoot me. I do have to pee, so I guess I should behave. He unlocks one handcuff, which lets me bring my hands down. I shake them and wiggle my fingers. It feels awesome getting the blood circulating. Getting up off the bed, I walk into the bathroom. Jett is immediately behind me.

"What do you think you're doing?" I whip around, stopping in the doorway. We're almost chest to chest. His closeness catches me off guard, and I have to step back to catch my breath.

"Coming with you to the bathroom." He shrugs.

"The hell you are. I can't pee in front of you."

"Sweetheart, there is a separate little room with a toilet. I'll wait right outside of that." He chuckles as he points in the direction of the toilet. "Would you rather have one of those fuckers in here with you?" he whispers into my ear, motioning toward the two thugs. The heat of his breath makes me shiver. I step back again.

Um. No. "Fine, cover your ears so you can't hear me," I huff.

Jett laughs out loud. A deep, sexy laugh. After I finish a much needed pee break, I come out of the room and wash my hands. My stomach grumbles. I wonder if they are going to starve me to make me talk. Man, I am really in a shitty situation. Jett leads me back to the bed and grabs the one hand with the cuffs still attached and locks it back to the headboard. At least this time I have one hand loose and my other hand is cuffed lower so it isn't directly above my head.

"Thanks," I say defeated and sit back against the headboard.

All three guys leave and a few minutes later Jett walks back in with a tray of food. He places it on the bed by me. A hamburger and sweet potato fries.

"Is it poisoned?" I ask snidely.

"I guess you're going to have to eat it and find out," he answers just as snidely.

It looks so good. I haven't eaten anything since breakfast and I'm assuming it's close to dinner, if not after. "What time is it?"

"Seven," he responds.

He sits on the chair and watches me eat. The food is really good. I *love* sweet potato fries. So much so that I might have moaned a little. I glance at Jett, hoping he didn't hear me. He has the sexiest grin on his face while he nods. Yep, pretty sure he heard me.

I notice that he shifts in his chair. Hmm… do I affect him as much as he does me? I can definitely use this to my advantage. After eating all my food, Jett takes the dishes and places them on the table.

"Is there a TV in here?" I ask.

"Do you think this is a fucking hotel?" He chuckles. *Asshole.*

"So if I get the pleasure of watching you all night as my entertainment, you could at least put on a show." I arch my eyebrow and smile.

"I could say the same to you." He smirks and winks.

Oh. I'm very competitive. *Game on.*

Smiling, I sit up a bit on the bed. His intense eyes are still on me, although I see a question in them now. He tilts his head while he crosses his arms. He's wondering what I'm going to do. I slowly lift my top. I am definitely comfortable in my body. My bra and panties are not much different than a swimsuit. His eyes get bigger as I get ready to lift it over my bra. I continue up and over my head. Even though one hand is cuffed to the bed, I'm able to hang my shirt on the headboard. I glance over at Jett with hooded eyes as I run my free hand over my breasts. My nipples get hard. Now he's fidgeting in his chair, adjusting himself. Then he gets up and storms out of the room.

Score one for Addison! I mentally high-five myself. I put my shirt back on and sit down against the headboard again. A few minutes later, Jett rolls in a TV. He's pissed. For a guy who seems to always be in control, he's not right now. This makes me very happy. After he plugs it in, he stalks over to me and throws the remote down by my side.

"There are fucking cameras everywhere in here," he whispers in my ear, "so stop playing a fucking game." His beautiful eyes bore into mine. The heat of his breath sends chills down my body. I'm irritated that he has this effect on me.

I grab the remote and turn the TV on and ignore him. I mindlessly switch channels trying to distract myself from a really pissed off Jett. "Do you like to watch anything?" *Besides me?* "On TV? *Bad Boys… The Enforcer… The Godfather?*" I try to think of any movies that might reflect the situation I am in.

He twists his lips as he leans forward in his chair and places his elbows on his knees. "You know, it really bothers me that you don't seem scared. You should be. You don't know what you have got yourself involved in here." I internally agree. I feel safe with Jett, but I'm not sure why. I definitely would have never stripped in front of Travis's other guys. Maybe if I was lying on that cellar floor I'd be a lot more worried. I hope my false sense of security doesn't come back and bite me in the ass.

"What the hell do you want me to do? I've told y'all who I am and why I was on the lawn. You don't believe me. So now I'm being held here against my will with a bodyguard who looks like *you…*" I motion up and down his body with my free hand "… and you're distracting! Sorry! I'm a smartass when I get nervous!" I throw the remote at his head and lie down. I blink back the tears. I'm not in the mood for TV anymore.

CHAPTER EIGHT

JETT

I CATCH THE remote flying for my head. What did *I* do? She says *I'm* distracting? I shake my head in disbelief. I'm the one who can't do my job because she's here. I'm just telling her like it is. I wish she'd just tell us who she is.

For fuck's sake! Now I made her cry. This girl is going to be the death of me. I've never *felt* so much in one day. So much for the plan of seducing her to get her to talk. That shit backfired. Instead, she's seducing me, doing that striptease. Her perfectly rounded breasts, flat, muscular stomach... I've never seen such an amazing body on a woman. My mouth watered seeing her hard nipples poke through her bra. Holy shit, I about lost a load watching her touch herself. And I might have if I hadn't remembered that the whole house was probably watching this on the security camera. I need to pull my shit together when I'm around her. I definitely don't want Travis to put one of his other goons in here to watch over her.

I don't know what Travis plans to do with her but it needs to happen soon. Maybe I can talk him into letting her go. He's hellbent that she's lying, and I'm not sure why. I don't like being kept in the dark.

She finally falls asleep. I get up and grab a blanket to lay over her. I bring it up to her shoulders and lean over and whisper, "I'll make sure nothing happens to you, sweetheart." I breathe in her scent, my hands itching to touch her beautiful hair. Holy shit, I've never had a woman grab my attention like she has.

It's only been one fucking day.

It has to be because she's off limits. Her long, dark eyelashes flutter as she dreams. Fuck, I hope she's dreaming about me. My eyes linger on her as she sleeps. Studying the outline of her body under the blanket, I have to force myself to leave. I could sit here all night and watch her. I turn the TV off and head out of the room before my hands take on a life of their own. I make sure to lock the door behind me.

* * *

"Travis, what the fuck?" I say, walking into his study. "You're not usually one to kidnap women."

"Jett, don't question me. She's lying. I need to know who she is," he responds, not looking up from his chair. "I gave you the task of trying to find out who she is and what does she do? She strips for you! You didn't seem to be talking much. I should be asking you what the fuck?"

Don't worry, I've been asking myself that since the second I saw her face.

"Really, Travis? You wanted me to have her continue? That's not gaining her trust. She was playing a game to see who would win." I sigh, running my hands through my hair.

"Well, we know you didn't win that round. Keep trying." He dismisses me. I walk out frustrated with the lack of information he's giving me.

Okay, I need a new game plan. I need her to gain my trust—and soon. Hopefully before my dick falls off from being sexually deprived. Maybe I just need to go out tonight, find one of my *friends,* and fuck that girl out of my system.

Walking back to my room, Joe stops me in the hallway. He's sporting a sadistic smile. I hate this guy. And I'm not in the mood to talk, especially to him.

"Holy shit, dude! Why did you stop her! I was getting ready to start stroking myself. If I could have ten minutes with her, I'd show her who was boss."

I can't stop my fist from running into his face.

CRACK.

"Fucking asshole! I think you broke my nose!" Joe screams. Blood rushes through his fingers as he holds his nose.

"Don't. Touch. Her." I growl before stalking back to my room. I definitely don't regret cold-cocking Joe. He deserved it talking about her that way. I don't care who she is, but I'm sure Travis won't be pleased.

I pull up her room on my computer's security feed. She's sleeping facing the camera. Damn, she gorgeous. Why can't I look away? What is it about this woman that has me in so many knots? I scrub my hands across my face, running them through my hair. I sit back in my chair and just watch her. How am I going to get her to talk? My head hurts, my dick hurts from being semi-hard all day, and now my hand hurts. I shake it open and closed making sure I didn't break it. Going out tonight is now the last thing on my mind.

Damn woman! And she thinks I'm distracting?

CHAPTER NINE

I WAKE UP confused. *Where am I?* Reaching for my face, I'm quickly reminded I'm still in this bed and still have handcuffs on. The sun shines into my room, making it a little too bright. I'm holding back tears thinking that Sydney is probably freaking out since I haven't called her. She's the only one who knows why I came to Chicago. Everyone thinks I'm on this wonderful vacation with a friend in Chicago. So wonderful, huh? I chuckle at myself, at the situation I got myself in. I cross my legs because I really need to pee. Like someone heard my thoughts, the door unlocks and opens. Great. Tweedledee and Tweedledum. Both are still carrying their guns. I figured Jett was behind them, but they come in and shut the door. Disappointment bubbles up.

What the hell, Addison? He's not going to be your hero.

Joe has a bandage on his nose and has two black eyes. I wonder whose fist he ran into? I'm about to ask but since he's hopefully here to let me go to the bathroom, I need to keep my mouth shut.

"Rise and shine, princess." I wince at his nickname for me. I'd rather he call me a bitch. Joe comes over and unlocks my cuff. "Don't fucking try anything, or from here on out you'll be using your bed as your toilet."

I stretch my arms. It feels good to be free. For a few minutes, at least. I take my time going to the bathroom and washing my hands.

I notice on the sink there is a brand-new toothbrush, toothpaste, and a hairbrush.

"Is this stuff for me? I didn't see it here yesterday?" I ask Joe, who thankfully didn't come into the bathroom with me.

"I don't know. Maybe your lover, Jett, brought them for you?" he says sarcastically.

My lover? What the hell is that about? I ignore him, opening all the new items. After a few minutes of washing my face, brushing my teeth and my hair, I feel much better. I look over to the shower and sigh. I really need a shower. I walk into the room dreading what's waiting for me and find Travis is back in his chair. Joe leads me to the bed and cuffs me again. He and his buddy then leave. I keep forgetting the other dude's name.

"Good morning, *Renee*," he says my mom's name with such contempt that it sends shivers down my back.

"Thank you for the food last night," I whisper, looking down for a second. I have no idea what his plans are for me, but at least he's not letting me starve.

Travis nods. He stares at me again, his eyes always assessing me, searching for the truth, but no emotions show on his face. "Are you ready to tell me your real name today?"

"It hasn't changed since yesterday. It's still Renee Pearson." I try to mask any emotion behind the name as I say it.

"How old are you, *Renee*?" he asks condescendingly.

Oh, shit. What did I tell Frankie to put down on my fake license? "Twenty."

Travis twists his lips, thinking hard about something. Then nods to himself but doesn't say anything.

"Why do you keep lying about your name?"

"Why don't you believe me?"

"Because I know you're lying."

"How the fuck do you know I'm lying!" I scream in frustration as I get up on my knees in bed.

"Because Renee Pearson is dead!" Travis jerks up as he yells. The chair falls backward.

If any words can make me feel like a knife has been stabbed into my heart and twisted, it was those. I slide down the back of the headboard. He knows. He knew my mom.

"Did you murder her?" I ask, my voice trembling and barely a whisper. I can't look at him.

Silence fills the air, answering my question.

Travis walks out and slams the door. I am immediately taken back all those years ago. I crumble into a ball and cry.

Not much later my door opens again and someone walks in. I don't want to look to see who it is. Jett comes around the bed and sits down with a tray of food. He brushes my hair away from my tear-soaked face with the lightest of touches.

"Where's my feisty sweetheart at?" he whispers.

"She died. Travis killed her," I reply in a deadpan voice. He winces.

The door opens again. I figure it's the two thugs or Travis coming back to kill me. At this point, I don't care. Jett gets up off the bed and walks over to whomever it is. I hear whispering and one of them is a woman. I sit up and brush away the tears. Hope immediately fills my head. There is an older women dressed in all black. She walks into the bathroom, but I can't see what she's doing.

When she walks out I look right at her. "Do you know I'm being held captive here? Against my will. Look! I'm handcuffed to a bed. How can you not help me?" I plead.

She looks at me with sympathetic eyes and sighs. "It'll be okay, I promise," she says softly and turns to walk out.

My mouth hangs open in surprise at the gall of that lady. "How does she know it's going to be okay? If I end up dead, I hope I haunt her for the rest of her life." I glare at Jett.

"And there she is. My feisty girl is back. Will you haunt me?"

Jett smirks and one of his dimples show. I don't know why my body immediately reacts when he does that.

"Why do you insist on calling me sweetheart?" I question. "And I wouldn't haunt you because I'm sure you have a house full of ghosts already."

Laughing that low, sexy laugh, he responds, "You are definitely right about the ghosts. The nickname? Your name isn't Renee, and you won't tell me what your name is, so I have to call you something." He shrugs.

Sweetheart is too personal, but I sure as hell am not going to tell him my real name, so whatever.

"Eat." Jett picks up a strawberry and brings it to my lips. I take a bite. The look on Jett's face tells me that he's enjoying this. He feeds me another bite of the strawberry. Strawberry juice runs down my chin but before I can grab the napkin, Jett swipes it away with his thumb and brings it to his mouth and sucks his thumb. The sensation from his touch sends a bolt of heat straight to my sex. Holy shit, it got hot in here. This cannot be happening. Why can't my body and brain come to an understanding? *Work together here, please!*

Scooting away from him, I say "Okay... I think I can feed myself." I grab some food and stuff it in my mouth. Jett needs to move off this bed. Right now. He gets up, shaking his head with a sexy grin, and moves to the chair. He sits there and watches me eat, grabbing my tray after I'm done, then leaves the room.

I'm bored out of my mind, trying to put together a puzzle with a ton of missing pieces. If Travis had my mom killed, he knows that I know, too, but he doesn't know who she is to me. What strikes me as odd is he has never threatened me. Maybe he's trying to see how I'm connected to my mom. I need to keep my guard up with Jett and not let the sexual attraction cloud my judgment. I don't trust him, but I can definitely use our attraction to my advantage.

* * *

I'm left alone for an hour or so, getting stiff and still reeling from my morning talk with Travis. Today has already been an emotional roller coaster and it's still morning. I need to get up and move, but seeing that I'm handcuffed to this bed, I'll have to improvise. I push all the pillows to the end of the bed and stand up. My cuffed hand moves up the metal rod. I run in place, thinking that I probably look ridiculous to anyone watching. The soft bed makes it a little difficult to run, but it's helping with the stiffness. I alternate running in place with jumps. Time is hard to determine, but I imagine that I've been doing this for a half an hour and have worked up a good sweat. I go into a split to stretch my inner thighs and bend over at the waist with both hands on the headboard. The door opens. I glance over my shoulder and see Jett frozen in place, flashing a devilish grin. I'm almost positive he is eye fucking me right now.

"See something you like?" I turn back around to face the headboard and lay my head on the bed. I'm still in my yoga pants so it's been easy to work out and stretch. Thank God I dressed for comfort yesterday.

"*Mmm...* you're very flexible," he groans.

He drops some bags on the bed. I sit up on my knees and he walks over to unlock my handcuff attached to the bed. This time he unlocks the cuff around my wrist, as well. He brushes my wrist. The electricity in his touch shoots all the way up my arm, straight down between my legs. I squeeze my legs closed and silently beg my body to stop reacting to him.

"Are you releasing me?" My voice is full of excitement.

"No. Sorry." He sounds sincere. "I brought you some clothes and toiletries so you can take a shower." He nods his head toward the bags.

I look through the bags and there is everything I need, plus a bra and panties. As if he read my mind while I'm searching the bag, he says, "I didn't pick those out. Melanie did." I give him a questioning look.

"Melanie is the lady who came in earlier," he answers my unasked question.

"Oh. I guess I should thank her." I shrug.

I quickly glance at Jett's gun, which is holstered on his hip. Even if I could grab it, I doubt I'd be able to get out of this room since we're being watched closely. There are cameras everywhere.

"Don't think about it," Jett warns. "You'd probably end up shooting yourself."

Seriously. I glanced at his gun for one second. It's those damn eyes. I'll let him keep thinking that I have no clue about guns though.

"I'm not sure what you're talking about. I've never touched a gun before. I wouldn't know how to *cock* a gun." I smile and try to sound innocent.

"It's not hard. Hold on tight, pull back, and it shoots," he says in a suggestive tone.

"Maybe you can *teach* me?" We have moved toward each other. We are inches apart. Frozen in place, I look up and our eyes lock. I go to put my hand on his chest but stop right before I touch him. The sexual tension between us is like a category-five hurricane, with the end result being total destruction. He looks down at my hand and back into my eyes. His eyes change, becoming serious and hard. I back away quickly, shaking my head back to reality, and turn around. I grab the bags and head toward the bathroom. He follows me but I can tell by his pounding, heavy, and rushed steps that he's no longer in a playful mood.

I whip around as he follows me all the way into the bathroom. "What are you doing? You are definitely not coming in here with me."

He grabs my hand and runs his fingers lightly around the red marks left by the handcuffs.

"Are you okay?" he asks quietly. He brings my wrist to his mouth and softly kisses it. I rest my hand on his face, and he leans into it kissing the palm of my hand.

Evacuate! Evacuate! My brain keeps telling me.

I step back, looking down at the floor. Jett lifts my chin to bring my eyes to his.

"You are the distraction." His tone is serious. Then he turns around and walks out, shutting the door behind him.

I need to get a grip. Yesterday he was an asshole and today I'm about to throw myself at him. *Why the hell am I throwing myself at a man who is helping hold me hostage anyway?* It's dangerous. Jett is dangerous.

Everything that I need is in the bag. The stuff I dig out is top-of-the-line. More yoga pants and a tank top. If I see Melanie again, I'll be sure to thank her for being so thoughtful to the prisoner. I let out a laugh. This situation is so bizarre. Then I remember the cameras in the bedroom.

"Jett? Are you out there?" I open the bathroom door and peek out. He's pulled the chair to the table in the corner and is working on a laptop. Hmm... very businesslike. I question my original thought that he is Travis's bodyguard.

"What's up, sweetheart?" he says, looking up.

"Um... are there cameras in the bathroom?" If he says yes, I am taking a shower in my bra and panties.

"No. But there's no way out of there either, so don't bother looking. And the razor will be taken away as soon as you're done," he responds in a matter-of-fact tone.

"Who do you think I am, MacGyver?" I laugh out loud.

"You're full of surprises, sweetheart." He smirks.

Damn, I wish he wasn't so hot. I close the bathroom door and get to my much-needed shower.

After an hour of pure bliss, I'm dressed and feeling so much better, even though I know what awaits me. I've never been more thankful for a shower. I open the door and walk out to find Jett still working on his computer. He slowly rakes his eyes up my body.

My face flushes from his perusal. Not knowing what to say, I blurt out, "Thank God for yoga pants."

CHAPTER TEN

JETT

I AGREE. *THANK fucking God for yoga pants*. Hell, I'll thank Melanie, too. Walking in to Renee bent over in a split, my dick immediately saluted. That girl has the best ass I've ever seen. Round and tight, and I'm sure even better naked. She must work out a lot to have that body. Which, by the way, is very entertaining to watch as she tried to get a workout in, handcuffed to the bed. I don't think my dick has relaxed in twenty-four hours. My dreams have been invaded by a girl with Caribbean blue eyes doing very dirty things with her gorgeous mouth.

When I saw the handcuff burn, I felt like throwing her over my shoulder and getting her out of here myself. I'm not sure where that anger came from, but seeing her in pain kills me. Her sexual banter is also killing me, but in a different way. Internally, I have to restrain myself from picking her up and slamming her into the wall and fucking her senseless. I've never been attracted to a person this fiercely before in my entire life. Such a twisted work of fate that the girl of my dreams is someone I can't have. Ever.

It pisses me off that I'm in the dark. Travis is keeping a tight lid on this whole thing. When he ordered a DNA test, it sent a red flag. I was surprised to see Melanie and even more surprised when she went in the bathroom and replaced Renee's toothbrush. Usually he has me do that type of stuff, not Melanie. Every time I talk to him about it, he tells me to keep doing what I'm doing: try to get her to talk.

Hating what I have to do, I get up from working on my computer to handcuff Renee to her bed. I'm going to have to talk to Travis about this. When I put the handcuff back on her wrist, I get a whiff of her hair. Holy shit, she smells good. Vanilla and cherry. Makes me want to devour her.

"Did you just smell me?" She asks with a huge smile on her face. She has the most beautiful, long brown hair, which makes her eyes pop. They are so bright you can see them from miles.

"*Mmm...* yep," I say, taking another whiff.

"Weirdo." She laughs. I love that sound. This whole situation sucks.

I walk away shaking my head, trying to escape the pull Renee seems to have on me. I walk into the bathroom and grab the razor. I hold it up and wiggle it in my fingers, lifting my eyebrows when I walk into the bedroom. She laughs and rolls her eyes.

I still don't have any idea how long her stay is going to be but since she is my main task right now, I figure I'll enjoy a little down time. This morning I went to the store and bought some things to keep us busy. I hop on the bed and dump out the contents of my bag: a deck of cards, Scrabble, and a few board games. She looks up with a huge smile on her face.

"Really? We're going to play board games today?" she asks.

"Well, I could watch you work out again," I wag my eyebrows and she blushes. Fuck, my dick just twitched. "Do you have something better to do today?" I tease.

"Since you put it that way, I guess not." She frowns and she sighs. Not the answer I was hoping for. I wonder what Travis would do if I just let her go. I'm surprised he's so interested in her. He has a lot of shit going on right now.

"Sorry. I can't let you leave, but I thought maybe we could play some games instead of sitting here staring at each other all day. Although, if you'd like to strip again for me, I definitely won't mind." I laugh when her eyes get huge. She playfully kicks her leg into my shoulder, pushing me over.

"Not going to happen." She smirks, picking up the deck of cards. "Five-card poker?"

Seriously? Why couldn't she have said Gin Rummy or Go Fish? A girl can't be this perfect. I adjust my semi-hard cock so it won't be so obvious. "But I can't play with just one hand…" She shakes her hand. Like I need a fucking reminder she's in cuffs. "You're in here, so where the hell am I going to go?" She furrows her brows.

"Alright, but you better behave." *Unless you want to not behave with me.* I lean over her on the bed to take the handcuff off. My chest grazes one of her tits, which makes my cock immediately hard. I hear her gasp.

"Jett," she breathes out. I look down at her heaving chest as she breathes heavily. Her tits push out more. I can see her nipples pebble. It takes everything I have to not lie down on top of her right now. She shakes her head quickly. "Can't happen," she whispers.

I push back on my knees, sitting back. "Fuck, Renee." I run my hands through my hair, groaning in frustration. Then I adjust my aching dick; I don't know why I bother. It's not going to stop aching any time soon. I jump off the bed and walk around. She just sits there and watches me with her arms wrapped around her knees.

"It's okay, Jett. We just can't," she says. "So let's play cards."

I sit back on the bed and shuffle the cards once my dick figures out he's not coming out to play and calms down. "How about we make this interesting? Whoever wins the hand gets to ask a question," I say as I deal the cards.

She looks hesitant at first but then agrees. With a higher pair than I have, she wins the first hand.

"How long have you worked for Travis?" she asks. Hmm… that's a weird first question.

"A year." She looks surprised but doesn't say anything else. She deals the next hand and wins again. What the hell? This is not going as planned.

"What did you do before this job?" She looks right into my eyes. It's like she trying to gauge if I'm being truthful. Her questions take me by surprise. Why is she so interested in my job?

"I did security. It was a company like Travis's." I pick up and deal the next hand. Finally, I win a hand. I hate to think I might be throwing away a question she might not answer, but it's worth a shot.

"What is your real name?" I ask, lifting my eyebrows.

CHAPTER ELEVEN

JETT IS VERY predictable. I knew this question was coming. I can't keep going with Renee. Even Travis knows that is not true. Good thing I've already come up with another name. I won't give my real name, so I need to say this one with confidence. With his security background Jett might be able to tell when I'm lying.

Looking him dead in the eyes, I respond, "Emily."

Never taking our eyes off each other, he responds, "I like Emily. It doesn't fit you though."

"I don't think Jett fits you either," I shoot back, raising my eyebrows. "I guess sometimes our parents miss the mark with our names."

"You don't like Jett?" He pouts.

"No, I like it. It's very sexy. But it's too simple. And I think you are a man of many layers." It's how I truly feel, but I hope my explanation gets him away from questioning me about my name anymore.

He ponders this for a while and nods his head. I pick up the deck and deal the next round. We continue playing for a couple of hours with many questions. Some answers are lies, some aren't. I try to not lie and just be vague. Like when he asked where I was from. I didn't see a problem with saying Texas. It's not like he is going to be able to hunt down an Emily in Texas. I'm also sure he made his answers as vague as possible, too. Seems he has a lot to hide, as well. I'm not sure how productive this game has been for him because I know the point was to find out more about me for Travis. It has been fun though. Something to pass the time. Something to keep my mind off how close we came to doing something we should not be doing. I've never been this attracted to a guy before, where a simple touch shocks my whole body into submission. I have to blame the situation for my feelings. Must be Stockholm Syndrome. This isn't reality. This isn't me.

"Thank you for this..." I look at Jett still sitting on the bed. "I know your job right now is to babysit me, but you've made my imprisonment a little less boring." I don't quite know what to say. I've only been here two days, but it feels like a week. My emotions are all over the place between Travis and Jett.

"Well, I'm glad I could bring a little excitement into your boring life." Jett lets out a loud laugh. He leans toward me on the bed and whispers, "I don't know where you came from or why you're here, but I wish we had met under different circumstances." He shakes his head before grabbing all the games and tossing them back in the bag then puts them on the table. He comes to my bed with the handcuffs and the look on his face tells me he doesn't want to do it. I just hold my hand out, knowing what has to happen.

"Me, too," I whisper, not sure if he heard me. What is with meeting beautiful men at the most inopportune times? I lie down on the bed, tired from my emotional day already. I fall asleep dreaming of a certain beautiful man with emerald green eyes.

* * *

My dream quickly turns to the day of my mom's murder. I'm transported back to sitting with my mom, eating brownies, and talking about my first breakup. The doorbell rings and I run and hide. She opens the door and I hear the gun go off.

NO!

NO!

NO!

Don't leave me again! She can't leave me. The man looks around, and I look right into his eyes. Emerald green eyes. Eyes that I know. He leaves in his car.

Mommy, please, get up! Please, get up! Mommy! Someone, please help me!

"Emily, wake up! It's okay. Shhh… it's a dream. Wake up, sweetheart."

I'm being held in a warm embrace as I finally leave the hell of my nightmare. I look up and see those emerald green eyes and jump back.

"Get the fuck away from me!" I scream. I'm shaking and can't make it stop. All I can think about are those eyes.

"Emily, look at me," Jett commands, but I can't. "Emily, please let me help." I shake my head no.

"Please, leave." I pull the bedspread over me to warm up my freezing body and add a safety barrier between Jett and myself.

Jett gets up and leaves. Turning before he gets to the door with a look of concern.

Once he's out of the room, I do my breathing exercises that my therapist taught me whenever I relive that day. I haven't had that nightmare in over ten years. I don't doubt that my morning talk with Travis is what caused this, but why did I dream that Jett was the one who did it? I know it wasn't him. He told me he was twenty-eight; he's only five years older than I am. Now that I've calmed down, I feel horrible. It's not like I can explain my dream to him, though. I'm burning up now, so I throw the comforter off. It's still light outside, but the sun is sitting low in the sky so I can tell it's early evening.

After a quick visit from Joe and his partner so I could make a trip to the bathroom, I'm back on the bed, handcuffed. They left as quickly as they came in. I don't know how much longer I'm going to be able to do this. As long as I'm handcuffed to this bed, there is no way I am getting out of here. At least I feel safe with Jett around, which might be his plan... get me to feel safe and trust him so I open up. The safe part, I feel. The trust part won't ever happen.

Realistically they can't keep me here forever. Why the hell am I still here? What does Travis want from me? Jett will eventually get tired of babysitting me. If Travis's plan isn't to kill me, I need to earn their trust that I really won't run when given the opportunity. I'm hoping my chance to escape isn't too far away though. I need to get as far away from Travis as possible, and soon—before my heart betrays me and decides to let Jett in.

Chapter Twelve
JETT

"WHAT THE HELL JUST happened?" demands Travis when I walk into his office. I had been in a meeting with him when Joe came running in saying our guest was screaming at the top of her lungs.

"She was having a nightmare." I sigh. "It must have been a horrible one because she was screaming for her mom not to leave her and to come back." I shiver, remembering her cries. It was heartbreaking seeing her go through that.

"What did she say when she woke up?" Travis questions.

"Well, that is the weird part. She looked at me with pure hatred. Told me to leave."

I look at Travis for his take on it, and holy shit, I think I see compassion in his eyes. I've never seen anything but cold, hard eyes from him.

"Travis, who is she?" I raise an eyebrow in question. The hardness returns. No signs of compassion anymore. This is the Travis that I'm used to.

"You know more about her than I do. I'm still trying to figure things out. All I've hit are dead ends." He walks over to his desk and sits down behind it. "So we know her name is Emily, she's twenty, and she's from Texas. That isn't a lot of information."

"Well, I thought I was getting close and hoped I could get more information out of her. After this afternoon, I'm not sure she'll ever let me around her again."

"Order a pizza and take her out to the patio. But make sure Joe and Bill are close by. And make sure she knows that if she tries to run, that's the last time she's going to come out of that room."

"So you want me to wine and dine her, huh?" I grin.

"Something like that," he says, curling his lips.

That I can do. Well, if she wants to see me again. I can't imagine what I did to make her look at me that way. It felt like the wind had been knocked out of me. I hope I never see that look of hatred in her eyes again directed at me.

I order the pizza and find the red wine that she told me she liked during our poker game. Out of all the questions I asked, thank God that was one of them because I am going to put that information to good use tonight. I have everything set up on the patio. All I need is Emily. I walk toward her room and start to get nervous. What if she doesn't want to see me? Shit! Well, I guess I'll deal with it if that happens. Joe and Bill are behind me, talking shit about how I have the lucky job. We'll see how lucky I am in a minute.

I lightly tap on the door and open it slowly.

"So you're knocking now? I'd get up to let you in, but, yeah… can't do that." She points to her handcuffs. She's smiling though. That has to be a good sign.

"I feel I should be waving a white flag. I'm not exactly sure if you want me to come in," I say, walking into the room just enough to shut the door. I don't need the two assholes in the hallway listening to our conversation. There is a monitor right outside the room so they can see everything but can't hear from where they are. I lean against the door with my hands in my jeans.

"Yes, you can come in." She sighs. "Look, I'm sorry. I haven't had that nightmare in a long time and it surprised me when I woke up in your arms."

She stares at me apologetically, but she doesn't offer any more explanation. I go over and sit by her on the bed.

"I have a surprise for you," I say. "But you need to understand a few things first: you cannot try and run or scream for help," I warn. "If you try either, we won't be able to take anymore fieldtrips." I smile and wink. Telling her she'll never leave this room again is a threat I don't want to make.

"You're taking me out of this room?" she questions.

"Yes. I think you need a break after the day you've had." I don't want to say a break from the morning with Travis or the nightmare, but that's what I'm thinking. "You're going to be handcuffed to me. And Joe and Bill will be right behind us the whole time."

"Oh, yay... Tweedledee and Tweedledum get to come," she says, rolling her eyes.

I throw my head back, laughing. Hard. That was fucking funny. "You always surprise me, Emily."

I've been on this Earth for twenty-eight years and I've dated *a lot* of women, but there has never been a woman who has invaded my thoughts as much as Emily has. Her eyes send an electric shock to my heart, jolting it awake. Her moods pull at the strings of my heart, dictating my emotions. When she's happy, I'm elated. When she's sad, I want to hurt someone. How can one woman come into my life for one day and have this much of an effect on me? I know how this ends, and it's not forever. I need my heart to go back into hibernation.

I walk up and unlock the handcuff and then lock it around my wrist. "Ready?" I pick her up off the bed. When I go to put her down, I slide her down my body. Our eyes never break their connection.

Then she had to go and bite her lip.

Well, if she questions the effect she has on me, my dick just made sure she knows.

Chapter Thirteen

IF JETT HAD any more room for me to slide down his rock-hard body and something else that was just as rock hard, I think I would have orgasmed. *Right there.* We're standing there staring into each other's eyes, inches apart, my body and head struggling internally. I can see the heat and yearning in his eyes. I'm pinned by his stare.

Jett breaks the tension with a low growl. "You ready?"

Ready for you to throw me on this bed and have your way with me. Yes, please!

Leaning down, he whispers in my ear, "Let's go before I do something I can't undo."

Chills break out all over my body. I almost push him back on the bed and say who cares. *Almost.* My head wins this round.

He puts his hand in mine where the handcuffs connect us and he leads me out the door. Joe and Bill—I finally learned their names—are standing there staring at us with big, goofy grins. Shit, I'm sure they witnessed our little interaction. I need to remember there are cameras everywhere. I suddenly remember I've never been outside this room… well, awake, at least. I look around, taking mental notes of every door, hallway, and window. It's a beautiful, modern house. I see other men around and look at each of their faces, searching for *the one* but never finding him. I haven't seen Travis since this morning and wonder why. Jett leads me outside into the backyard. The backyard is huge but the fence back here is solid brick. There's a fountain and beautiful trees surround the property. The landscaping and gardens are immaculate and taken care of very well. The air smells of roses. The sunset is the backdrop to a gorgeous, clear night sky. I can't say that I've ever seen such a beautiful sight.

Then reality sets in. I'm a prisoner in this exquisite picture. Jett is watching me take everything in. "What do you think?"

"Hmm... what do I think?" I look at him suspiciously. "Is this like my last meal?" I wonder if he'll know I'm referring to the meal that a prisoner gets on the night of his execution.

His gaze becomes serious. "Emily, I won't let anything happen to you." His jawbone is tense as he pulls me into his body. He leans down toward my ear. "I promise."

The lock and key protecting my trust breaks open a little. I believe him. I don't know why, but I do. This doesn't change anything. I still need to get out of here. Jett pulls me over to a blanket on the perfectly manicured grass. I don't think I've ever seen grass this green. On the blanket are a couple boxes of pizza with a table right next to it and two wine glasses with my favorite bottle of wine.

"Wow," I say as he guides me to a spot on the blanket.

"I didn't know what kind of pizza you liked so I got a veggie and a meat one." Jett sounds nervous. All I can do is sit and watch him. I don't know exactly what to think of this. I feel like I'm on a royally messed-up date with an amazing guy who makes me feel things I shouldn't be feeling, yet I'm a prisoner of this house and handcuffed to him. He's not letting me go or helping me escape, so he's not much better than Travis. But my body betrays me. I've never been so torn internally about how I should feel about someone.

"Don't overthink this, sweetheart." Jett glances at me as he fills my wine glass. "I wanted to do something to help you forget about the situation you are in, at least for one night." He smiles warmly. Damn those dimples!

"So, you're going to get me drunk? This will definitely help me forget," I reply playfully, taking a drink of my wine. Jett laughs and shakes his head. The wine tastes absolutely divine. I point to the veggie pizza when he opens both boxes. This is nice. Definitely a good distraction from the prison waiting for my return. I try to ignore the sinking feeling that I will be back there soon.

By the time we are done eating, the sun has finally set and the stars are out in full force. I lie back on the blanket and stare up at the sky. Jett lies back with me and we watch in silence. He entwines his fingers with mine.

I point to the sky. "Look, a shooting star."

"What are you going to wish?" Jett glances over at me.

"Hmm... let me think about that," I say sarcastically, looking back to him. Those beautiful green eyes lock with mine and in that moment my wish isn't to be free. It's that we'll meet again *when* I'm free.

Jett sits up and pulls out his phone. Sam Hunt's "Take Your Time" begins to play and he places the phone on the table by our half-empty wine bottle. He gets up on his knees, which causes me to rise as well.

"Let's dance." He lifts me up with his free arm.

"I don't think I have much of a choice, do I?" I giggle, feeling the wine's effects. Already standing with his arm around my waist, he brings my body flush against his.

"Nope." He flashes a devilish grin.

I put my arm around his neck, and he pulls our joined hands up to our hearts. I can feel his heart pounding as we sway to the music. The touch of his thumb rubbing lightly at my back ignites a fire that quickly spreads through my body.

"I didn't tag you as a country boy?" I say, playfully.

"There is a lot you don't know about me," he responds,

peering down at me. We stare into each other's eyes until I can't take the intensity anymore. I lean my head into his neck. My five-foot-eight body fits perfect in his tall frame. He smells like spice, woods, and masculinity. He hums along with the song then softly sings about wanting to get to know me. I'm not sure if they're just lyrics or that's how he feels.

Holy shit. This beautiful man can't be anymore perfect. A perfect man who I can't have. I must have pissed off the gods in another life. He stops singing and hums again. The song ends but another one starts. We never stop dancing; our bodies continue to melt into each other's. I look up and his eyes trap me.

"You're so beautiful." His voice is low and gravelly.

"You're devastatingly beautiful," I breathe out.

"So what should two *devastatingly* beautiful people, who have an unexpected pull that can't be explained and can't be together, do?"

"Be devastated," I whisper.

I go back to my spot, resting my head in his neck. I breathe in a smell that I hope to never forget. He places a kiss on my head and pulls me in tighter to him.

CHAPTER FOURTEEN
JETT

SOMETHING IS DEFINITELY wrong with me. I don't even know her real name. She said it so confidently I almost believed her, but I *know* when someone is lying. I didn't share this information with Travis though. I need to find out what his plans are with Emily. We're on day two and he hasn't shared anything with me. I'm supposed to be his right-hand man.

I haven't wanted a girl this bad… ever. She has me so wound up, it's on the verge of becoming painful. I've gone out with a few girls while I've worked for Travis but never anything serious. They know what I want: no strings and no expectations. Nothing and no one has ever distracted me enough that I don't care anymore about my job—until her.

"Sweetheart, it's best we go back inside." I need to try and stop this. Holding her tightly, her body rubbing against mine, feeling her heat is driving me insane. I need a cold shower for a fucking hour.

I grab my phone and down the rest of my wine. She does the same, and I lead her back inside. As we pass Joe and Bill, I tell them I no longer need them tonight. They hesitate but see that I'm not messing around. Emily is handcuffed to me so she's not going anywhere. I bring her back to her room, and she lets out a long-winded sigh. Shit. I hate doing this.

"I'm sorry," I whisper. Truthfully, I'd rather take her back to *my* bed.

"It's okay. I know it's your job," she replies with a flat voice.

We get in the room and I take off the cuffs. Both of them. She can't get out of the room so there isn't any reason she should be cuffed to the bed. I'll be sure to tell Travis, and I don't fucking care what he says. She opens her mouth but then snaps it shut. I shake my head. *Don't ask.*

"I'm going to the bathroom." She walks away but stops before she hits the door. She looks over her shoulder smiling and says, "Thanks."

I sit on the bed and wait. When she comes out, she walks up and stands in between my legs. My hands are itching to grab hold of her and run them all over that body. Instead, I stand up. We're inches apart. Her beautiful tits barely touch my chest. Our eyes dance around each other. My gaze drops to her lips, where she's biting.

Fuck. Me.

Before I can stop myself, I grab her and lift her up. I slam her against the wall and crush my mouth against hers. There is no slow and sweet. It's hard, fast, and full of need. Legs wrap around my waist. She opens her mouth for me and my tongue darts into hers.

I get lost in our kiss. The need to be closer to her overcomes me. Her fingers thread through my hair. My hands find her ass and squeeze. Holy shit, her ass is perfect, round and hard. I push her warmth against my dick that's straining to get out of my jeans, rubbing and grinding my hips. Her legs squeeze, pulling us together. The welcoming heat of her pussy urges my dick to come out and play. And damn is he trying his hardest to escape.

"Jett. Cameras," Emily gasps during our kiss.

"Can't see this wall," I breathe out. I move my mouth to her neck, tasting and nipping her jawline.

I can feel the quickness of her pulse on my lips. She grinds her pussy against my throbbing erection. A low growl erupts from my lips.

BUZZ-BUZZ-BUZZ

The vibration from my phone in my back pocket shocks me back to reality.

Distractions.

"Fuck, Fuck, FUCK!" I yell as I put her back on the ground and walk away. I need to step away before I really fuck this up. I pace the room with my hands on my head. She leans against the wall like it's holding her up, staring at me with those hypnotizing eyes. I've lost control. I never lose control. Losing control can get me killed. So why does one look from her make me lose all control.

"*This* can't happen!" I growl, motioning between us. "You. Can't. Happen. *Fuck, Emily*. I feel like an asshole who is taking advantage of you in this fucked-up situation! Why can't you just tell us who you are so you can leave!" I bark out in frustration, throwing my hands in the air. As soon as the words are out of my mouth, I regret them. Logically, I know she needs to leave. Soon. But selfishly, I want her here. With me.

She stands tall and walks toward me. "You think I want to stay here, locked in this room? I *don't know* what Travis wants from me. I do know why he sent *you* in here, though." She knowingly looks at me with a raised eyebrow. "So, if you feel like an asshole, that's between you and your boss. But let me be clear, if I weren't a willing participant, you'd know it." She turns and heads to the bathroom. Looking over her shoulder, she whispers, "Good night, Jett."

Chapter Fifteen

I NEED TO put space between us. My body feels like an inferno, and Jett is the only one who can extinguish it. I sit on the tub, trying to catch my breath.

Breathe, Addison.

He's just a man, a really gorgeous man, but nonetheless a man. A man I've known for a whole two days. This is not me. I've had sex and a few boyfriends, but I never slept with any of them right away. *I guess captivity brings out the inner slut in me.* A laugh escapes my lips. I cover my mouth with my hand to stifle any more laughs.

I don't know why I stood between his legs when he was sitting on the bed. His eyes were so full of need and pulled me to him. I'll blame the wine. Or maybe him singing to me or holding me close when we danced. I crave his touch. My whole body drips with desire. Need. And I know for damn sure that he feels it, too.

But he stopped.

He's stronger than I am.

Jett tells me a muffled goodnight through the door. I rub the wrist that has been in a handcuff for two days. It feels good to be able to walk around, to be free—from the bed, at least. I go back into the bedroom. The table that Jett had been working on earlier has some bags on top of it. I didn't notice those when we walked in.

I was a little distracted.

The bags are filled with clothes, in my size, of course. There are quite a few different pieces, which I'm thankful for but begs the question how long they plan on keeping me here. The more I think about it, it's a good thing Jett and I stopped when we did. My focus needs to be on getting out of here, not on a guy whom I will never see again. I pull out a pair of cotton shorts and a T-shirt, along with a pair of panties, and head for the shower.

Later that night as I lie in bed, memories of our "date" flood my thoughts. Jett promised me that I will be safe, that he won't let anything happen to me. He seems sincere, but I can't trust him.

So why am I okay with giving him my body?

He *is* the only one here who seems to be on my side. *Addison, don't be fooled by lust.* He's not going to be my knight in shining armor. Travis has placed Jett in my company as my entertainment while they figure out what they are going to do with me.

I want to believe that it's not an act, but I would be stupid to act so naïve. I need to be smarter about this. Nothing will keep me from being free, even a gorgeous, green-eyed man who can light me on fire.

* * *

I wake up feeling refreshed. It probably helps that I'm not tied to the bed. Melanie walks into the room as I sit up.

"Good morning, Emily," she says with a bright smile, placing breakfast on the table.

"Not sure it's so good. I *am* still being held a prisoner," I say sarcastically. I wonder if she knows that she's an accessory to kidnapping? She's dressed in all black again. She's a beautiful, older lady, probably in her sixties.

She frowns. "I am sorry about that. I do hope that you are being treated well. Travis is a powerful businessman, but he doesn't make it a habit of kidnapping women." Her answer makes it seem like she has known Travis for a long time.

"How long have you worked with Travis?" My stomach growls as I walk over and sit down at the table.

Surprisingly, she sits down with me, glancing at me with loving eyes the way a grandmother would look at her grandkids. I look away from her. It makes me miss my own grandma. Makes me wish I had spent more time with her before she passed away. "I've known Travis since he was born. I was his nanny." She smiles. I can tell she adores Travis. "He's really not a bad man."

"Could have fooled me. Usually *nice* guys don't keep women locked up against their will." My sarcasm is back.

"Not that I agree with what is going on, but I do know that he has his reasons." She smiles genuinely at me.

Reasons? What the hell kind of reasons? Making sure he finishes the job he started thirteen years ago? I wonder if she knows he had my mother killed? I wonder if she would think he was such a good *man* after that?

"I'm sorry. I can see that I upset you." She stands and squeezes my hand. "Please let me know if there is anything that I can get you to make this easier." She begins to leave.

A quick thought of taking her down runs through my mind. Now that I know what it looks like outside this room it helps, but I'm sure Tweedledee and Tweedledum are right outside. And could I really hurt this lady? If people would just be a little meaner, I would have a lot more will to fight. This is what confuses me the most. I've read many cases of kidnapped victims and their stories when I was in college. *This* is not what is supposed to happen. I am thankful, but it confuses the hell out of me.

I'm still eating as the door opens again. There's a flutter in my stomach hoping it's Jett. My eyes dart to the door. *Control yourself, Addison!*

I drop my shoulders in disappointment but quickly hitch them up again as Travis walks in. I cross my arms and offer a fake smile. I'm sure I come across as a bitter juvenile.

"Emily, how are you this morning?" Travis asks nonchalantly.

Oh, just perfect, jackass. I squeeze the chair arms to keep me in place and stay quiet.

"I see that Jett has taken off the handcuffs. I do hope you won't cause any problems with your newfound freedom." He smirks. There is a warning in there.

I laugh. "Would you like me to thank you? Why are you keeping me here?" I ask, looking at him dead-on.

He smirks. *Asshole.* He walks toward the door but stops right before leaving. Not even turning around, he says, "I didn't kill her." There's a hint of pain in his voice. And with that he walks out.

What? Did I hear that right?

One statement and my head feels like it's going to explode with unanswered questions. He didn't kill my mom? Does he know who I am? If he didn't kill her, why is he keeping me here? Question after question fills my head. Why couldn't he have stuck around to answer a few of them! The need to move around has me jumping out of my chair. Exercise has always helped clear my head. Looking around, the room is fairly large so I put on my tennis shoes and run around the room. I stop every ten minutes and do push-ups, sit-ups, lunges, and squats before running again. I really want to do some kickboxing, but I don't want them to figure out exactly how skilled I am. I might need to use those skills in the near future. I make a mental note to ask for a clock.

After what seems about an hour, I'm sweaty and thinking a lot clearer. I pull out more clean clothes and take a quick shower, concerned about anyone entering my room unannounced.

Back at the table I pull the deck of cards out of the bag Jett left. I play solitaire. I'm bored. I laugh to myself, thinking I'm a high-maintenance prisoner. The things you learn about yourself in certain situations is interesting. So far I'm a slut and high maintenance.

Totally opposite of my normal life.

My thoughts return to Jett. I wonder if he'll ask Travis to

assign someone else to me. I sigh. That would suck. It would definitely be easier to think about planning an escape without him around, but I would miss him.

His hardness. His softness. His eyes. His smile. His touch. All of *him*. I drop my head on the table and release a loud sigh of frustration. I'm so screwed.

A couple hours of solitude, just like my card game, and I'm bored out of my mind. Hmm… Melanie did say that if I needed anything to let her know. I know there are cameras in here, so I stand in front of one of them. "Hello? Can you please send Melanie in?" I ask directly into the camera. I feel a little stupid, but I'm sure someone is watching. A few minutes later, the door opens.

Melanie walks in with a big smile. "You called?"

"Um… Jett doesn't seem to want to play with me today?" I laugh at my own little joke. "I'm bored. Are you busy? Would you like to play a board game with me?" I say anxiously. I don't like to be alone in here. I *guess* I should be a little thankful, but I'll never tell them that.

"Sure," she says as she sits across from me. "What are we going to play?"

Chapter Sixteen
JETT

"TRAVIS, I CAN'T do this anymore," I bark out when I see him in the kitchen getting lunch. I've been avoiding *her* room all morning. "I have a job to do, and I don't have a fucking clue why you're keeping Emily here."

After I left her room last night, I took an hour-long cold shower. It didn't do a damn bit of good. Instead, I got myself off thinking of how her body felt wrapped around me, the fucking heat of her sex begging me for relief. I'm sure had I not stopped, I would've fucked her seven ways till Sunday. Dammit, just thinking about her gets my dick at full attention. I adjust myself and turn my attention back to Travis.

He's smiling at me.

"What the fuck is so funny?" I demand.

"I knew a woman once who grabbed my attention like no other woman could. It was like she hypnotized me."

So much for trying to hide it.

"Every time I was around her, I couldn't think of anything else. I would have given my life for her."

"What happened to her?" I'm curious because I've never heard of Travis being married or having a girlfriend.

"She left me because of my job. She felt it was too dangerous. And I'm not an idiot, I know it is. So I let her go." His voice turns cold. "I agree, I think it's best you focus on your job." His answer surprises me.

It's what I want, so why do I feel like someone just ran over my puppy?

"You're *not* going to let Joe near her, are you?" The words come out harsh. There is no way in hell I'd let that fucking happen.

His smirk is back. "No. She seems to have bonded a bit with Melanie. I'll have Melanie *entertain* her for now." He chuckles.

I'm glad someone thinks this is funny. I sure as hell don't. I don't know how I'm going to concentrate on work, but it makes me feel better knowing Melanie is with her.

As I grab some coffee to try and get some work done, Travis stops me before I can leave. "Jett, Emily is here for a reason. You may not know why, but there *is* a reason. So think with your head and not your dick if you plan on helping her." That was definitely a threat. If Travis is threatening me, then Emily's importance to him is worrisome. What does he want with Emily? I might need to do a little digging myself. I've stayed out of it up to this point, but it's time I step in. I just have to be careful; one bad move and I might be six feet underground.

I walk into my office and sink down in my chair. Before I start looking into Emily, I need to actually do some work. Curiosity gets the best of me. I turn on all six of my screens and pull up Emily's room on one of them. She's playing Scrabble with Melanie. I breathe a sigh of relief knowing that she isn't alone. Seeing her again has my dick twitching. I can't watch her all day or I'll be jacking off under my desk. Thinking back to Travis's warning, it makes me wonder who she really is. I do know that if Emily's life is in danger, things will fucking be done to get her out of here. I made her a promise that I would keep her safe, and I plan on keeping that promise.

* * *

It's dinnertime and thoughts fill my head about last night. I've kept myself busy with work so I haven't looked at Emily all day. I click on the keyboard and pull up her room. She's lying on the bed, reading a book. Surrounded by white with her hair falling down around her face, she looks like an angel. She has gorgeous, long hair. Hair I'd love to pull back in order to give me access to that beautiful, long neck of hers. Why can't I get her out of mind?

Her door opens and Joe walks in with her dinner. I immediately sit up straight, taking notice that Joe is by himself. That motherfucker will die if he touches Emily.

Chapter Seventeen

JOE WALKS IN and closes the door behind him. He has my dinner and places it on the table. I'm a little surprised his sidekick isn't with him. I put my book down, thankful that Melanie has given me something to do while I am by myself. Joe walks toward me. I sit up in bed wondering what the hell he's doing. The look in his eyes sends chills down my back.

"I guess your boy toy got tired of you." He chuckles, continuing toward me.

I want to say something back, but I don't want to agitate him. Maybe he'll get his snide comments in and leave. I hop off the bed and plant my feet. I'll be ready if I need to defend myself.

"Maybe you just need a real man to show you how it's done," he spits out, standing right in front of me. I can smell nicotine and whiskey on his breath.

I can't hold back anymore. "You fucking touch me and I'll kill you," I say through gritted teeth. I quickly see that he has his side-piece holstered.

He laughs. "Bitch, someone needs to teach you a lesson." He throws me on the bed, his body following. He pins my arms to my side. No way, asshole. I bring my knee up with as much force as I can and kick him right in the balls. He doubles over, falling off the bed in pain. "Fucking bitch!" he yells, holding his dick. I go to grab his gun but the door flings open making me jump back. Jett is on Joe before I can blink. He picks him up and throws him against the wall. Jett and Joe are about the same height, but Jett has as much muscle as Joe has fat.

"You so much as look at Emily again, I swear, I. Will. Kill. You," he says, grinding his teeth. Jett punches Joe square in the jaw. With a loud crunching sound, I am pretty sure he broke it. Two more guys who I've never seen come in and grab Joe, dragging him out of the room. Jett paces the room again, muttering a curse. *Or a few.* His normally emerald green eyes are raging black. I can see the rise and fall of his chest with his erratic breathing.

"You *know* I had him. I didn't need any help." I chuckle, trying to break the intense air surrounding us. He doesn't laugh and just stares at me. I can see his jaw is clenched.

"I need to go. I'll be back later, I promise." His voice is still filled with anger. I don't have a chance to respond before he walks out, slamming the door behind him.

Glancing at the dinner that Joe brought in, I decide it's probably not a good idea to eat it. Who knows if he drugged it? I lost my appetite anyway. The smell of nicotine still lingers in the air. I shiver in disgust, needing to wash his smell off me.

When I come out of the bathroom Jett is sitting at the table looking at the uneaten food. "Why haven't you eaten?" he asks. His eyes are back to emerald green, but I can still see the concern in them.

"I was afraid if I did I'd be dead by the time you came back." I shrug. He grabs the food, gets up, and leaves.

Well, that went well.

I turn on the TV to get my mind on something else while lying back in the bed. Jett returns about an hour later. I know how much time has passed because I now have a clock in my room, again thanks to Melanie. He has food with him. Jett walks over to the table and pulls out Italian food and places two plates on the table. He pours a glass of water at each setting.

I guess no wine tonight?

The smell takes me back to only four nights ago when I was enjoying my dinner with Marco. It seems like weeks ago. Although Marco was sweet, flirty, and had a very defined body, he's not Jett. Just looking at Jett has me winding up.

"Eat with me?" Jett asks, pulling me from my thoughts.

Dinner smells awesome. Nerves having calmed down, I'm really hungry now. I turn the TV off and sit down, glancing at Jett. He's trying to act calm, but his eyes show something entirely different. His jaw flexes as our gazes trap one another.

"I guess I should thank your for spying on me," I say, twisting my lips and cocking an eyebrow. I want to bait him to talk. His intense stare is hard to escape.

"Anytime." He clears his throat, his lips curling up slightly revealing his dimples. My stomach flutters. He starts to grab my hand that rests on the table but rears back. Awkward silence surrounds us. I grab my fork and eat. The food is amazing. A small moan escapes my mouth as I pull my fork from my mouth. I peek up at Jett and see him staring at me. His eyes are filled with lust. I saw those same eyes last night.

"Would you not do that?" He exhales through gritted teeth, adjusting himself in his seat.

"What? It's *really* good," I respond playfully with a knowing smile. He lifts his eyebrow and smiles.

"Want a taste of mine?" He lifts a piece of meat from his plate and brings his fork to my mouth. I open and he seductively pulls the fork out.

Holy hotness.

I don't remember if it was good because the look on his face as he watches me eat has me fidgeting in my seat. My sex tingles as my body starts to hum.

"Do you have any idea what you do to me? You're going to unravel me." Jett leans in closer. "You're taking something that shouldn't be yours to take. I feel like I can't stop the freight train that's about to collide head-on."

"Then don't," I answer in a whisper. I hear what he's saying. Hell, I've said it myself, so why do I want to see the result of the impact?

He leans back. "It's not that easy. I'm not supposed to be here tonight. But fuck if I was going to let Joe lay a finger on you. I already broke his nose. You'd think he would have learned."

"Maybe he'll get the message now." I smirk. "I know why you broke his jaw, but why did you break his nose?" I ask, tilting my head, raising a curious eyebrow.

Jett grunts. "He runs his mouth too much."

That I can agree with. "So why aren't you supposed to be here?"

"It's getting too complicated. This. Us," he says, looking down at his food.

I sigh. "Then why are you here now? You're definitely not un-complicating things." Warmth spreads through me as he looks my body over with hungry eyes. I exhale sharply, licking my lips. "I'm going to have to take matters into my own hands if you keep looking at me like you want to eat *me*," I breathe out.

He leans over and whispers in my ear. "*Mmm...* Emily, I would like nothing more than to have a taste."

Holy shit.

I've never had my body heat up so fast yet have goose bumps all over. I can feel the wetness of my arousal. I wiggle in my seat. The friction of my pants rubbing against me is about to make me explode.

"You can't say shit like that if you're not going to follow through." My breath catches as his hand comes up my thigh, antici-pation roaring through me.

The door suddenly opens, making me jump. It's like all the

sexual tension in the air falls to the ground. Jett moves his hand from my thigh and casually stands up.

It's one of the men from earlier who dragged Joe off. "Jett, Travis needs you."

Jett turns around with a smirk. "Well... saved by the bell. I'll talk to you tomorrow, Emily," he says in a playful tone. "Sweet dreams." He wiggles his eyebrows and then turns and walks out the door.

I groan out in frustration.

I should write a letter so if they find me dead in the morning, they know it's because I combusted from sexual frustration. If I were at home, I'd pull out my trusty bullet to satisfy myself, but there is no way in hell I am going to masturbate in this room.

Needing a distraction, I turn the TV on. Not soon after, I fall asleep dreaming of Jett. Although, in my dream we don't stop.

CHAPTER EIGHTEEN

WAKING UP TODAY I feel like a trapped animal. Today is day four and there is no end in sight. Feeling depressed, I make my way to the shower and get ready for my non-exciting day.

Walking out, I'm surprised to see Travis sitting at the table. Breakfast is spread out and he brought me an iced chai tea latte. I have it in my hand so fast I don't bother asking how he knows about my favorite drink.

"That good?" Travis laughs, revealing a smile that reaches his eyes.

I pause from guzzling down my drink. *Weird.* Travis seems to be in a good mood. The few times I've seen him, he's never been happy. Intense, angry, questioning… yes. Happy… no.

"Yes, it's *that* good. Thank you. But how did you know it was my favorite drink?" Thank God it's a venti.

"Jett."

Oh, yeah. Our card game of many questions. I can't believe he remembered. I sit down and grab a pastry. I peek up at Travis and see he is staring at me. His stare isn't intense though. There's a warmth to it today. It shakes my core. Something's changed.

"So, are you going to let me go today?" I'm certain it's a no, but maybe I'll wear him down and maybe he'll actually do it one day. He seems like he's in a good mood, so maybe.

He warmly smiles at me. "Emily, I want to tell you a little story."

I guess that's a no.

"I fell in love a long time ago with the most beautiful woman I'd ever seen. She was an angel to my darkness. I was drawn to her immediately. I wanted to change for her. I would have done anything for her. Our love story was like none other. It was truly magical."

What the hell? This is definitely random and very unlike the Travis I met over the last few days. Maybe he needs a friend. Damn, he doesn't need to hold me prisoner for this. Maybe he is telling me this to warn me about Jett. *Don't worry.* There is no me and Jett outside this place. And *that* is my number one goal. To be free again.

"I didn't know you were married?" I knew he wasn't from researching him on the Internet. Actually, he'd never been married, which I found kind of odd because he's a really good-looking older man.

He chuckles. "I'm not."

"Okay." I try to sound interested, but I really couldn't care less.

"After we were together for six months, the most wonderful time of my life, things happened that were out of my control. I wasn't able to leave my business and she left me." He frowns and looked down.

"I'm sorry?" Does he want compassion from me? Not going to happen, dude.

He looks back to me. "But I saw her again the other day."

Why does he want to talk about something personal with me? I don't care who he saw the other day. I don't care about his love life. I wish he would leave me alone or I don't know... let me go. He's ruining the small excitement that I'm getting from drinking my tea.

"Look, Travis, I'm not sure why you feel the need to walk down memory lane with me right now, but I don't like you. I'm really confused as to why you think that this is a good time to tell me your life story. Do I seem like someone who gives a fuck? You are holding me against my will and won't let me go."

He laughs, nodding his head. The asshole actually laughs.

"You may have her looks, but you definitely don't have her soft demeanor." My head shoots up, my eyes wide open. What the hell? He has my attention now. And he is fully aware of it.

"Four days ago I saw her lying in that bed," he says pointing to *my* bed.

I look at the bed and then at him. I start breathing heavy as my heart beats faster. My eyebrows pull together out of confusion and anger but nothing comes out of my mouth.

"You look so much like her. An *exact* copy. When I walked into the room, you were still asleep. With your hair spread around your head, I thought I was seeing things. It knocked the wind out of me," he breathes out, "but then you opened your eyes. It was like I was looking into *my* eyes."

No... no... no. I was shaking my head. There is no way. *No fucking way!*

Travis continues ignoring my panic. "When they brought me your driver's license, I saw the name Renee Pearson. It was like my world came crashing down on me."

"No! You killed her!" I scream. "You did *not* love her!"

"I. Did. Not. Kill. Her." He calmly pronounces each word. "She held my heart captive. The day she left, she took it with her. She obviously took other things of mine, as well."

"I am not yours!" I stand up and shout. "I saw the man's car that killed my mom and it was *your* car!" I scream, pointing at him.

He winces, confusion on his face.

"That's right, asshole, I know it was you!" I'm frozen in place. Tears stain my face.

"Emily, I swear to you, I did not kill your mom." He remains seated, looking up at me with pain in his eyes. He grips the chair so hard his knuckles turn white. "When the police came and questioned me about the murder of Lana *Renee* Pearson, part of me died with her. I found out who did kill her and made him pay with his life." The coldness in his voice gives me chills. "What I don't understand is I have seen the police report and *no where* did it mention a witness, let alone a child witness."

"I was ten! I don't have a clue why I wasn't on the report. I was there. I saw the man walk up to my door, point a gun to my mom's head, and pull the trigger," I cry out. "And even if you didn't pull the trigger, it is still your fault."

"Yes, it is," he whispers and drops his head into his arms. "And I live with that regret every day." He looks up. "And now finding out about you…" He chokes up with tears in his eyes.

"NO! You don't know that." I hold my hand to my heart. It's beating so fast I can barely breathe.

"Yes, I do." He keeps his eyes locked with mine. "When I saw the name on the driver's license I knew it wasn't a coincidence that you looked exactly like her but with *my* eyes. At first I was angry, thinking someone was playing a game with me. I had to find out, which is why I did a DNA test."

"You bastard! You've kept me locked up in this room so you could see if I was your kid? Well you win father of the fucking year!" I seethe, throwing my hands in the air. I can't stand it anymore.

I run to the bathroom and slam the door, needing to release some of this anger. There is so much bottled up inside. I scream at the top of my lungs till I can't anymore. Falling on my knees, I curl up on the floor and cry. I don't know how long I've been on the floor, but warm arms wrap around me and pick me up.

Jett.

He carries me to the bed, gently lying me down. I feel his hard body lie down behind me. He holds me tight with his strong arms.

"Shh, sweetheart. It'll be okay," he whispers softly into my ear.

Wanting to tell him to fuck off, that no, it won't be okay, but words don't come out when I open my mouth.

I must have fallen asleep because I wake up burning. Trying to toss the blankets off of me, I find I'm still being held tightly by Jett. I turn around to face him and soft, emerald green eyes meet mine.

"Hi." He smiles, showing off those dimples.

"Hi," I squeak out, closing my eyes.

I'd say my life has never been so messed up, but unfortunately my life has been nothing but messed up. When will the hits stop coming?

"Want to talk about it? Tell me what's wrong?" he speaks softly while brushing my hair out of my face.

I guess Travis didn't tell Jett. I don't think I can tell him either.

"I don't want to talk about it right now." I sigh, closing my eyes again, knowing if those eyes grab hold of me, I'd tell him everything.

"Okay, we can just lie here." His hand picks up mine and tangles our fingers together, resting them in between us. We lie there for a couple hours more. So much is going through my mind. Travis is my father. My father is a very powerful and dangerous man. *Wonderful.* Now I understand my mom's decision to leave him. A lot of good that did. I need to get out of here. Travis needs to let me leave. Maybe since he knows that I'm his *daughter*, he'll let me go now.

Jett is absently rubbing his thumb on my knuckles. I focus on that, no longer wanting to think about Travis. I need Jett to help me forget. I quickly swing my leg over his body and straddle him. I lean down and kiss his perfect lips. Begging him to let me in with my tongue. His mouth opens as he brings his arms around my waist, pulling me into him. I gently suck on his tongue, moaning into his mouth. I can feel him getting hard underneath me. He quickly picks me up and turns me over so he is now on top, pressing into me.

"Emily. We *can't* do this right now," he grunts, pulling my hands out of his hair and holding them above my head. "You're dealing with something I don't understand. I can't be your distraction."

"What the hell? You've been my distraction for the last three days. Distraction from this prison. I should have been thinking of how to get out of here the entire time, but instead I was thinking about you. How much I want to feel you inside me, filling me. How twisted is that?" I exhale. He still hasn't moved. His body and his eyes have me pinned.

"Emily, I've never wanted anyone so badly in my entire life. I would like nothing better than to slam my dick into your sweet pussy. Feel how hard you make me?" He rubs his dick on my sex. I tremble.

I think I just had an orgasm.

"I think about you all the time. I've jacked off more these last three days than I have in years. And it fucking isn't working. It's not enough. But I can't stop feeling like I'm taking advantage of you being locked in here."

"You wouldn't," I breathe out.

"When you leave here, I can't have you thinking that you didn't have a choice."

I laugh. He cocks an eyebrow. "Seriously, how many women have told you no?" I ask.

"Well... that's not the point." He chuckles. "Please know that I'm not telling you no because I don't want you, because *good Lord, Emily*, you are unraveling me more and more everyday." He kisses me softly. He sits up pulling me with him. I'm straddling him again.

"Do you want to tell me why you were screaming at the top of your lungs this morning? I mean, holy shit, do you have a loud scream." He flashes a smile.

"I was releasing some pent-up anger. I would have rather beat the shit out of something, but nothing was in there." I shrug, twisting my lips. "No, this is between Travis and me. I need to talk to him. Can you get him for me?" I ask.

I need to find out what his plans are. I also want to know more about him and my mom. I only had ten short years with her, and I love when people share stories about her. If Travis was the love of her life, and it seems she was his, I want to know more.

"Are you sure about that?" Jett questions.

"Yes," I sigh.

Jett lifts me off the bed and carries me into the bathroom, sitting me on the sink. He kisses me passionately. Deeply. Not forced, not rushed, but with more feeling than our previous kisses. He bites the bottom of my lip and stares directly into my eyes. With his hands on both sides of my head, he leans his head against my forehead and sighs.

"Fate can be so fucked-up sometimes." He kisses my forehead and walks out.

Welcome to my life.

Chapter Nineteen

I'M SITTING AT the table reading a book when Travis comes into the room. He walks over to the other chair and sits down. It's a quiet couple of minutes before either of us speak.

"Did you know that when I met your mom she told me her name was Renee?" he asks.

Well, shit. No. If I had thought that my mom ever used her middle name I would not have used it on my fake license. But it makes sense now about how he reacted when he saw it. I shake my head.

"When she finally told me her real name, I had already fallen in love with Renee. So that is what I always called her. She didn't stop me, so it stuck." I can tell how much she meant to him. His eyes shine with so much emotion. "We met in Mexico. I was on a business trip and she was on a vacation. She had graduated college and was there with some friends. The first time I saw her we were at an outdoor bar right on the beach. Her beauty caught my eye immediately. I watched her the entire night. I felt a little stalker-ish, which was so unlike me." He chuckles but then continues. "I usually went after what I wanted, but she kind of scared me. I was a cocky bastard back then; if I wanted something, I got it." He smirks. "But I was so afraid that she would reject me, so I watched her, how she smiled and talked to everyone. Everyone immediately liked your mom."

I hang on to every word he's saying about my mom. I believe everything coming out of his mouth. Everyone loved my mom.

"I couldn't get up enough courage to talk to her that night, so I went back every night, hoping she would be there. And every night I would leave regretting not talking to her on the first night because she wasn't there. On the fourth night I told myself this would be the last night: if she wasn't there, it wasn't meant to be. But she was. I had never been so nervous about approaching a girl… ever. I finally found the courage to ask her to dance. When she spoke to me, she had the softest, kindest voice. I thought I was dreaming. We danced and talked all night long. I wanted her to myself, so I got her to take a walk with me on the beach. We talked for hours about anything and everything. I had never met anyone like her. She was only in Mexico for two more days, so I asked her if I could take her on a date the next night. Here I was only two years older than your mom but a very powerful man already, and I truly thought I would cry if she didn't say yes. She already had the power to destroy me, and she had no idea."

When Travis says that, I remember what Jett said to me.

I'm destroying him.

Our situation is different, though. He doesn't love me. We have explosive sexual chemistry, but that doesn't mean we can't live without each other. He doesn't even know my real name. The reality of it all is that we aren't going to end up happily ever after. He's a means to an end.

My heart hurts just thinking that.

Travis continues telling me the story of their love affair. As fate would have it, they lived within an hour of each other so they continued their relationship when they got home. "Your mom was going to move in with me. We had it all planned out…" his voice softens "…but my business took a hit from one of my enemies.

There was retaliation and your mom witnessed how dangerous my world was. She told me that she couldn't do it. She couldn't move in with me." He sighs. "I couldn't argue with her. How could I put this angel of a woman in my hell? It wouldn't have been fair to her so I let her go. I let her walk away."

I knew right then how much he loved her. As much as I wanted to blame this man for the death of my mother, I couldn't. He thought he was taking her out of his world by letting her go.

"How did they find out about her? Whoever it was," I ask quietly.

"One of my men betrayed me." He closes his eyes, his jaw tense. "I never thought she'd be targeted. Ever. If I had, I would have had someone watch her. There were very few people who knew about her. But when a car of mine had been used, it was obvious to me who had done it." He pauses. "I didn't even know where she lived. When she left, she took my love with her. She broke me. I was angry that she didn't want to be with me. I went through a destructive period in my life. If it wasn't for Melanie, I'd probably be dead right now."

The confusion reflects on my face. My eyebrows cinch together.

"Melanie was my nanny growing up and has been more of a mother to me than my own flesh and blood. She's been an employee of mine ever since I started in this business. She manages the house," he explains. "She knew your mom, too. She loved your mom very much. She's the one who got me to understand why she left."

Melanie knew my mom. "Does she know that I'm her daughter?"

"She knew the minute she saw you. She actually yelled at me for having you handcuffed to the bed." He chuckles under his breath. "I've been in this business a long time; trust is not something I give out freely."

Tell me about it.

"I needed to know for sure." He tries to justify his action.

"I get that. I've been lied to my whole life. Trust is earned, not given," I say, glancing up at him.

"What made you come here? You're not a naïve girl. Maybe a little too ambitious at times, but I see where you get that now." He warmly smiles.

I'm not sure I'm ready for him to start picking traits that I got from him. It's a little too early so I ignore that comment.

"I knew my mom's killer was never caught. I'm the one who gave the police the license plate numbers so I found out that it belonged to you. After I grad—" I stop midsentence. I don't want to tell him my life. I might not ever be ready for that. "After I had some free time, I decided I'd come check you out."

He doesn't question why I stopped but asks, "And what did you expect to do if I was the one who killed your mom?"

"I saw the face of the killer. I knew it wasn't you. I thought maybe one of your guys had done it. I was going to see if I could get a look at your men and then go to the police if I saw him," I explain. Coming out of my mouth, it even sounds juvenile. "*I don't know.* I wanted to do something. My mom was dead and her killer never paid for what he did." I sigh.

"Oh. He. Did," Travis says with coldness in his voice.

"So you say," I respond. I'm glad the asshole got what he deserved, but I plan on going into law enforcement. I know the rules and vigilante justice is frowned upon.

"I'd like to have a chance to get to know you," he says cautiously, twisting his lips, warmth entering his eyes again.

"What if I told you I wanted to leave?" I ask.

"I already let your mom go and she was murdered because of me."

"But no one knows about me," I quickly reply.

"*I* don't know that," he says in frustration. He gets up and paces the room. "I don't know what to do. I find out that I have a daughter. I've missed twenty-three years of your life already. I want to know everything about you."

"So you want to keep me prisoner?" I stand up in protest. "How noble of you to make sure I stay safe. If you keep me here, I'll be in more danger than I am out there where no one knows about me. People will start to ask questions why I'm here. *My people* will question where I am."

"I'm not going to keep you *locked up in the this room*. I want you to stay with me. When you leave the house, I'll know you're safe because you'll have a bodyguard."

Here is my out. My way to escape. I'm going to have to agree so I'll be able to leave this room. "Can I think about it?" I try to sound defeated.

"Of course." He walks over to me and I think he's going to give me a hug but instead stops short. "I really hope you can learn to trust me."

Travis turns to walk out, locking the door after him. For now I'm still a prisoner. I really don't think he's going to give me a choice. I understand how he might feel after losing my mom, but this life is not mine. It's not part of *my* plan. My plan is to take guys like Travis Stein down, not have him as a father. And though we share the same DNA, I don't have to acknowledge him as my father. I can leave here without so much as a glance and never regret that decision.

My mind switches to Jett. I might not ever regret leaving here, but I will regret what I have to do to leave. I have to use Jett. I have to remember he's a means to an end. And hopefully that end is tomorrow.

Chapter Twenty
JETT

"EMILY WILL BE staying here indefinitely," Travis tells me as we are having our daily meeting.

"*And* she's okay with that? Because I'm pretty sure she wouldn't agree to that." I stand up. This can't be happening. "You may do a lot of shit, but since when did you think keeping a prisoner was a good idea?" I'm pacing again. Shit. I'll never get my job done if she's here.

"Jett..." his voice is laced with warning "...don't question me."

"Travis, I've backed off, letting you do what you feel you need to do, but this is a little fucked up, even for you." I fall into the chair and slump down. I need to figure out his game here. This isn't like him.

"I thought this would make you happy?" He smirks. "You seem to have taken a liking to Emily. I can't fault you. She's a beautiful girl. Reminds me of someone." He chuckles. I feel like I'm looking at an imposter. Travis doesn't laugh.

"Fuck, Travis. I don't deny that she's beautiful." The most beautiful woman I've ever known. "But I feel like I'm taking advantage of her since I'm sure she's out of her mind being held prisoner. *We* are not happening."

"She's not afraid. She's a tough girl. If she didn't want you, I'm sure you'd know it. I'd tell you to ask Joe about how that feels, but you won't get that chance." My eyebrow shoots up glancing at Travis. "Joe took a business trip to New York."

"I don't want to know," I respond, shaking my head. I'm a little surprised I didn't kill him myself. Thinking about him throwing himself on Emily has my blood boiling. When Emily joked that she could have taken care of herself, I almost believed her.

"Emily will be able to leave her room, but she will not be able to leave the property. I need you to make sure of that. You are head of security and I trust that you'll see to it."

My day keeps getting better and better.

"Yes, sir." I stand up to leave.

"Jett… just don't get her pregnant. It complicates things." He laughs as my mouth hangs open.

"Okay, *Dad*…?" I feel like an adolescent right now. I'm sure my dad said the same thing to me when I had my first girlfriend in high school. He laughs harder at my response. "Holy shit, Travis, I don't know what the hell is going on but we *do not* need to have the birds and the bees discussion." I turn around and walk out shaking my head.

Emily can't stay. She doesn't belong here, and I know *she* doesn't want to stay here. The longer she's here, the more complicated things get. She's a distraction that I can't have right now. I need to make some phone calls. She'll have her freedom soon. Now I need to figure out a plan so Travis doesn't suspect me of anything.

* * *

I've looked in on Emily throughout the day on my monitor. She's still locked in her room. I thought Travis said she was going to be able to leave. I need that to happen to get my plan in place.

Our last night together. I should make it easy on both of us and stay away, but I can't. I can't stop thinking of her. I'm a selfish man. I want her for myself tonight, knowing that after tomorrow I'll never see her again.

It's almost dinnertime. I pick up the phone to call in an order at a favorite restaurant of mine when someone knocks on my door.

"Jett?"

"Hey, Bill. What's up?"

"Um… Travis said that only you and Melanie are allowed in Emily's room from now on," he nervously tells me.

"Okay?" I'm not sure where he is going with this.

"Well… of course, we've been watching her like normal," he quickly adds, "and she… um… she went into the bathroom over an hour ago and hasn't come out at all. Travis and Melanie went out for the night, so I don't know if we should be concerned."

"Thank you for telling me." I pull up her room on the screen and the bathroom door is shut. She isn't anywhere in the bedroom. "I'll go check on her."

Emily, what are you up to? I know there is a window in the bathroom, but there are bars on it so there isn't a way to escape that way. At least, not that I know of.

Chapter Twenty-one

I'M STARTLED AWAKE. I'm lying in a lukewarm bath. This bathtub is huge, my dream tub. I need to relax and plan my escape. I hold up my hand, looking at my wrinkled fingers. I must have been in here for a while. I'm not sure what woke me up though.

"Emily!" Jett screams my name as he comes barreling in the bathroom. I jump at his entrance. "Oh, shit! Sorry," he says as he quickly turns around, putting his hands in his pockets.

Damn that man is so gorgeous. Especially when he's blushing or wearing his typical black shirt that clings to him perfectly and shows off his broad shoulders and muscular back or those dark jeans that show off his perfect ass. My stomach flutters seeing him standing there and him knowing that I'm naked. Desire tickles deep down to my core. I stand up out of the water. I can see his muscles flex with the increase of his breathing.

"Can you hand me my towel, please?" I breathe out.

He grabs my towel as I step out on the bathmat. He holds it behind his back to hand it to me. "Here." I quietly snicker at his politeness.

"I was hoping you could *help* me dry off?" I say suggestively. I can see him take deep breaths. "Turn around, Jett," I softly command. He slowly turns around.

"Demanding little thing, aren't we?" Jett growls. His eyes slowly rake over my body, drinking me in. When they meet my face, I can see the heat in his eyes, black pupils overtaking the beautiful emerald color. He walks toward me opening the towel. My pulse quickens. He bends down and starts with my feet. Tingles explode in every part of my body. I can feel the heat in my sex, the anticipation of him touching me. He moves at a deliberately slow pace. I need to remind myself to breathe.

When he moves up my thighs, his face is so close I can feel his hot breath on my sex. When he moves the towel in between my legs, his fingers slightly sweep across my folds. I tremble. He groans. "Emily, you are so beautiful."

To my disappointment, he continues his ascent. When he gets to my breast, he cups my breast in his hand, still using the towel. On his knees, he moves the towel so now his large, strong hands are massaging my breasts. He brings his mouth to one and starts sucking, flicking and biting my taut nipple. His mouth is burning hot on my bare skin. I gasp. My hands fist his hair and I arch my back. I can feel the wetness of my arousal, moaning out in pleasure as I get closer. I'm wound so tight, it won't take me long to explode.

"Not yet, sweetheart. *Patience.*" He flashes a devilish grin, continuing his way up my body with the towel. He drops it on the floor when he stands up. I had braided my hair before I got into the tub and pinned it up. I reach up to unpin it and then start to take out my braid.

"Keep it in," he says as he brushes his lips on the corner of my lips. The kiss starts out soft and sweet but quickly turns into a hot and demanding kiss. Our tongues explore, sucking, teasing. He grabs my braid and forces my head back, kissing down the sensitive part of my neck. He lets go of my braid and brings his eyes to mine.

"You are the sexiest woman I've ever laid my eyes on. Do you have any idea what you do to me?" He turns around before I can answer and walks away. "Stay right here," he demands as he walks out of the bathroom.

I'm not fucking going anywhere.

He's only gone a minute before he comes back in. He lifts me up and I wrap my legs around him. With my naked body, I can feel his erection through his jeans. He kisses me again as he guides me into the bedroom. I freeze. "Jett, I'm not into giving shows. Well… to anyone but you." I smirk.

"I'm glad it's only me who you want to put on a show for…" he grins "…but don't worry. I'm head of security, I've got skills."

"Oh, I bet you do," I murmur. "How about you show me some of those skills?" I ask playfully.

"You don't have to ask me twice." He throws me on the bed and is immediately climbing on top of me. His fingers find my sensitive nipples, pulling and twisting, sending an electric current straight to my sex.

I tug on the hem of his shirt. "You're a little overdressed." He stands up and quickly pulls it off with one hand.

Oh. My. God. His chest and stomach are perfectly sculpted. *Definitely in the wrong business.* I sit up and slide down off the bed, getting on my knees. I need to see the rest of him. I unbuckle his belt and undo his pants. I slip my fingers beneath the band of his underwear and brush the top of his dick. He gasps audibly. I slowly take off his pants and boxer briefs together. He kicks them off. I lick my lips as I watch his dick twitch. I look up at him as I slowly run my tongue down his sensitive vein.

He groans, "Sweetheart, that feels awesome. Put your lips around my cock. I want to feel you fuck me with your mouth," he commands. I've never been the type of woman to be dominated, but something about Jett demanding me excites me.

My tongue playfully licks the top of his thickness before I open up and slide his whole cock into my mouth. My tongue rubs his shaft as I suck him hard. I massage his balls with my hands as he lets out a growl. I moan as I continue my assault on his cock, taking it all the way back into my throat before bringing it back out.

"Holy shit. I'm not going to last long if you keep doing that," he growls. I continue, wanting him to lose control. His hands grab my hair. I wrap my hands around to his ass. His perfect, hard ass.

"Em, I'm going to come," he hisses as he tries to pull out, but I grab his ass and push him into my mouth as far as he'll go while leaning against the bed behind me, moaning. He comes undone and I taste the salty liquid shooting down my throat. He pulses as I suck out the remainder of his release.

"Fuck, woman! I thought I was going to show you *my* skills," he says as he pulls me up off the floor. I run my hands up his taut chest to his hair as I kiss his neck. "Sweetheart, you are one sexy woman." He pulls my mouth to his, sucking on my bottom lip before biting it. "It's my turn," he says as he pushes me onto the bed.

I giggle. "You were taking too long. I had to move things along." I smirk.

"Oh, is that right?" he asks, kissing his way down my stomach. "Well, don't plan on me rushing. I want to enjoy every inch of your pussy." His tongue wets my folds as he finds my sensitive clit. I arch my back off the bed, moaning. "Mmm... so responsive." He flicks his tongue against my clit again. "You are so wet. So ready for me."

I moan again. "Only you, Jett. So ready for you." *Did that come out of my mouth?*

"That's right, sweetheart. Only me." He continues the torturous movement of his tongue. Slow and then fast, working his way down in between my folds to fuck me with his tongue. My hips match his movements. "You taste so sweet. So perfect."

"Jett, please," I beg him, needing a release. "More."

"You need to learn to be more patient, sweetheart." He chuckles. "I told you, I want to enjoy every inch of your pussy." His tongue starts back at my clit as he inserts a finger. Moving inside me, pressing against the spot that sends me pulsing. "You're so tight, so fucking hot. My dick is twitching wanting to be buried inside of you."

"Oh, God, Jett," I scream.

His two fingers fuck me as his mouth wraps around my clit, sucking and flicking my clit with his tongue. He groans and the vibration sends me over.

I explode, the heat so intense. "Jett... Jett... oh, God... Jett!" I squeeze my eyes shut and scream. My orgasm pulses around his fingers, soaking him with my release.

Major fucking skills.

"*Mmm...* so good, sweetheart." He kisses up my stomach to my breast and starts sucking and nipping again, his other hand assaulting the other. His path of kisses continues to my neck. My body is already on the edge again. His mouth finds mine, and I welcome his tongue as we kiss deeply. I can taste myself on him, and I moan out. I move my hips, rubbing against his hard dick. I can feel him at my entrance.

"Jett. I need to feel you inside me," I say wantonly. He stands up and grabs his pants, taking out a condom. I lift my eyebrow and smile.

"What?" He flashes his sexy grin. "A man can hope." He mumbles something about the birds and bees but shakes his head and chuckles. I stare up at him, wondering what he was thinking. "Never mind." He laughs, ripping open the wrapper. He has it on within a few seconds. Kneeling in between my legs, he pushes them farther apart. I can feel the cold air where I am dripping wet.

He intertwines our fingers together, pulling them above my head, kissing me softly on my forehead, nose, and then my mouth. His kiss is passionate and slow. Doubt immediately starts to surface. It isn't supposed to be like this. A quick fuck, that's it. A way to extinguish the sexual spark we've had all week. This feels like it's more. Am I promising Jett something that I can't give?

"Emily. Look at me. Where'd you go?" Concerned emerald eyes find mine.

"Jett," I sigh. "If I was to leave tomorrow, would you still want this?" There is a flash in Jett's eyes, not sure if it's fear or surprise, but it changes quickly. He can't know about my plan.

"Sweetheart, don't overthink this. We're enjoying the moment. I want *you* tonight, no matter what happens tomorrow, next week, or next year." His voice is seductive and sexy as hell. Tonight will always be ours. The heat in his eyes burns deep within me. I lose myself in them. I would do anything for this man in this moment. I've never given so much of myself to any one man.

A man I met four days ago.

A man who doesn't even know my name.

A man I'll never see again.

The need to feel him inside me is almost too much to handle. "Show me exactly how you want *me*." I grind my hips again. He squeezes our hands together.

"So impatient," he growls as he thrusts his cock inside of me. We both gasp as he's buried completely. He pauses, allowing me to adjust. I nod as I slowly move my hips. "Fuck, Emily!" His jaw clenches as he puts his forehead on mine. I can see the control slipping from his lust-filled eyes. "Emily, I've wanted to be buried in you the last four days. I don't think I can go slow," he murmurs.

"I'll take whatever you can give, Jett," I breathe out. He ravages my mouth in a heated, demanding kiss as he pulls out and thrusts back in. Over and over. I moan into his mouth. The sensation of him stroking my insides has my body trembling. He sits up on his knees, bringing my legs up against his chest. The change of position has me screaming out. My back arches off the bed as he continues his punishing pace. I grab the headboard, pushing as he thrusts deeper. A low guttural growl escapes his lips.

"Em, you're so beautiful." His eyes linger on my body. "Come for me, baby," he commands as he applies pressure to my sensitive clit. I scream out his name in ecstasy as my climax rips through my body.

Jett's release follows right behind as he grabs my hips,

slamming into me. He yells out my name as his whole body trembles. He falls on top of me, our breathing out of control. Pushing up on his elbows, his gaze is full of emotion. He leans down and brushes a kiss on my lips. My eyes close, relishing the soft touch of his lips. My heart aches that I might not ever feel his lips again. This was a mistake.

A beautiful mistake.

A tear escapes from my closed eyes. I feel his thumb brush it away. "I'm sorry, Em," he whispers.

I open my eyes and look right into those beautiful emerald green eyes. "I'm not." My breath hitches. "Jett, I don't regret *this*. I don't regret *you*. I regret our *ending*." I pull him down to me, bringing his lips to mine. I pour all my emotions into this one kiss. It's soft. It's heated. It's rushed. It's slow. It's love. *Devastating love*. It's goodbye.

He pulls out of me and the feeling of loss shakes me to my core. He takes off the condom and throws it away then climbs back into bed, pulling me into him. "Don't think about the end," he whispers into my ear as he strokes my hair away from my face.

It's all I *can* think about.

Chapter Twenty-two

I WAKE TO Melanie walking in my room. I immediately look to my side, searching for Jett. My heart pounds, afraid that I will find him there. I slowly release the breath that I'd been holding when I find the other side of the bed empty.

I let out a big yawn and stretch. Thoughts of last night come flooding back as I feel the delicious soreness between my legs. Blushing from my thoughts, I glance up to Melanie, hoping she's not watching me. I see that she's brought my favorite chai tea latte. I peek under the covers and I'm surprised to find myself dressed. Jett must have dressed me because I have no recollection of dressing myself. I guess great sex really takes it out of you. I laugh as I get up and walk over to the table.

Melanie watches me as I suck down my drink. I release an appreciated sigh. "This drink," I say as I shake the cup only filled with ice now, "may only take me a few minutes to drink, but for those few minutes everything is right in my life. So, thank you."

Melanie warmly smiles as she places her hand over her heart. "You look so much like her, Emily. She was so beautiful and youthful. She made Travis a better man. I thought for sure if anyone could save Travis, Lana could." I can hear the love in Melanie's voice when she talks about my mom. She sighs, and I know where her thoughts are. Her eyes gloss over as she pulls me in for a hug.

"I'm so sorry, Emily." We share a silent moment before she turns to leave.

When Melanie leaves, my emotional ups and downs from the last twelve hours leave me feeling mentally drained. I curl up in bed. The cool sheets feel refreshing and allow me to relax and drift off to sleep.

I wake not much later to a quiet, *almost* peaceful room. The brightness shines into the room giving a false sense of tranquility, because outside this door is anything but. Sitting up, I glance around the room, taking in a deep breath. Today is the day I try and leave this prison. A small laugh escapes my lips as I think about the oxymoron using the word prison. I'm surrounded by luxury. Throwing my head back on my pillow, I think about the last five days. I thought coming here would give me an idea of who killed my mom. Instead, I find out who my father is, have a whirlwind affair with a bodyguard—a *hot bodyguard*—and, of course, find out the man who did kill my mom is dead. Not bad for a week, I think, as I spontaneously laugh. I'm sure whoever is watching me thinks I'm losing it.

After I shower and quickly dry my hair, loosely wrapping it in a bun, I wonder if my door is still locked. I walk over and reach for the door handle but then hesitate. The anticipation has my heart beating a little faster. Beyond this door is my freedom. Freedom away from Travis. But that also means freedom from Jett. A part of me hopes that the doorknob won't turn, which is the *exact* reason I need to leave here soon. Jett may seem perfect, *but he's the wrong kind of perfect.*

I grab the cold door handle and twist. It turns and I hear the click as I pull it toward me. I blow out the breath I didn't know I was holding and walk into the empty hallway, looking both directions. Not knowing where to go, I hear a door open at one end and Jett comes strolling out. My whole body heats up looking at him. He's wearing low hanging basketball shorts and a black T-shirt.

His eyes run over the length of my body. My body temperature spikes when I see his lust-induced, emerald green eyes sparkle. I get anxious and fidgety. My hands need something to do, so I take out my bun and redo it, like it's in need of fixing.

When he approaches, I shyly say, "Hi." I look up to the ceiling and roll my eyes in embarrassment. *What the hell, Addison.* I sound like a prepubescent teenager. I'm a confident, independent woman and this man makes me feel like I'm sixteen all over again. I clear my throat, straighten my spine, and look into his eyes and try again. "Hey."

Jett laughs and shakes his head as he grabs my hand. "Let's go show you around." Walking down the hallway, we pass door after closed door. We walk in silence, hand in hand. Jett leans over and whispers, "I feel the same." I look at him confused. He smiles his sexy grin, displaying those dimples. "When I saw you standing there looking gorgeous, I had to keep myself back from running to you and taking you back into your room. Emily, I don't know what you're doing to me, but I haven't stopped thinking about you since I left your room last night." He rights himself and continues walking like he said nothing important.

My heart skips a beat, and I sneak a look up to him. He looks down at me and winks. My heart hurts. What started out as a means to justify the end is starting to be a need with no ending. My need has morphed to an insatiable hunger.

Reality hits me. I need to move faster on my plan. As soon as a window of opportunity presents itself, I need to follow through. As much as it'll hurt me to leave Jett, he's a small part in the big picture.

"Where are we going?" My voice comes out high pitched and rushed. *Really, Addison!* I'm all over the place this morning. Jett assesses me with raised eyebrows and twisted lips. I wave him off and steady my voice, ignoring his inquisitive stare.

"So? Where to?" I say as I walk, pulling him with me.

He lets go of my hand and crosses his arms. His stare pins me in my spot. "What's going on in that head of yours, Emily?" He questions like he's interrogating me. His eyes don't miss a thing.

"Nothing, Jett," I say trying to convey confidence. "It feels weird to be out of that room, and then you... after last night... I'm all out of sorts this morning." I sigh.

"We can go sort things out, if you'd like." He moves in quickly, pressing his body against mine as he leans down and kisses me softly on the lips.

I jump back in surprise, caught off guard. "Jett," I warn. "This is so wrong on so many levels. I'm a prisoner in this house. People will think I have Stockholm Syndrome," I say seriously and hold up a hand to stop him from coming closer.

Offering a bemused smile, he answers, "You can always say no, sweetheart. Let's go." He grabs my hand in midair and pulls me into the kitchen. Say no *to that body*? I don't think anyone in their right mind could do that.

Looking around at the beautiful kitchen with picturesque windows facing the patio, I say, "I already ate this morning. Melanie brought some food." Jett grabs some eggs and bacon from the fridge. He's a sight to see cooking in the kitchen. I sit on one of the bar stools and study him as he continues to make breakfast. The muscles in his back flex whenever he moves. I'm appreciating the backside of his body, remembering exactly what that body did to mine last night. A quiet moan escapes my lips.

He slowly turns and the corner of his mouth twitches. "You keep looking at me like you want to eat me," he growls. "I don't care who knows about us, I will throw you on that table and have a feast myself." My whole body trembles, and I clench my thighs together trying to find the friction I'm all of a sudden in need of. I look to the table and I'm not sure I care either. Jett has a devilish glint in his eyes. He walks—or more appropriately stalks—toward me.

I hop out of my chair, grabbing onto the counter. "Jett. You wouldn't," I say, giggling, and try to tame the beast about to attack. He keeps walking around the island toward me. I slide around the other way, keeping hold of the counter like it's going to protect me. His walk increases to a run. I scream and laugh as I keep running around the counter, away from him. We both slow, still opposite of each other, his beautiful emerald green eyes never leaving mine.

I'm trying to gauge his next move in this playful game of cat and mouse. I arch my eyebrows, taunting him a little. "How hungry are you?" I breathe out. He audibly sucks in a breath.

"Woman," he warns, the devilish grin still on his face.

I'm bouncing on my feet trying to predict which way he'll run, but I seem to have misread him. He instantly jumps over the counter and grabs me as I dramatically squeal in surprise. He wraps his hand around my back pulling me into him. Our body's mold to each other. I instantly feel his arousal.

"I'm starving," he says as he bites my earlobe then sucks it into his mouth. He wraps his hands around my hair and tugs, giving him full access to my neck. My lips part and my breath quickens as he alternates biting and sucking. I can feel the slickness of my arousal already. He whispers, "The real question is if I'm going to throw you on the table and feast on that sweet pussy…" I release a sigh, his lips barely hovering over mine "…or do I take you right here, bury my cock in that tight pussy of yours that's begging me to fuck you hard and fast again?" He crushes his lips to mine. He pushes his erection into me. My hands wrap around his hard-muscled arms, trying to hold onto him while he devours me with his kiss.

The sound of someone's voice brings us back to reality. "I hate to interrupt, but I think the bacon is done."

We break apart quickly and look to see Travis standing in the kitchen, displaying a wide grin, chuckling. My face flushes with embarrassment. *Oh, fucking hell!* I whip around, unable to escape Jett's embrace quick enough.

"Um…" I try to think of a reason to get the hell out of the kitchen. Fast. "I forgot to…" Why can't I think of *something*. "Whatever. I just need to go." I throw my hands in the air. I speed walk to my room, shutting myself back into the prison I couldn't wait to get out of. Damn distractions!

* * *

Half an hour later, enough time to calm my racing heartbeat, I hear a knock at the door. I look at the door expecting it to open but it doesn't. Hmm, weird. Then another knock. I guess since I'm not a prisoner *in this room*, I get the luxury of privacy. Novel idea.

I answer the door only to find Jett leaning against the door-jamb. My heartbeat might have calmed down, but the sexual tension between the two of us is anything but calm. Damn, that man is gorgeous. His arms are crossed, which shows off the muscles in his biceps.

I turn around to walk back into the room. I hear the door shut but can tell he is still in the room by the way my body reacts. He fixes his eyes on me. "Jett, we can't do this," I say, turning away from him. I know that if I look at him I won't be able to stop him. I'm about to continue when I feel his hard body right behind me.

He sweeps my hair to the side before he bends down to whisper, "I'm sorry, Emily. I haven't been able to stop thinking about you since the day you showed up in this room, but when I'm in the same room as you, I can't stay away from you. I know this is a bad idea, but fuck, Emily… there's this chemical reaction when we're together that I can't explain. It's melting things inside of me. Things that were frozen. Things that should stay frozen. "

I shake my head. "Why couldn't we have met somewhere, *any-where*, but here?" I turn to face him. "This isn't *my* reality, Jett. I have a life outside these walls, one that I actually like." He lowers his forehead to mine. He breathes out a big sigh.

"Yep," he says in a strangled voice. We stand there for a couple minutes in silence. I immediately feel the loss of his body when he steps back. His jaw clenches with his hardened expression. His hands are fisted into his shorts pockets. I crack my knuckles out of habit; it's something I do when I'm nervous. "So, I was going to go for a run around the property. Would you like to come?" he quietly asks as his expression softens.

"Sure," I say, looking down at my bare feet, "but I'll need to put on my shoes." Maybe exercising will help clear my head.

"I'll meet you in the hallway. I need to grab my gun." I tilt my head and twist my lips. Understanding my confusion, he answers, "Travis doesn't like us leaving the house without our guns. Even if it's still on his property…" he smirks "…you never know when unexpected guests might drop in."

I playfully push him toward the door. "Ha, ha. Cute."

We're outside stretching and Jett tells me that there is a dirt track around the compound. He uses the term *house*, but compound is more realistic. We set our stride, keeping up with each other. I can feel Jett's gaze on me, so I glance up meeting those emerald green eyes. Assessing.

"I'm in the dark here, Emily." He sighs. "I still have no clue why you're here. Travis demands that you stay here, but why?"

I look forward, continuing to keep up with him but remaining quiet. A few minutes pass and I whisper, "I can't tell you." He doesn't press the issue anymore.

We continue our run in silence, only hearing the pounding of each step. My Jett-induced fog lifts with each step I take and clarity rears its ugly head. Reality sets in that Jett has never mentioned helping me leave. He works for Travis. Travis demands I stay. Have I been stupid not to see what's going on? I knew from the beginning Jett was playing me, but he sounds so sincere now. Is he trying to make me fall in love with him so I don't leave?

My pace increases, as does my anger. Jett keeps in step with my pace, glancing at me from time to time. As we make our way around to the side of the house, I realize that we are going to run in front of the house. Right by the bushes where I know what is waiting for me on the other side. My heart pounds. Shaking out my hands to calm my nerves, I glance around to make sure I don't see any other men.

"Want to race?" I say as I run ahead, gaining a small lead.

"Come on, sweetheart, show me what you got," Jett teases, smacking my ass as he passes me. I don't want to catch him, but I want him to think that I am trying. I see the spot. The spot that hopefully will be my way out as much as it was my way in. The hope that Jett doesn't connect the two makes what I'm about to do more crucial to get right the first time.

Five.

Four.

Three.

Two.

It's now or never.

"Shit!" I say as I fall to the ground. My knees hit the ground and I roll. One of my knees is bleeding, but my adrenaline masks any real pain. The fall needs to be believable. Jett comes back running.

"Em, are you okay?" Jett is sincerely worried. He bends down and inspects my knee.

"Shit, it hurts. I think I twisted my ankle." My words come out pained. While he inspects my ankle, I inspect his gun. He's wearing a shoulder strap holster. My stomach twists at what I'm about to do. He stands up and gets ready to lift me off the ground. "Wait, let me see if I can stand first." Instead, he grabs my already waiting hand and pulls me up.

I use the momentum as I swing my knee into his groin area.

As he drops screaming in pain, I swiftly grab his gun on his way down. "FUCCCKKK! What the hell, Emily!" Jett's words grate through his clenched teeth. He looks up at me but stares into the barrel of a gun. His gun. "Emily, put the gun down," he demands, trying to stand up. "You're going to hurt yourself." I smirk, internally laughing. I know my time is limited before Travis's other guys come running. I'm sure they have been watching. We're far enough away from the house that I will still have a two-minute head start before they can make it to me.

Jett must see what's about to happen. My hands grip the gun as blood runs down my leg. There is no other way. My heart aches, knowing what's about to happen. It hasn't had time to catch up with my head. *I'll never forget you, Jett.*

"Emily, don't!" Jett's voice rises and his words are rushed, "Tonight I'm—"

I don't wait for him to finish. Anything he says is only trying to keep me here. I pull the trigger. Jett lets out a grunt and falls to the ground. I spin around and run, holding onto the gun. I don't look back in fear of seeing what I did. I don't have time for regret or apologies. Right before climbing over the fence, I hear Jett scream, "I can't believe you fucking shot me!"

The adrenaline flowing through my body has me running faster than ever before. I run to my car, assuming it's still there.

Oh, Shit! What if it's not?

Chapter Twenty-three

MY HAND SHAKES as I unlock my door. I let out a huge sigh of relief as I drive away in the opposite direction. Looking through my rearview mirror, I keep expecting someone to be following me but no one is. I drive an hour before I'm sure and pull over at a rest stop. Letting my head fall back in my seat, I let out a loud scream that I'd been holding on to since I left. I beat my hands on the steering wheel as I break into an uncontrollable sob. My mind is racing, trying to decipher the tears. Anger. Relief. Remorse. Heartbreak. It can be any one of them or all of them combined.

My cell phone is dead, so I plug it in and wait for the Apple logo to pop up. A flow of dings lets me know I've been missed. I'm not surprised to see over fifty texts and numerous missed calls. Most are from Sydney. I thought I had my emotions under control before making the call, but when I hear Syd's voice the dam breaks.

"Addison?" Syd asks when all I can do is sniffle. "Addie, you need to let me know this is you."

"It's... me," I stutter as I press my hand to my chest, trying to stop the ache.

"Oh, my God, Addie. It's been five days since you last called. I've been freaking out. I was so close to calling the police and coming to look for you myself. Please tell me that you're okay."

Okay? Not even close. I struggle to speak, trying to find the right words. How do I explain my last five days? Chewing on my cheek, fighting the sobs wanting to escape, I scream out, "*Fuuuuckkkkk*!" That's all I've got.

"Well… based on the fact that you're not telling me to call the cops, I'm thinking you are not in danger. Which is a good thing, because we both know how great of a fighter I am. We'd probably both end up dead." She giggles and it makes me smile. It's just like her to try and lighten the mood. My silence is her affirmation that something is definitely wrong. "Seriously, though. Addie, come home. Do you need me to come get you?" She would in a heart-beat. She's been my rock since I was ten. Someday, I'll be hers, maybe when *fate* stops hating me.

I breathe out a long sigh. "No, I'll be okay. As much as I need you right now, maybe the drive will be good for me to fig-ure out what the hell just happened. It's complicated. So fuck-ing complicated, Syd. But I'm safe. I'll tell you everything when I get home." My emotions have turned off. They've been shocked into submission.

"Addie, I love you. Please text me at every stop you make," she pleads.

"I will. I'll probably stop for the night and be home tomorrow. Love you, too, Sydney."

* * *

I collapse on the bed of my hotel room. I'm exhausted. I stopped again in Mt. Vernon, at the same hotel I stayed at five days ago. It's familiar and as hard as I tried to drive farther today, I just couldn't. My thoughts are mangled together and no longer make sense. I need a reset button. My thoughts turn to dreams as I drift off to sleep.

I startle awake, dreaming about Jett. One minute we're mak-ing love, the next I'm shooting and killing him. It's close to reality, but I know I didn't kill him. It takes a few minutes to calm my raging heartbeat. Regret forges its way in my head, which pisses me off because *I* was the one being held captive. I shouldn't feel bad for doing what I had to do to escape.

The room is dark but I can see the sun slicing through the middle of the drapes, its rays illuminating the dust particles floating in the air. I roll over and grab my phone to see what time it is. My stomach growls reminding me its dinnertime. Leaving the hotel sounds tiring. Take out, it is. I open the drapes and the sun bursts through, warming me up. I look down at the traffic. People are just now getting out of work, heading home. Simple life. I long for the simple life.

Twenty minutes later, there's a knock on the door. Relief that my food is here turns to surprise as I answer my door. My eyes widen as I do a double take.

"Hello, beautiful." Marco smiles. He's holding a bag of food. I can smell it from here. It smells delicious. My stomach growls again, telling me to hurry the hell up and let the man in. I'm holding the door half open, still shocked to see him standing there. Remembering I just got out of bed, I run my fingers through my hair, making a quick brush through.

"Marco," I say, stalling for a moment, "This is... a surprise. How did you know I was here?" I furrow my brow as I tilt my head. After the week I had, my bullshit meter is at capacity.

"Oh. I'm sorry." He looks to the floor before looking back to me. "The hotel manager and I are friends. After you left on Monday, well... you know guys, we talk." He sports a Cheshire Cat grin. "He noticed you were staying again so he called to tell me. I was hoping you'd come to my restaurant." His lips twist. "He texted me when you called down to the front office for takeout. I decided to try my luck and bring you your food instead." He lifts up the bag in his hand.

Okay, I know there has to be some laws broken in that conversation. This is the last thing I need. I let out a huge sigh. "I'm sorry, Marco. I don't want to be rude, but I've had a week from hell and I won't be very good company right now."

"I make a good listener," he says.

I can't believe I'm considering letting him in. Marco was very easy to talk to on Monday. Maybe some company will be good for me. Take my mind off of Jett and Travis.

"Okay." Marco's eyes shine as he smiles bright. "But no more calling me beautiful. The flirting that happened on Monday won't happen tonight. If you come in here, it's just to talk as friends. Also, since you *guys* talk, I'm sure you know my name already." I tilt my head as I quirk an eyebrow.

"*Addison.*" He smirks. "Only friends. I promise." I open the door wide and he walks into the room. I chuckle and shake my head closing the door. He sets out dinner on the coffee table. It smells divine, but I immediately think about Jett and our Italian dinner. Marco takes a bottle of wine out of a bag, accompanied by two wine glasses and holds them in the air, giving me a questioning look.

Sitting on the couch, I nod. I could drink a few of those. Bottles, that is. He makes me a plate with a little of everything on it. I sit on the floor and scoot to the table. The wine placed in front of me is drained in one gulp.

"That bad, huh?" He glances at me, filling my glass again. "So, it seems it did not go as you planned."

Rolling my eyes, I say, "That's the understatement of the year. And yes, it's that bad."

I bring a fork full of ziti to my mouth, not wanting to talk about my week. I can't even tell if the food is good because my thoughts have consumed my entire body. I'm eating purely on autopilot. I eat only enough to make my stomach happy.

"I'll try not to be offended that you're not eating my food." Marco smirks, eyeing my uneaten plate of food.

"I'm sorry. I'm sure the food is wonderful, I'm just not that hungry." I sigh.

Marco attempts to make small talk, but I can't bring myself to *want* to talk. All I'd like to do is go to sleep. Wake up to a new day. It probably won't be a better day, but it'll be new.

"Marco, thanks for the food and trying to make me feel better, but I think I need to call it a night," I say, standing up and throwing away our plates.

"Addison, I'm sorry for just dropping by," he says, bagging the uneaten food. When he's done he stands in front of me, lifting my chin so we're looking into each other's eyes. "If you ever need anything, let me know. I may be from a small town, but I know lots of people." He winks before turning to walk out the door.

What?

He knows people? Who says that?

I laugh, thinking I probably just had dinner with the head of the Italian mafia. I laugh even harder at the absurdity of that idea. I've had too long of a week. I don't even bother closing the curtains before passing out on the bed.

Chapter Twenty-four

SYDNEY THROWS HERSELF on my bed, adding a lot of drama flair to her fall. "I can't believe it's that time already."

"We've spent almost the entire month together since I got back from Chicago. I can't believe you're not pushing me out the door," I say, plopping down next to her.

She rolls to her side and looks up at me. "Are you sure you're okay? You know… about the Travis and Jett thing?"

I twist my lips and slowly nod. "I don't have much of a choice. I'm not going to ever acknowledge that Travis is my father, and Jett… Well, there's nothing to say about that. It wasn't ever meant to be." I shrug. She sits up and hugs me.

"Okay, we're done being sad. Let's go party." Syd jumps up, grabbing my hand and pulling me up with her. Aunt Amy and Uncle Ted are throwing me a *NYC or Bust* party.

Excitement bubbles through me and I squeal, which surprises even myself because I'm not usually a squealer. After a few rough weeks of dealing with what happened in Chicago, I've put it all behind me and now I'm ready to move on. At least that is what I keep telling myself. I left there unscathed, maybe a little broken-hearted and really confused about Travis, but physically I wasn't hurt. And I'm thankful for that. I do find myself looking over my shoulder a little more often. I can't do anything about it if Travis finds me, so I'll deal with it if or when that happens.

Dressed in my favorite denim cutoffs, black New York City tank that I bought last summer, and boots, I walk into my aunt's backyard. She and Ted moved to a small town between Austin and San Antonio when I went to college. She wanted to still be close to me but away from the big city. They have a beautiful house on a ranch in the country. Ted retired from the force shortly after I came home from the hospital a few months ago, so now they spend their time fixing up their house and land.

Twinkling lights hang across her backyard, the warm breeze gently swaying them. It looks like hundreds of stars dancing to the music of the band. I notice some friends from college two-stepping on a dance floor right in front of the stage.

"Addison!" Amy yells from across the lawn when she sees me, motioning me to come over.

"Amy, the backyard looks amazing. You really didn't need to do this much," I say, giving her a hug. I pull back and continue looking around. "I can't believe how beautiful everything looks. It's almost magical."

"Addie, I would do anything for you. You have given me so much." She reaches out to grasp my arms. Her eyes gloss over.

"Amy, stop," I say, my voice cracking with emotion. "You're the one who took in a child and raised her like your own. You gave up so much for me. I can't..."

"I didn't give up anything, Addie. Please, don't ever think that," she says, shaking her head. "Your mom gave me what I couldn't have, and I have never regretted taking you in."

We embrace in another hug; it's tight and emotional. Focusing on the glittering lights, I make a wish that someday I'll find a way to show Amy how much I love her and how much I appreciate everything she's done for me.

"You guys are making me cry! I love you both. You're like

Reese's Peanut Butter Cups: they always come as a pair and you can't have just one so you equally love both." Syd grabs both of us, joining in on our hug. We laugh at her. She's a nutcase sometimes. "But I thought this wasn't a goodbye party."

Amy wipes her tears away and smiles. "It's not. You girls go have fun."

Syd grabs my hand and pulls me to the dance floor. The band plays a fast song, so we start to swing dance. We both try and turn at the same time, causing us to die laughing as we untangle ourselves.

"You're supposed to be the man and lead *me*," Syd cries out between laughs. My cheeks hurt from laughing so hard.

"I *have* to be the man. If you were, you'd chop my head off," I say trying to catch my breath and massage my cheeks so they stop hurting.

"How about you dance with a real man?" A familiar voice startles me from behind. I whirl around to see Frankie, a huge smile plastered on his face.

"Frankie! You're here!" I'm surprised to see him. Mainly because, well... he's Frankie. And how in the world did Amy know how to get in touch with him? He wraps his arms around me, picking me up and swinging me in a circle.

"Your cool aunt invited me. Howard found me and told me about the party. I couldn't miss my chance to say goodbye to my hot guardian angel," he says, winking at me.

I can feel the warmth creep up to my cheeks. "Well, I'm glad you came. So, are we gonna dance or what?" I say, grabbing his hands. He smoothly glides me across the dance floor, twirling me all around. Feeling dizzy, I grab onto Frankie's shoulder to steady myself. "Whoa. Let's two-step for a bit," I say, giggling. "Obviously, your leg is doing better." I catch Ted's gaze fixated on us as we pass him. I laugh and roll my eyes knowing this is killing him that I'm dancing with Frankie. He's fully aware who Frankie is, which is why I'm even more surprised Amy was able to invite him.

"Sure is, Add Cat. A little gunshot ain't gonna keep me down, sweetheart." I *know* that Frankie is the one talking, but when he says that, it's Jett's voice that I hear. I shake my head, squeezing my eyes shut. Holy shit, I'm not even drinking yet. "Addison?" Frankie stops dancing.

I open my eyes to a concerned Frankie. "Sorry. I think I spun around a little too much. My head is still spinning." Thankfully the song ends and we walk off the dance floor.

"Well, Add Cat, I'm going to take off. I just wanted to be able to tell you goodbye. I'll miss seeing you at the DC," he says, jutting his chin out. I furrow my brows together.

"DC?"

"District courthouse," he says slowly like I'm supposed to know.

"Oh. Right. I'm so behind on my street lingo." I laugh. He pulls me in for a quick hug. "Thanks for coming, Frankie. I'm sure I'll see you again. Just stay out of trouble between now and then," I say, squeezing his muscled bicep.

"Only for you, Add Cat." He smiles his panty-dropping smile and winks before turning to walk away. I stand there admiring his backside. He is one gorgeous man. I feel something cold touch my arm, snapping me out of my gaze.

"He's like Dwayne Johnson hot," Syd says, fanning herself after handing me a Corona. I slowly nod, bringing the cold drink to my lips. We both watch as he gives my aunt a hug and leaves. "It's a shame that he's a bad boy."

"A damn shame," I breathe out.

The rest of the night is spent laughing, dancing, and reminiscing with all my friends and family. Syd and I even get up and sing with the band a couple times. There is nothing that could have made this night better. As the night ends, I get emotional telling everyone goodbye. After all I've been through in my life, the love that I feel from these people makes me believe that the good in this world far outweighs the bad. I wish my mom was here with me, but I know that she's watching over me with a smile.

"She'd be so proud of you," Amy says, reading my mind as she wraps her arms around my waist. We both stare up at the twinkling stars in the pitch-black sky.

"She'd be proud of you, too," I say, giving her a kiss on the cheek.

"When do y'all leave?"

"Monday morning." Syd is helping me move my stuff to New York in Jeff's SUV, and then he's flying there in a week to drive back with her.

"I have to give you something so don't let me forget tomorrow before you leave," she says quietly still staring at the stars.

"Amy..." I hesitate. "Is everything okay?"

"Oh, yes, sweetie. I didn't mean to worry you. It's nothing bad." She reassures me, slightly brushing my cheek with her hand. "Go, finish saying your goodbyes. I need to clean up a little."

* * *

"Mmm... I'm going to miss your cooking," I mumble with biscuits and gravy in my mouth. Amy laughs. I can't cook worth a darn. I seriously burn water. Amy tried to teach me numerous times but finally gave up.

Thank goodness Syd is a great cook. Although, I'm not quite sure what I'm going to do in New York. I've never lived without a personal chef.

Amy takes a seat at the table, watching me eat. "I'm really going to miss you, Addie," she says, smiling.

"Me, too. But this gives you a reason to come to New York City," I say, grabbing her hand. "There is so much I want you to see there so don't wait too long."

"I won't, sweetie. I'd love to come out. Maybe for Christmas?

I'd love to see New York City then. Or Thanksgiving… for the Macy's parade. Or New Year's Eve," she says excitedly.

"*Probably* not all in one year. You'd hate New York by then, but we'll do them all."

I finish eating my food and push off the table to stand up. Amy grabs my hand, stopping me. "Wait, you sit. I need to give you something. I'll be right back." She picks up my plate and drops it off in the sink on her way out of the kitchen. I think back to the day I thought she was giving me a car. I shake my head.

Boy, did I have that wrong.

The scraping of the chair pulls me from my thoughts as Amy sits down across from me. She's smiling a genuine smile. I breathe a sigh of relief; my memory made me wonder if this was bad news again.

Amy fidgets with a manila envelope that she has laid on the table. I sense that she's nervous but whatever it is it's not bad. I tilt my head, lifting an eyebrow, waiting for her to start.

"Addie. Don't be mad." She laughs, taking a pause. She flicks up the corner of the envelope. The noise distracts me so I look from her hands to her face, back to her hands. Waiting.

"Spit it out, Amy," I say, tapping my hand on the table.

"Okay, okay. When your mom died, her insurance policy left you a trust." I nod, already knowing this because I received it on my eighteenth birthday. "You only received the first part."

"I don't understand." I furrow my brows.

She slides me the envelope. Now it's my turn to toy with the envelope. I look at the envelope and then to Amy. I don't know what I'm waiting for, but I'm nervous as hell. I close my eyes and take a deep breath.

When I was eighteen I received two hundred thousand dollars, which I still have over half that left. That is what I'm using to find a place in New York City. I also received a letter from my mom that she had written to me when she set up the trust. I had to stop taking it out and reading it so often because the paper was starting to thin and rip at the folds. After that, I laminated it to make sure it wouldn't get ruined. The letter was the most important thing, much more than the money.

My breathing picks up. "Is there a letter?" My voice cracks as anticipation takes over my senses.

"Open it, sweetie," she whispers.

I'm afraid.

I'm afraid there won't be a letter.

I'm afraid there is.

This might be my last lifeline to my mother. I drop my head on the envelope still laying on the table, stretching out my arms and setting my palms down flat on the table. I slightly tap the table, trying to calm myself.

This is ridiculous, Addison. Open the damn envelope.

After a few minutes, I sit up straight and pick up the envelope. Slowly, I pull together the gold brads and slip open the flap. I hear the locusts buzzing outside the window. I think they're all chanting for me to hurry the hell up. I look up to my aunt, her mouth curving into a smile. I pull out the contents of the envelope.

My heartbeat races as I look through the papers. I'm looking for one thing and one thing only. Tears well up as I see what I'm looking for. A small envelope with my name written on the outside. In her writing.

Mom.

I drop the rest of the papers and hug the envelope against my chest. I squeeze my eyes shut, forcing tears to escape down my cheek. Hearing Amy stand up, I open my eyes.

"I'll give you some privacy to open your letter," she says, wiping away tears that have stained her cheek. I exhale loudly.

"Please stay," I say, grabbing the hand she placed on my shoulder. "I want to open it later. Stay with me while I look at the rest of this?" I ask, peering up to her.

She smiles and sits back down. I gingerly place the letter back on the table, running my finger over my name. Warmness spreads through my body knowing her hand touched the pen that wrote that. I swipe my tears away, ready to see what else was in the envelope.

Glancing through the papers, I have to read through the legal jargon to get to the important stuff. When I find what it is I'm supposed to see, my eyes almost pop out of my head. My head snaps to Amy. "Eight hundred thousand dollars?" I say in disbelief. She gives me a lopsided grin.

"Keep reading."

I look back down, scanning the document. It seems my mom had a million-dollar trust set up for me if she ever died. It explains the amount I received on my eighteenth birthday and how the rest would be given to me at either my college graduation or my twenty-fifth birthday, whichever occurred first. I keep reading, wondering what my aunt was referring to. I flip the pages until I'm done reading the trust. There's one paper left that wasn't attached to the rest.

It's a statement. My eyes roam the page until it spots a number.

"HOLY SHIT!" I scream, jumping out of my chair almost knocking it over. My hands are shaking as I look to my aunt. She's beaming. "Is this right?" She nods. "What the hell am I going to do with this much money?" I say, shaking the statement in the air. She laughs.

"Well, New York *is* kinda expensive."

"Not *that* expensive." I keep reading the total, thinking I misread it. But it hasn't changed. "Why is it so much?"

"Well, it's been in a financial investment account for thirteen years, untouched." She shrugs.

"I don't even know what to say." A flush of adrenaline tingles through my body just thinking that I'm a millionaire.

"Now you can do whatever you want." Amy stands up and walks over to me, pulling me in for a hug.

"Huh. I am doing what I want. I love forensics and can't imagine doing anything different," I say. "This money isn't going to change my mind. But... maybe now I can buy a really cool apartment in the city." Excitement races through me just thinking about it.

Syd and I looked at so many places online for me to live. I found an apartment, not too far from work, but it's a room. Literally. Like one whole room and each wall has a different part of a whole house. Kitchen on one wall, bed on another, and couch on the other. Thank God I'm not claustrophobic. We laughed at how our tree house growing up was bigger than my apartment. I sigh. Thank God I only signed a three-month lease. I wanted to make sure I like the area before committing to a year lease.

"You can do whatever you want. You deserve it," Amy says, leaning over and kissing me on the cheek.

* * *

"Oh, my God!" Sydney screeches. "My best friend is a million-aire." She wiggles in her seat. We're on our way to New York, and I just got done telling her everything that happened yesterday.

"Whatever," I say, rolling my eyes.

"What are you going to do with all the money?"

"Well, first thing I'm going to do is pay off Ted and Amy's mortgage. For all she has done for me it's the least I can do." My face beams knowing I can do that.

"You know what she'll say about that, right?"

"That's why I'm going to do it without her knowing. I'll talk with my financial advisor and have him get all their information; he'll write a check directly to the bank." I smile mischievously.

"Sneaky." She narrows her eyes and laughs. "Okay, then what?"

"*Hmm.* I'm going to keep my job. Of course, you probably already know that." She nods her head, staring ahead, driving. She knows how much I love what I'm doing. "I'm thinking I want a better apartment where I can actually walk into different rooms. Oh, and not be able to see my kitchen when I pee." We both giggle. "So I'm hoping you'll come back in a couple months and help me move again," I say in a questioning tone. Her lips twist, and I can tell she's calculating when that will be. Being a teacher, things have to be planned around holidays. I already know this, so I add, "It'll be Thanksgiving. I'll fly you and Amy out together. We'll have so much fun."

"I don't even know why you ask. You know I'll be there."

Chapter Twenty-five

A year later

"HI, ADDISON. WHAT can I help you with?" asks Cheryl as I walk up to her desk.

"Hi, Cheryl. I need to drop off these case files to Damon. He's expecting them on the Reeves's case," I reply.

Cheryl, the executive assistant of the New York FBI office, is the first person everyone sees when walking into the office. She's beautiful and one of the sweetest people I've ever met. We have become friends over the past year and have gone to happy hour a few times.

"How about I let you pass them off to him..." I wink at her "...it'll give you a reason to go talk to him," I say in a whisper. She blushes with just the mention of Damon. I keep trying to get her to make a move, but she's too shy.

I look past Cheryl's desk to admire the group of agents talking. I don't know what it is about the male agents in this office, but I think the job requirements state that you have to be tall and gorgeous. Dave, the tallest of them, had asked me to go on a date when I first started. My heart, unfortunately, hadn't healed yet. I think I bruised his ego. He didn't talk to me for a couple months. *Typical male.* An unfamiliar agent standing next to Dave catches my attention. He's not looking in my direction. I can only see his back side. His stance exudes confidence. The wide span of his back to his thin waist, muscular arms, and his perfect ass, that man has the perfect body. He lets out a boisterous laugh, clapping Dave on the back and then he turns around. I gasp, slapping my hand to my mouth.

What. The. Hell.

Jett?

There is no way that could be Jett. I saw him on TV, getting arrested with Travis Stein, my father, a month ago. Oh, shit! He's looking over here. I duck down in front of Cheryl's desk.

"Addison... um, is everything alright?" Cheryl leans over her desk, looking down at me.

"Yes. I thought I dropped something out of my purse. Hey, I just remembered I have an appointment so I have to get out of here. Can you make sure Damon gets those files?"

She nods. "Are you sure you're okay?"

I'm *sure* I look like a total idiot, not wanting to stand. Good thing there's a partition right behind Cheryl's desk. Hopefully he didn't see me.

"Yes, I'm good. Thanks for your help, Cheryl. Lets do girls' night soon," I quickly reply as I rush out the door. I hold my hand to my heart; it's beating too fast. It hasn't been this alive in a year.

Since our office works really close with the FBI office, I know every agent there. Well, I know all but one, but he's always been out in the field. Oh. Shit. Agent Aiden Roberts. I never met him because he was on assignment when I started at the forensics office. It can't be. Can it? Is Jett Agent Aiden Roberts? I practically run out of the FBI building and just start walking.

Oh, Fuck!

I shot an FBI agent.

On purpose.

This cannot be happening. I never thought I'd ever see him

again. I slept with the guy then shot him. Okay, so I grazed him with a bullet, but still… I'm sure he didn't appreciate it. And now I know he is an FBI agent.

Shit. Shit. Shit.

Addison, pull yourself together. Obviously, I'm not going to quit my job so we'll eventually run into each other. This means only one thing: I need to go see him. Get this whole thing under control before it spirals into a huge mess.

Our night together has been one night I have never forgotten. He was perfect in every way, except he worked for the wrong man. My father. He probably wouldn't even remember me, but I'm sure he has that nice scar to remind him everyday. Not exactly the way I want to be remembered. What will he do when he sees me? He has to know why I did what I did.

When I get back to my office, I fall back into my chair. Harper comes walking over to me. "Addison, you're back already." The surprise is evident in her voice. I usually take my time catching up with the guys whenever I get the chance to get over there.

"Yeah, the guys were in a meeting so I dropped the files off with Cheryl," I lie. "Hey, you want to get a drink after work today?" I desperately need a drink. Maybe it will help calm my nerves.

"Definitely!" Harper replies. "Hey, did you see Agent Roberts? I hear he's back. He is one of the hottest men alive. A huge playboy though."

"Nope, I didn't see anyone I haven't seen before." It's the truth, but I secretly agree, he is gorgeous. Hmm… a playboy, huh?

"That's too bad. Don't worry, you will. You can't miss him. He is beautiful. It's a little unfair to the rest of the men in the world. Every woman takes notice when he walks into a room. Maybe your picky self will approve." She laughs. She seems to think I am too selective. No, not picky, just hung up on the wrong guy. Wait… well, actually it's the guy she's talking about. What the hell am I going to do?

A few hours pass quickly, not that I get much work done. That's it. I'm going to his office tomorrow. Get this out in the open and out of the way. That way there will be no surprise encounters. It'll be better for both of us. I really hope Travis never said anything to him about me being his daughter. That might cause some problems. I lean my head back against my chair, rubbing my temples. The department knows about my mom and my aunt, but they have no idea about Travis. I let out a deep breath. There's nothing I can do about it right now. I'll just have to see how this plays out.

Harper interrupts my thoughts. "Addison, let's go get our drink on. Find you a man." Harper thinks it's her life mission to find a guy for me. Finding a man is the last thing I want to do tonight. I already found one today that I'm not sure what to do with.

I grab my purse. "Let's go. O'Malley's?"

Chapter Twenty-Six

AIDEN

"DAMON, ADDISON DROPPED these files off for you. Said you were expecting them." Cheryl hands over a few files to Damon while he's sitting in my office.

"When was Addison here?"

"She dropped them by about fifteen minutes ago, but she had to go suddenly. Acted really weird. I told her I would make sure you got the files," Cheryl replies.

"Thanks, Cheryl."

"What's up with you and Cheryl?" I ask Damon when she leaves. She had that *look* in her eyes when talking to him.

"Nothing. Not sure I want to go there with someone I work with at the office. She is hot, though, if you like shy girls." He shrugs. "It's too bad Addison left. You need to meet this girl. She is gorgeous. Legs that go on forever, beautiful blue eyes, blonde hair, curves in all the right places but a rock solid body. She can kick my ass, so I'm a little scared of her." Damon laughs. "She would be perfect for you. She works over in the forensics crime lab for NYPD. She's been working there for almost a year."

I narrow my eyes. Since I've been back, he's taken on the role of matchmaker. I'm just not interested. Well, except for one. I sigh. I wonder if she thinks about me as much as I do her. It sucks that I didn't find out her real name.

I still can't believe she fucked me and then shot me. Damn, I don't think I've ever had that hot of sex before and then was even more turned on when she shot me. The way she handled that gun was impressive. And her body was amazing. The girl that Damon is talking about has nothing on Emily. *Shit... whatever her name is.* I just need to forget about her.

"If she's so hot, why haven't any of you guys tried to pick her up?" If she's seriously as hot as he says, I'm surprised the guys haven't eaten her up.

"We've tried. Well, I haven't... Like I said, she scares me a bit. I like my girls not so independent. When she first started, the guys drew straws to see who was going to get to ask her out. I swear the first time she walked into the office, the entire group yelled dibs. You'd think we were all fucking horny teenagers. Dave drew the long straw, lucky bastard, but when he finally asked her out, she said no. I don't think I've ever known a woman to turn down Dave. After that, everyone was afraid to ask her out."

"I like my women willing. Not sure she sounds like my type." No one seems to be my type lately. Someone seems to have broken me.

"Willing to what? Shoot you?" He smirks. "Aiden, you need to forget her. Move the fuck on. There are millions of women out there. Beautiful women."

Could you tell my dick that, because he seems to be on a hiatus? And the messed-up part is I'm not too upset about it. But, I definitely need to forget about her.

Damon knows what happened between Emily and me. He knows she shot me, too, which he had a nice long laugh about. *Fucking asshole.*

I still want to know why she was there. Travis kept that secret to himself. I had to stop bringing her up to him; I was going to get fired before I had all my shit together to take his ass down. He'd get pissed whenever I mentioned her. I told myself that I'd find her after I was back home, but I've been hitting a brick wall every time I find a lead. I need to move on. It was one night. One. Fucking. Night.

Shit. Move on, Roberts. You're never going to see her again.

I am ready to get back to my normal life. "Let's go get a drink after work".

"Definitely. Let's go find you one of those beautiful women," Damon replies, "I'm glad I have my wingman back."

"What the fuck ever. I'll let you believe that tonight though," I say, laughing. "I haven't been to O'Malley's in forever. Let's start there."

Chapter Twenty-seven

HARPER AND I head to my apartment for a quick change. Since I live right in the city, we always use my place to get ready. I slip on my black skinny jeans and a cute, sleeveless white shirt, letting my hair hang down with some loose curls. The brown color in my hair has finally faded. Now it's my natural dark blonde with highlights. I freshen up my makeup with a little mascara and lip gloss and I am ready to go.

"I'm so jealous of you and your body," sighs Harper. "Seriously, I need to work out with you."

"Harper, you're gorgeous. You get attention like no other girl I know, so I don't know what you're complaining about," I reply.

"You're a badass. I want to be like you when I grow up." She laughs. "You're beautiful *and* can kick ass."

"Whatever, gorgeous, let's go," I say as I put on my three-inch black heels. At work we're always in our white lab coats or wearing vests and tennis shoes when we're out in the field. When we go out at night, I like to wear my high heels. Feel a little sexy.

The bar is two blocks from my apartment so it's a quick walk. It's a beautiful night out. I love the city at night with all the lights. I never feel in danger walking around Manhattan, but then again, I usually carry my gun. Tonight I plan on drinking so my gun stays home. O'Malley's is used to its patrons carrying guns since most are NYPD police officers and FBI agents.

My feet stop moving on their own. What if Jett... Aiden is there? I didn't think about that.

"Addison, what's wrong?" Harper says as she stops walking and looks back at me.

"Um... nothing," I say, catching up to her. "Sorry. I was making a mental note about something I need to do later." He probably won't be here. I mean, he's been back for a month and I haven't seen him out yet. Let's hope he doesn't decide that tonight's the night he goes to O'Malley's.

* * *

"Harper... Addison!" Vinnie yells as we walk into O'Malley's. Vinnie is the bartender as well as the owner's son. I have been coming to this bar with Harper for about six months so we have gotten to know him really well. "Get over here, my gorgeous women."

We walk over to the bar, and he leans over giving us each a big hug and a kiss on the cheek. "What's it going to be tonight?" he asks.

"Let's start with a lemon drop," I reply before Harper can answer.

"Whoa, girl... really?" she questions.

I shrug. "Yeah, why not."

"Hmm.... what is up with you today? You have been acting weird ever since you got back from dropping those files off to Damon." She narrows her eyes at me. "You've been in dreamland all day and now you want to start off with shots. That is not like you... at all. Spill it."

"Really, it's nothing. I saw someone today who reminded me of someone from my past. It got me thinking. That's all," I say casually.

"Is the someone a him?" she questions. "Come on, I want juicy details. You get to hear about me all the time. It's time I hear an Addison story." She pouts.

She makes me think of Sydney. Syd is always telling me I'm a closed-off person, that I need to share more. I just don't like to kiss and tell.

"Yes, it's a him and you know I don't like to give juicy details." She pushes out her bottom lip. "Okay... here's a little. He's probably the most gorgeous guy I've ever seen. We had a short fling and some amazing sex but that was it."

"What! Did the asshole leave you? Because if he did, he is the dumbest idiot I've ever heard of. When someone finally gets your attention, they better do everything in their power to keep you," she says as her eyes widen and she puts her hand on her hip.

I laugh at her. "No, he didn't leave me. I had to leave him. I don't want to talk anymore about it. Please?" I sigh.

"Fine." She huffs. "Let's drink to our past and look forward to our future," she says as she lifts her shot.

"I'll drink to that." Smiling, I lift the shot and quickly down it. Although, my future is a little uncertain right now. "Another one, Vinnie." I need to stop thinking about tomorrow.

We drink another shot, and Harper pulls me to the dance floor. It's not a big dance floor, but we make it work. We both love to dance, but Harper demands attention when she dances. When I dance, I don't care who is watching. It doesn't take long before she has the attention of several men. Harper eats it up and dances with more seductive movements. Typical Harper.

We stay on the floor for the next song. I spin around toward the bar, debating if I have enough time to run and get a drink first. The song starts, making my decision for me. I'm getting into the beat when I feel a body behind me. I can tell it's a tall, strong, hard body. He moves fluidly with me, staying with the beat. I feel his hands grab my hips, squeezing them.

He whispers into my ear, "Please tell me I'm not fucking dreaming." Chills break out all over my body.

Aiden.

CHAPTER TWENTY-EIGHT

AIDEN

"WOW, O'MALLEY'S HAS expanded," I say, walking into the bar. The last time I was here, it was a small hole-in-the-wall pub, but now it's much larger.

"Yeah… I guess it happened right after you left. It's been about ten months since O'Malley remodeled. He added a small dance floor and a couple more tables. It's definitely become the place to go after work," Damon replies.

We head to the bar and I see Vinnie. I haven't seen him in forever. He pretty much runs this place. His dad owns it, but Vinnie is the one who does most of the work. The place has been on this corner for over twenty years.

"Vinnie, how the hell have you been?" I ask when he sees us.

"Aiden! What hole did you come out of?" he says, shaking my hand.

"Work. But I'm back for a while. The place looks great. You and your dad are doing well, I see. And the dance floor is a nice addition, especially seeing how it brings free entertainment," I say, looking toward the dance floor. There's a group of women on the dance floor, all being watched by every guy in the place.

"Holy shit, if we would've known that…" he says pointing to

the dance floor "…we would've done that a long time ago." I nod in agreement. "What'll it be tonight?"

Damon and I order our beers. People from NYPD who I haven't seen since I got home come over. It feels good to be back. I missed this place. New York City is my home. It's hard to be away from everything you know and love for two years of your life. I know it's my job, but it doesn't ever get easier. Usually, it's great to get back and forget about the fictitious life I lived, but this time there is still one piece I can't seem to forget. I close my eyes and pinch the bridge of my nose. I *need* to stop thinking about her.

"Vinnie, another shiner!" I yell.

There are lots of women here tonight. I only need one to help me. Help me forget. I haven't had sex since *her*. How can I be so hard up for a woman I knew for five days and slept with once? And then she shot me. What the hell is wrong with me?

"Isn't that Harper from forensics?" I ask, leaning against the bar and point to the dance floor.

"Yep, that's her, and she's with Addison. You can't see her face, but I'm sure that's her. They're usually here together. Not many women have a smoking body like that." He eyes the other woman on the dance floor.

I tilt my head, bringing my beer to my lips, wondering if I do know her. Her body is familiar, but she isn't facing us so I can't be sure. She has long, beautiful, blonde hair and I definitely agree, she does have a body that I wouldn't mind doing things to. Those black jeans make her legs look impossibly longer and her ass is perfect. She's gorgeous from behind. My dick twitches. Holy shit! I actually want to give it a high five, excited that he's not broken.

Damon and I stand there and stare as she dances, swaying those hips. I adjust myself to hide my semi-hard dick. Harper is beautiful, too, but she isn't my type. She likes attention from men and tries a little too hard to get it. I wish Addison would turn around so I could see her face.

I get my wish when the song ends and another one comes on; both women stay on the dance floor. Addison turns and looks my way, but she quickly turns back around.

What the fuck? My eyes go wide and I almost drop my beer. I shake my head. Am I seeing things?

"What's the girl's name who Harper is with?" I ask Damon, not believing my eyes. I know he said Addison, but I need to hear it again. That was definitely *Emily*. I memorized her face. And those eyes… they haunt my dreams every night.

"Addison. Isn't she gorgeous?"

If he only fucking knew.

"What?" asks Damon.

I mumble a curse under my breath. "Her eyes are so fucking blue," I respond quickly.

"Oh, I know. I've never seen eyes that turquoise blue before. They're hard to look away from. I'll introduce you to her when she comes off the dance floor. Right now, I'm enjoying the show too much." He chuckles.

As Damon continues to watch, I look around noticing every guy watching her on the floor. Heat spreads through my body as I make fists. I can't explain it, but all of a sudden I want them to stop watching her. This foreign feeling of jealousy shocks the hell out of me.

I notice a couple of guys heading their way. My spine stiffens. I know what's about to happen. I can't stand here and watch another guy go after the one person I've been dreaming and fantasizing about for almost a year. My nerves stop me. I don't know if she even liked me. Shit, the last thing she did was shoot me before running off.

Setting down my beer, I push back my nerves and catch up with the guys heading straight toward them. "She's with me," I hiss, pointing at Addison. I'm already primed for a fight. They look at me and size me up before nodding and retreating. My eyes are laser-focused on one thing: Addison. Everything ceases to exist as I walk toward her. I slide up right behind her, pulling those perfect hips to mine.

Her scent takes me back. I could never forget that smell. I squeeze her hips as I grind into her. I bend down and whisper, "Please tell me I'm not fucking dreaming."

She spins around immediately. We stop moving and stare at each other. I narrow my eyes, expecting to see a look of surprise but it never comes. Instead, she flashes her beautiful smile at me.

"Hi, Aiden," she says quietly, tilting her head to look up to me.

She said my name. *My real name.* How long has she known? If she knows who I am, why hasn't she come to talk to me? Was I really just a way for her to escape? She's staring up at me, and I can't move. Hypnotized is an understatement.

"Hi," I murmur.

My eyes flicker to her lips, and she licks them. That fucking does it. I slam my lips to hers, and she opens them for me. Our kiss isn't soft; it's heated, necessary. My tongue explores her entire mouth, and she sucks on it lightly. I growl into her mouth as I feel her body melt into mine.

"Well…" coughs Harper "…Addison meet Aiden."

I reluctantly stop kissing her. Damn. I look around at Harper, who has a huge smile on her face. I notice Damon standing right beside her. Both of them are staring at us with mouths gaped open, wondering what the hell just happened. Shit, I don't think I know myself.

I look back at Addison, and she smiles. She reaches up and touches my shoulder softly where my scar is from where her bullet grazed me.

"I'm sorry," she says as she looks at me with guilt in her eyes.

I chuckle. "I'm glad you missed."

I'm not sure what I said to make her laugh, but she does. She grabs Harper's hand and pulls her off the dance floor. I watch them head to the bar.

"I'm so confused," Damon says, still standing there with me.

"What the hell just happened? I thought you didn't know Addison. Then you're dancing with her like you own her. Then you kiss her like you're fucking her with your mouth. And then she's saying sorry for something on your arm." He glances at my arm right when he says it. I can see when the light bulb goes off in his head because his eyes get wide.

"Is Addison... *Emily?*" he asks. I nod slowly. Then he starts laughing. Why is everyone laughing at me? This is not a funny moment.

"If Addison was the one who shot you, she didn't miss." That's all he says before he walks back to the bar, too, shaking his head and laughing. I'm standing there, sure I look an idiot, wondering what joke I missed.

CHAPTER TWENTY-NINE

HE ACTUALLY THINKS that I missed when I shot him. I didn't mean to laugh, but it was funny. I'm sure once he figures out why, he'll be thankful I only grazed him.

"Okay, girl. What. Was. That?" asks Harper. "You're not the type to kiss a random guy. Especially a kiss like that. Damn, I felt a little naughty watching you guys." She fans herself.

I sigh. We do have explosive chemistry. At the time though, it was something that couldn't be, but are we getting a second chance now? What will happen when he finds out why I was actually there? I don't think I can tell him the truth if he doesn't know already. I still can't believe he was an undercover agent. Our entire time together was based on lies. And now there is still this huge lie looming over us. Backing away from him is the only way I can save myself from getting hurt. *I need to breathe.*

"I need to get out of here. I'll tell you, but not here." We walk out and go back to my apartment.

* * *

"So, last summer before I came to New York, Aiden and I met, but we were both going by different aliases for different reasons. I'm assuming he was undercover, now that I know that he's FBI. I didn't know then. We had a short fling and then we went our separate ways," I explain.

"It doesn't look like *he* wanted to part ways. Now it's starting to make sense. You saw him earlier today didn't you?" Harper asks. "That's why you were acting so weird." She knows the answer to her own question. "I have so many other questions. First, why were you going by an alias?" In our line of work there are never too many questions. I should expect nothing less from Harper.

"Yes. He obviously didn't see me. I was going to go to his office tomorrow to get this whole awkward situation out of the way. It's not like I can ignore him. We'll be working together sometimes," I say. "Last summer I had to figure some stuff out so I used an alias. I did what I needed to do and then I left. Unfortunately, meeting Aiden wasn't part of the plan," I say vaguely. I can't tell her the whole truth.

"So, what's next? It looks like you both are still hot for each other. It's obvious whatever was started isn't finished. And you two are hot together. Definitely a power couple. You're two of the most beautiful people I know. You'd seriously have beautiful babies with the most beautiful eyes." I laugh. Harper's a little dramatic, at times.

"First, we are not having babies. Next, I don't think we'll work out. Our relationship, short as it might have been, was all based on lies. Yes, our physical attraction is out of this world..." my whole body reacts when I think about it "...but that's not enough." I sigh.

"So are the rumors true?" Harper asks, lifting her eyebrow.

"What rumors would those be?"

"You know... that he's huge." She holds up her hands like she's measuring something.

"Oh, my God!" I throw a pillow at her, laughing.

"Come on! He can't be perfect *everywhere*!" She giggles.

"Oh... he is perfect... everywhere," I say with a huge grin.

"So what are you going to do?"

"*I don't know.*" I throw myself back into the couch. "I have a past. Things that need to stay in the past," I answer, staring up at the wall.

"We all have skeletons, Addison." Yeah, but mine is an actual person in a jail cell. Put there by Aiden. "But, like you said, it's in the past. Why can't it stay there?"

"I wish it were that easy." I blow out a breath.

"Well, if you ever need to talk, about anything, you know I won't judge. And I'll always keep what you say between us." Harper stands to make her way into the bathroom.

"Thanks, Harper." It's still hard for me to trust people. Syd is the only person who knows everything about me.

* * *

"You two look like shit." Our boss, CJ, stops us before we get to our desks. Harper spent the night last night, only we stayed up talking about what I'm going to do. "You better get some caffeine in you because I need you both out in the field today. We had a person go crazy and kill four family members this morning. Go get your shit together and I'll brief you in my office in fifteen minutes."

After a quick dose of coffee, I'm doing much better. I put on my Crime Scene Investigator vest on my way out the door. Harper and I take the crime scene van. Once we get there, we grab our kits. The press is here with grieving friends and family. We're so used to the chaos it doesn't faze us anymore. My job is dedicated to the people who have been murdered, finding who did this and bringing them to justice.

The crime scene is gruesome. The parents and two kids have been murdered. It looks like a home invasion with furniture upturned and smashed. Harper and I get to work immediately. There is no need for discussion. Nothing we can say can reverse this horrendous act, but we can hopefully help find out who did it before they do it again.

After an hour of tagging and taking pictures, I run out to the van to grab some more tape. I notice a couple of black SUVs pulling up.

And so it begins. I release a quick breath, knowing this would happen.

I'm not surprised to see Aiden and Damon get out of one of the SUVs. Aiden spots me and struts over. I shift from one foot to the other. Before he can say anything, I ask, "Why'd they call in the feds?" It isn't normal for the feds to be called for this type of case.

"They think it might be a serial killer, so they called us in to help." He shrugs and looks me up and down, causing my body to react. *Which it shouldn't be doing.* "You look good." He flashes a sexy grin, revealing his dimples.

"Thanks." I twist my lips and tilt my head. I could definitely say the same for him.

"All you need is a gun and then you won't have to steal one if you need to shoot someone," he teases.

"Maybe *someone* shouldn't have made it so easy for me to steal." I laugh and turn around, walking away with a little more sway in my hips than usual.

"Touché, Addison," I hear him chuckle behind me.

I only see Aiden a couple of times after that. He is definitely a sight to see. His arrogance is evident in his powerful stride and the straightening of his back, which causes him to appear taller, but when he talks to people, he makes them feel at ease. It's that damn sexy, deep voice. He is a confident, beautiful man. My heart flutters the couple of times our eyes meet.

Harper and I get back to the office a little after three. It's been a long day. We unload and enter all of our evidence in the lab. As we're working, one of the techs sticks her head in.

"Hey, Addison, looks like you have an admirer," Kenlie says.

I look up from the computer, confused. "What are you talking about, Kenlie?" Harper shrugs.

"Have you been by your desk since you came back?" Kenlie asks.

Harper and I look at each other and both make a fast dash to my desk. We round the corner, and there on my desk are two dozen beautiful red roses.

Harper looks at me. "Is it from… you know who?" she asks with a squeal.

"Oh, my God, did you just squeal? I don't know who it's from," I say, walking over to pick up the card attached to a stick.

"I don't know you, but I want to."
Aiden

I stand there staring at the card. Tingles spread through my body, remembering that night. Harper grabs it out of my hand and reads it. "Wow…" She breathes out, fanning herself with the card.

"Well, you'll be even more wowed when I tell you what it means. When we were together, or whatever you want to call it, one night we danced to Sam Hunt's 'Take Your Time.' That's what he sang to me," I say softly. Of course I skipped the part about being handcuffed to him.

"Addison! You missed a few details when you told me what happened. You made it seem like it was a one-night stand." I wish it had been. Do I? The sparks that we had definitely have not gone away. Just the sight of him has my body humming, craving his touch. When those eyes catch mine, they penetrate deep into my soul, making me question things, but I can't give him my heart fully just for him to tear it apart when he finds out who my father is.

"It's complicated." I sigh as we head back to the lab.

"Do you like him?" she asks.

"Yes. No. Yes. Shit! See, I can't even decide if I like him. We don't know anything about each other."

"Exactly. He obviously wants to know more about you," she

says, wiggling her eyebrows, pointing back to my office. "Listen, I've known Aiden for six years, and I've never seen him go after a woman. *Ever*. He has always put his job first. Women come and go. Shit, we all thought it would be a cold day in hell if we saw him settle down. Addison... *it's getting cold in here*," she says, laughing, rubbing her hands over her arms acting like she is freezing.

"Shut up." I laugh. "He doesn't know how to handle a woman who doesn't throw herself at him."

"I don't think so, but you keep telling yourself that." She grins.

CHAPTER THIRTY

AIDEN

I'M LYING HERE in bed and can't think of a damn thing other than Addison. What is it about this girl that has me actually *thinking* of wanting more? I can't be pussy-whipped from one fucking night. The sex was amazing, but I don't even know her. After a quick search on Google, I found out she won first place in some national action-shoot competition when she was younger. That explains why everyone was laughing. She hit me exactly where she was aiming. She's not like any other girl. *Yeah, she's not falling at my feet.* Is that why I'm so intrigued? I run my hands through my hair, kicking the sheets off me.

Seeing her in the field the other day, I couldn't keep my eyes off of her. Thankfully she only caught me looking at her a couple of times. I had to keep my distance so I could actually do my job. How fucked-up is that? I need to get my head on straight. Work has always been my number one priority. Women come second. So why the hell can't I get her out of my mind?

I can't believe I sent her flowers. Cheryl helped me because I sure as hell haven't ever sent a woman flowers. That was three days ago and I haven't heard anything from her. I feel pathetic waiting to see if she'll contact me. How's that for karma. I'm sure every girl I screwed over would be enjoying this. I know Damon is. *Asshole.*

I blow out a breath. It's Saturday morning and I can't stay in bed all day. Maybe I can pound out some of this frustration at the gym.

* * *

"Hey, Aiden, glad to see you're back," Stacy says as she winks at me. Stacy's the receptionist at the boxing gym. "Damon got here a little bit ago," she says, pointing to the gym. I'm walking out of the locker room when I see Damon. He flashes a huge smile.

"You don't have to be that happy to see me," I joke.

"Oh, you just made my day." He laughs, but I can tell he's up to something. "You remember Tony, right?"

"Yeah, he's kicked my ass a few times." Tony is the Krav Maga instructor at the gym. A lot of the agents like to spar with him because he's brutal.

"Well, some of the guys are watching him and another person spar. It's pretty intense. You should come see." There's that fucking smile again.

We walk over to the mat and I freeze. There's Addison and Tony rolling around on the floor, sparring. Addison jumps up in defense. She's wearing leggings that go right below the knee with a sports bra, showing her gorgeous, muscular stomach. Her ass is perfect and her breasts glisten with sweat. Tony jumps up and catches her legs, bringing her to the floor. My instinct to help her kicks in.

"Don't do it," Damon says, holding my arm. I stay put, crossing my arms. "She can take care of herself."

"So I've been told," I say, remembering when Joe jumped on her. I ball my hand into a fist thinking of that asshole.

Addison uses her legs to grab hold of Tony and throws him over her. This woman is going to unhinge me. Fucking bolt by bolt. I've never been so turned on to the point of pain before.

"She's a powerhouse," Damon says, leaning over to me. Suddenly, I want to kick Damon's ass and every guy watching. The caveman in me wants to grab her and take her away and yell "mine!" What the hell is wrong with me? Why am I so jealous of everyone all of a sudden? I've never had to compete for a girl. Ever.

Addison is back up in her fight stance. She glances my way and catches my eye. In that exact moment she doesn't catch Tony coming for her. She goes down hard. Shit! I start to run out there to see if she's okay, but I know if that was me, I'd be pissed, so I stay.

I see her slowly get up and hear Tony ask, "What the hell was that, Addison?" She shakes her head and apologizes. They both go to the side of the mats and talk. Everyone watching disperses. I'm hesitant to go talk to her. Dammit, I hate this feeling of insecurity. I walk toward her while she's putting her stuff in her bag.

She peers up at me with those beautiful, Caribbean-blue eyes. "*Still* a distraction," she says, laughing, shaking her head.

"I'm impressed." I flash a grin.

"Oh, are you?"

"Heck, yeah. I want a turn." I wag my eyebrows.

"You want to spar?" She looks at me suspiciously.

"Hey, I need to redeem myself." I smirk. "You caught me off guard."

"I guess that's what happens when you're distracted." She shrugs, a smile tugging at the corners of her mouth.

She picks up her bag and starts to leave but pauses, turns around, and says, "Thanks for the roses. They are beautiful." *Not as beautiful as you.* As she walks away, she looks over her shoulder and says, "I'm an only child."

"Okay?" Her random comment confuses me.

She doesn't look back, but I hear her say, "You wanted to know more about me." Then she exits the gym.

I thrust my fist in the air. She's not shutting me down. Time to up my game.

* * *

"You want me to do *what*?" Damon asks in surprise when I tell him my plan.

"You fucking owe me." I stare at him.

"For what?"

"Stephanie."

Damon chuckles. "Oh, yeah. That." He owes me big time. He asked me to hook up with this girl so he could get her hot friend. I didn't mind helping… she was cute, but holy shit, she was psycho. She stalked me for a year. Like crazy stalk. I'm a fucking FBI agent and I was scared.

"I'm sure you'll get something out of this, too." I smirk.

"You're starting to concern me. You never chase women." Damon looks at me like I've lost my mind.

"I wish I could explain it. Something about Addison has been making me go out of my mind." I sigh. "I have all these *feelings* I don't know what to do with."

CHAPTER THIRTY-ONE

I AM SO excited! Sydney is coming to visit me next week. I haven't seen her since last Thanksgiving when I moved into my new apartment. I miss her so much. I haven't had a chance to tell her about Aiden. She's going to freak out, probably tell me that fate brought us back together. She believes in all that fairytale crap. My life is far from a fairytale. Fate hates me. She dangles things within reach, tempting me, only to pull it back and say *"fuck you."*

I push off my couch and wince. I'm a little sore from sparring with Tony yesterday. The hit that took me down caused a nice bruise on my ass. Damn Aiden. His emerald eyes grabbed hold of me, and I couldn't move until Tony knocked the hell out of me. I need a nice hot bath with Epsom salt for my aching body.

As I'm about to get into my bath, my phone dings. I run to get it just in case it's work. It's from a number that I don't recognize.

Unknown: I grew up in North Carolina

Someone has the wrong number. I put my phone down and sink into my bath. All the tension in my muscles release. My mind takes me back to a bath I took last summer, the night Aiden and I had sex. Goose bumps spread across my body as I remember him drying me off. The feel of his smooth, thick cock in my mouth. His glorious mouth on my clit, tongue fucking me. My body heats up, and I can feel the swelling sensation in my sex. My hand trails down my stomach to my clit. I start to rub, feeling the intensity increase. With closed eyes I imagine it's him touching me there. I move toward my entrance and insert a finger. I moan. I can feel my orgasm getting close, getting ready to explode. Oh... oh... Jett! I scream out as a rush of heat is sent through my body and my sex pulses around my finger.

Did I just scream out Jett? Oops.

Harper calls me, wanting to do lunch. I dress casual, throwing on some jeans and rolling them up to make them capris then pair it with a white, V-neck T-shirt. It's a beautiful sunny August day. Not too hot. I catch a cab to our favorite French bistro in Tribeca.

I walk into the restaurant and notice Harper already seated at a table.

"Hey, girl," I say as I sit down. I grimace.

"I heard you might be a little sore today," she teases.

I furrow my brows. "Word travels fast. Since when does anyone care about Tony taking someone out? It happens all the time," I say.

"It's not that you were taken out... it's *why* you were taken out." She winks.

Was it that obvious? In my mind it all happened so fast I didn't think anyone noticed. I sure as hell didn't think everyone would gossip about it.

"Seriously, why is everyone making it a big deal?"

"Girl... everyone sees how you and Aiden look at each other. *Brrrrr.*" She pretends to shiver.

"Very funny. Hell hasn't froze over yet. Aiden and I are not a thing." I'm not sure if I'm saying that to convince Harper or myself. My phone dings again. I grab it out of my purse.

Unknown: I have one sister. Katie.

"So weird." I glance up to Harper. "I'm getting these random texts from someone I don't know," I say, showing her my phone.

"Hmm… I only know one person with a sister named Katie." She looks at me and smiles at my questioning expression. "Aiden."

"What? Why would he…" My mouth drops open and my eyes go wide. Aiden. Of course. Harper has a cocked eyebrow, waiting for me to continue. "Yesterday at the gym I told him I was an only child. He was confused so I told him that he wanted to get to know me and then I left." I shrug.

"That boy wants you bad. Are you going to respond?" The excitement in her voice makes me laugh.

Me: How did you get my number?

His response is quick.

Aiden: Sweetheart, I'm FBI.

I roll my eyes and show Harper. "He's so cocky." I snicker.

"That's what I hear," she responds, giggling.

"Oh, my God, we are not back to talking about his dick," I whisper and roll my eyes. We enjoy the rest of our meal and then go do a little shopping after.

"Oh! My best friend, Sydney, is coming to town on Friday. I want you to meet her. You'll love her. Let's plan on doing something fun Friday night," I say.

"Fun! I can't wait to meet her."

* * *

Today isn't quite as busy as Monday was. I'm enjoying the downtime from the hectic chaos yesterday. I was in the lab the entire day. We found some prints that might help us catch a lead on the murders from last week. The FBI is heading the case now, so we're getting our information together to pass off to them. I'm typing out our findings when Kenlie peeks in my office.

"There are two very *fine* agents here to see you," she says.

I get up, laughing, shaking my head. Whenever agents come over to the office all the women gawk. The men in the office always puff their chests out and wonder what the big deal is.

Our offices are set in a square with the lab in the middle, surrounded by glass, and an open area in front of it that we call the bull pen. The techs sit there. When I walk out of my office, Aiden and Damon are waiting for me in front of the bull pen. They are a sight: two gorgeous, muscular men exuding authority by just standing there. It's funny because I'd heard many stories about these two before I found out who Aiden really was. And the trouble they got into. I'm carrying the folder with all of the information we have collected so far.

As I walk up to them, Aiden says, "Hey, beautiful," and winks.

I feel the heat crawl up my face and blow out a breath before handing him the folder. "Here is everything we have on the Monroe case." He smiles at me. There's an awkward silence. Of course, people are glancing our way. I stick my hands in my lab coat pockets. "Well, if that's all you need... I should get back to work." I turn around to walk away.

"Addison, wait." I stop and turn around. He clears his throat. "Have dinner with me Friday night." He fiddles with the file in his hands. I've never seen him nervous. He's usually a confident man. Then he flashes his dimples and it makes it really hard to decline his offer.

"I can't. I have a friend coming into town that day." I look around as people talk in hushed voices, watching us. *Great.*

"Tomorrow night then?" he asks.

"Aiden, I don't know." I sigh. I hear Damon mumble something but ignore him. "Let me think about it and get back to you." I'm still trying to figure out where this can even go. And I don't want to lead him on. He nods his head, so I turn around and walk away.

The sound of a deep, sexy voice singing stops me.

What the hell?

Turning around slowly, standing in all of their sexiness, is Aiden and Damon in aviator sunglasses, singing, "You've Lost that Lovin' Feeling" to me.

And there's the confident man I know.

Someone has watched *Top Gun* too many times. A laugh escapes my lips. Everyone who wasn't already watching our exchange is being drawn out from their office by their singing.

All I can do is stand with my hand over my mouth, which hangs open. Harper comes up to my side and whispers, "Holy shit." Every girl is glancing from me to the men with their hands on their hearts. *Oh, my God.*

If it wasn't bad enough that I have two guys serenading me, now the whole office decides to join in at the chorus. Even Harper. I swear someone is going to pop out with a hidden camera and yell "GOTCHA!" This is insane. CJ, my boss, is leaning in her door-way with her arms crossed. She looks over at me and I shrug and mouth, "*Sorry.*" She laughs and shakes her head.

When the guys finish, everyone yells and claps. Aiden stands there with his arms open, aviators still on and panty-dropping smile. "*Please go out with me,*" he mouths.

CJ puts a stop to all the chaos. "Okay, everyone, *High School Musical* is over. Get back to work. Addison…" she looks my way "…go deal with *Maverick and Goose.*"

I walk toward Aiden and Damon, and I laugh at CJ's comment. Damon winks and leaves, but not before he's stopped by several women in the office. Aiden stands there lifting an eyebrow with a sexy grin that displays his dimples. My breath catches from just that one look. "You're insane," I murmur. I don't know why he has this profound effect on me. I don't have any control over my body when he's near me.

He leans down and whispers in my ear, "Insane for you." The heat of his breath gives me goose bumps that trail down my entire body. "So…?" He tilts his head so he's right in my face. His lips are a breath away from touching mine.

"I'm afraid what you'll do next if I say no." I laugh nervously as I step back and try to regain my senses. His eyebrow goes up like that was a challenge. "Okay!" I say before he actually does do something else. "Yes."

"Pick you up at seven tomorrow night." He smirks before turning and walking away. I stand there and stare at his ass for a minute.

Harper walks up and interrupts my gawking. "Girl, I don't know what to say. I think I fell in love with him," she teases. "That boy will stop at nothing to get you. You must have a golden vagina."

"You did not say that!" We both laugh. "Please tell me someone got that on video," I call out.

Numerous people say at once, "I did!"

CHAPTER THIRTY-TWO
AIDEN

IT'S CRAZY HOW many women are calling, asking me to marry them. The guys busted our balls the second we got back to the office; a video was shared with them before we even got back. And now *everyone* has seen that video. Damon is definitely enjoying the attention.

All I care about is one woman. The look on her face was priceless. And to top it off, everyone joined in. That wasn't part of the plan, but it was awesome. Tonight is our date. I've never been nervous about a date in my life. I'm not sure when I became a fucking girl with all these feelings. That's not true. I know the exact day.

The day I met Addison.

I know I'm not the only one feeling this attraction. I can see it in her beautiful blue eyes, but she's pulling back. I know our situation isn't typical, but fuck typical. She will be mine again. And I'm not letting her go this time. Well, I guess I didn't let her go last time... she fucking shot me.

There is a new Italian restaurant down the street from her place where I made reservations. I heard it was phenomenal, and I know that Addison likes Italian food. My dick twitches remembering her moaning while she ate Italian during her stay with Travis.

Damon walks into my office and sits in one of my chairs across from my desk. "Holy shit, dude, our video is going viral!" he says. "Maybe we need to take our act on the road." He puts his aviator glasses on with a shit-eating grin.

"You're crazy. Don't quit your day job." I throw a wadded up piece of paper at him.

"Hey, don't mess with the face. I could have movie offers soon." He chuckles. I didn't think his ego could get any bigger than before. Fuck was I wrong.

"Dude, you were just the back-up singer." I laugh, totally messing with him.

"Whatever, ass. That's okay. This back-up singer has women lined up. You know that if Addison doesn't work out, there are plenty of women wanting to lick your wounds." He wags his eyebrows.

"Addison will come around," I say. Because I won't stop trying until she does. Starting with our date.

* * *

I arrive at Addison's place at seven sharp. The doorman calls her before allowing me to go to her apartment on the third floor. This place is really nice. There is no way she can afford this working in forensics. I shrug. *It's not like I know anything about her.* I'm hoping that changes tonight. I want to know everything about her. I remind myself that I need to take this slow.

When she answers the door, I inhale sharply. She is gorgeous. I slowly rake my eyes up and down her body. A groan escapes my lips as I try to control my raging desire for her. She's wearing black leather pants and a white scoop neck shirt that shows off the tops of her fantastic breasts. Three gold necklaces graze the top of her chest. Her hair is long with loose curls. I want to grab a hold and pull her to me. My fingers twitch to reach out and hold on to her for dear life.

"Are you going to stop eye fucking me soon?" she says in a

breathy voice. Those blue, hypnotic eyes are so intoxicating that I can't look away.

"Sweetheart, we need to leave. Right. Now. Or we're eating in," I say.

So much for trying to take things slow.

She puts her hand on my chest and pushes me out of her doorway before closing and locking her door. "Not going to happen." She laughs. "Where are you taking me?"

"I guess since it won't be back into your apartment..." I wink "...I'm taking you to a new Italian restaurant that opened up a week ago. We can walk from here. It's a couple blocks away."

"Oh, is it Bella Mistero?" I nod my head. "I've heard great things. I've been meaning to try it. You know I love Italian food," she teases. My dick might not survive tonight.

I intertwine our fingers as we walk to the restaurant. I can't explain why, but everything about us feels right. I've never held hands with any other woman, but this feels as natural as breathing. Anytime a woman wanted a relationship, I immediately backed away. I've never had the time, patience, or need to be with a woman longer than a few hours. Until Addison dropped into my life. Literally. Now there seems to be a piece missing, and I want her to fill it.

"How's your ass?" I chuckle, glancing back to look at her ass. A mighty fine tight ass. I resist grabbing it.

"My ass is fine," she answers with a questioning tone, brows furrowed.

"Mighty fine," I quip. "But I was talking about the hit you took from Tony."

"Oh. It's alright now... a little bruised."

"I can always kiss it and make it better," I say, wagging my eyebrows. She shakes her head and laughs.

Walking into the restaurant, the savory aroma of garlic and basil greets us. Addison inhales deeply, closing her eyes, moaning.

I will feed her Italian everyday just to watch this reaction. I lean over and steal a quick kiss. Her eyes open wide. "Sorry, I couldn't resist," I say.

"It's okay, it just surprised me," she says, blushing.

As I'm telling the hostess my name I hear, "Addison, is that you?" I look at a tall guy walking up to her, proceeding to pick her up in a huge hug. Who is that? Then I hear him say, "My beautiful mystery woman."

Who the fuck is this guy? My beautiful mystery woman?

CHAPTER THIRTY-THREE

"MARCO," I SAY as he lifts me up in a hug. When he puts me down it's slow, and he doesn't release me. This is a little awkward. I can already feel the atmosphere changing with Aiden right by my side. I think I hear him growl. Stepping out of Marco's arms, I glance at Aiden.

"Beautiful, what are you doing here? Do you live in New York now?" he asks, clearly ignoring Aiden.

"Yes. I've been here for almost a year. Is this your place?" I look around, confused.

"It is. I've always wanted to come open a restaurant here in the city. And what luck I have… it's where you live," he boasts. Shit, that was definitely a growl coming from behind me.

"Marco, this is my friend, Aiden." I introduce the two. Friend doesn't seem to sit well with Aiden. He glances at me with a forced smile before returning to Marco.

Aiden puts his hand out. "It's nice to meet you, *Marco*. So how do you know Addison?" They're having a testosterone-fueled handshake battle right now. Both have their chests puffed up, staring each other down. I roll my eyes. *Men!*

The hostess telling us our table is ready couldn't have come at a better time. Aiden leads me to our table with his hand on my back. He pulls my chair out for me to sit before taking his own to the side of me. I look around, fidgeting with my napkin. Between the awkward silence and the intense gaze burning a hole in me, I reluctantly look at Aiden. "We're friends." I sigh, feeling I have to justify Marco to him.

"Who us? Or you and Marco?" he responds. It's not what I meant, but if he wants to be a jealous asshole about it, I can play that game.

"Well, actually, *both*." I look him square in the eyes. His jaw clenches. "Marco and I are friends. It's never been anything more than that. I met him last summer during my… *travels*."

"You know that he wants you, right?" he asks. I know Marco flirted with me both times I saw him, but to say he wants me based on the five-minute interaction is a stretch. We've only seen each other twice, and I haven't seen him in over a year. "He called you *his* beautiful mystery woman. Why?"

"He probably saw that I was with you and being a typical man, Tarzan beating his chest, laid claim. You fell for it, beat your chest back, and now you're in a pissing match," I say sarcastically. I don't need to tell him about the mystery part. He can probably figure that out himself.

"This is the last thing I'm going to say about Marco because I don't like the guy. It seems a little too coincidental that he ends up in the same place that you're living and names his restaurant after you." His smile is gone as he glances over to Marco, who is watching us as well.

"What are you talking about? His restaurant isn't named Addison?" What the hell is he talking about.

"Do you know what Bella Mistero means in Italian?" I shake my head.

"It means 'beautiful mystery,'" he replies, raising an eyebrow.

That is a coincidence. There is no way he knew I was living in New York City, but I'll think about that later. We've spent too much time talking about this already.

I get ready to change the subject when two women around my age come over to our table. "You're the guy who sang 'You've Lost that Lovin' Feeling,' aren't you?" And then they look at me. Oh, boy. "Yes! And you're the girl he was singing to. Oh, my God, that was so romantic. And obviously you said yes," one girl squeals out. And unfortunately it's not a quiet squeal. Everyone is watching us. Aiden can see how uncomfortable I am and throws his head back, laughing.

"Yes, girls, I'm that guy. And she did say yes." He winks at me with a huge, sexy grin, showing off his dimples. Jealous Aiden is gone. Thank God.

"Well, if she doesn't work out, call me," she says as she slips him a piece of paper with her number on it.

My mouth falls open. I'm so shocked, I'm speechless. I grab his hand on the table and smile up at her.

"That won't be necessary. You can leave now," I say rudely, not smiling anymore when I meet her eyes. They huff and walk off saying how much of a bitch I am. *Really? I'm the bitch?* I take a deep breath and look back at Aiden. He has the cockiest grin on his face. Then he beats his chest and says "*Ahahahaaahaaa.*"

He pulls my chair toward him and whispers in my ear, "Next time my cock is balls deep in your wet pussy and you're screaming my name, you will be *mine*. And I. Don't. Share." Hot tingles shoot straight down to my sex. I can feel the wetness in my panties as I wiggle in my chair. He looks at me with those beautiful emerald green eyes laced with lust.

"Neither do I." I pick up the paper with the phone number and rip it into little pieces.

"Well, now that we have that out of the way, we can enjoy our dinner." He grins.

* * *

Our dinner ends up being rather quick, unfortunately. We talk a little about our day but are continually interrupted by Marco. Very conveniently, Marco is our waiter and anytime we start a new conversation he comes over to *check* on us. I know it's pissing Aiden off, so I eat fast. It goes from bad to worse when we head out the door and Marco hugs me, saying, "If you want Italian, you know where to find me," and winks. I'm pretty sure he wasn't referring to the food. And with Aiden growling again, I'm almost positive he got that, too.

"Okay. Where to next?" I walk out the door, tugging Aiden's hand, trying to prevent any confrontation between the two guys currently staring each other down.

"I don't like the guy," he grumbles as we walk down the street.

"I got it, Tarzan. Let's forget about Marco. Where are we going now?" I smile up at him, pulling him to a stop. With my heels I'm a few inches shy of him, so I slowly bring my lips to his and softly kiss him on his perfectly shaped, soft mouth. I can feel him relax. Marco is a beautiful man, but my feelings are so different with Aiden. Feelings that I'm not sure I can follow through with, but right now Marco isn't part of the equation. I pull back and smile at this gorgeous man in front of me.

"I'm sorry, Addison. You have fired up feelings in me that I have no idea how to handle." He leans his forehead against mine and takes a deep breath. "Okay, let's go." He grabs my hand and we walk back toward my apartment. I hope he doesn't want to follow through with his previous plans on coming in; I'm not sure I'm ready for that. Even if my body is screaming at me how stupid that decision is, we need to take this slow. We still don't know anything about each other.

As I'm about to question him, we stop at a gorgeous, sleek, black BMW with dark tinted windows. He reaches for the door and guides me in. He's at the driver's side within seconds and slides into his seat, flashing me a devilish grin. Boys and their toys.

"Very nice," I say, rubbing my hand across the soft black leather. "What, you're too good for the subway?" I tease. I don't own a car, like most people in the city. There is no room on this island for people *and* cars.

"Hey, I love the subway, but I love my car more." He chuckles. "I don't drive it often in the city, but I can't impress you if I take you on the subway."

I laugh. "Do you think I'm that shallow?"

He grabs my hand and glances at me. "Not at all, Addison. I do think that you're one of the most independent, stubborn, *beautiful* women that I know. And I'll do anything to make you like me." His eyes soften.

"I do like you. I wouldn't be here if I didn't," I say, squeezing his hand in mine. He pulls it to his lips and kisses the top of my hand. It's such a sweet gesture. The walls that I have firmly built up over the years are slowly coming down.

Aiden pulls over when we get to Central Park and jumps out. I always feel uncomfortable getting out of a car when I'm on a date: do they want me to wait for them to open my door or do I just get out? I decide to get out on my own.

Walking around the front of the car, Aiden stops in his tracks when he sees me getting out. He nods his head and laughs. "Figures." He pulls a blanket out of his trunk before grabbing my hand and leading me toward the park.

* * *

The sun is setting, resulting in a beautiful sunset. Pinks and oranges paint the sky. Aiden has found a quiet spot on a hill. It looks like there is going to be a concert tonight. We're far enough away from the crowd so it won't be too loud. The weather is perfect. It's the beginning of September, and I can already feel the weather changing.

"This is nice. Surprising, but nice," I say to Aiden as he sits on the blanket. Truthfully, I'm relieved that he didn't plan an extravagant date. I like sweet and simple.

"Surprising?" he asks with a raised eyebrow.

"Well, all you went through to get the date, I'm... surprised. It's a good surprise, though." I smile at him. "And come to think of it, let's talk about your newfound fame."

He laughs out loud. "Can you believe that shit? I will never live this down. Damn YouTube." He leans back on his elbows, straightening out his muscular legs. He is one gorgeous man. He has his typical dark jeans on that fit him oh so perfectly and a black button-up shirt with the sleeves rolled up to his elbows. He should be on the cover of *GQ* magazine. "You should see how many marriage proposals I've received. Even from Australia." He wags his brows and grins.

"Oh, I hate that I'm getting in the way of *all* your marriage proposals," I say, taking off my shoes and leaning back on my side. I prop my head on my bent arm and glance at Aiden. "Maybe I should go in case one of your fans shows up here. I'd hate to cramp your style," I tease. I have a feeling that Aiden hates this attention. In fact, I'm not sure how he expects to go undercover anytime soon with that out there. My thoughts are quickly interrupted when Aiden throws himself on me. I let out a scream. "What are you doing?"

"You aren't going anywhere," he whispers into my ear.

A couple passes us, but the guy stops and asks, "Are you okay, lady?" He must have heard me scream. Aiden looks up at him with a shit-eating grin and is about to reply, so I take this opportunity to push up and flip him over onto his back, now with me on top.

"Yep, I'm good," I say, laughing. The guy laughs and turns to walk away but not before we hear him say, "You better keep her."

"*Mmm...* I plan on it," Aiden says to me. "But right now, I need to get you off of me or we're going to be hauled in for indecent exposure." I can already feel his hard bulge against my thigh. There's a fire in his eyes, so I know he's not kidding. I slide off to the side of him and lie on my side again. He turns toward me and adjusts himself. "Goddamn, woman, you're so sexy," he whispers as he brushes my hair behind my ear. "So, I have to ask, is this your real color or are you a natural brunette?"

"This is my real color."

"Good, I like it better," he says as he plays with my hair. "So tell me about you. *The real you.* I'm not exactly sure our little get-to-know-you card game last summer was... accurate." He laughs.

"Um... most of it was true. But I intentionally left out things where I would have had to lie, I guess."

"Are you from Texas?"

"That, I am. And I know now that you're from North Carolina." I giggle, remembering his random, one-line texts.

"Are your parents still there?"

I take a deep breath. "My mom died when I was ten," I say as I bite on my lip.

"...and your dad?" he asks. I look down and act like I'm removing dirt from the blanket.

"He died in a car accident when I was one." I look back up at him. He can't know that Travis is my father, so I go with the story that I was told for more than half my life and hope he doesn't figure out I'm lying. I hate lying. I've been lied to my whole life. I've always tried to be an honest person. His brows furrow, and I can tell that he's thinking about what to say next. That's usually what people do when I tell them.

"I'm sorry, Addison." And there's the typical response. He continues. "That had to be rough."

"My life has definitely been a roller coaster. One hell of a ride. My aunt took me in and raised me. She's wonderful and has done so much for me." I fall to my back and stare at the sky. I hate seeing pity in people's eyes when I talk about my mom.

"How did your mom die?" he quietly asks. I've never hidden that my mom was murdered, but I don't think I should tell Aiden. He could easily start digging into my past and put two and two together, especially since Travis Stein was labeled a suspect in my mom's murder at one point.

"Can we not talk about this right now. I'd hate to ruin our evening. Someday I'll talk about it, but not today," I say, still staring at the sky.

He puts his hand on my face and turns it to look right into his eyes. "I'm sorry. We don't need to talk about it." His thumb softly touches my cheeks before he leans down and kisses me. The kiss is a lot like our earlier kiss, soft and sweet. He leans his forehead against mine, and we stay silent for a minute.

I can hear the concert in the background. Darkness has surrounded us and streetlights illuminate the walkways. It's a beautiful night, and I'm in the arms of a beautiful man. I'm not sure where we are headed, but I won't ever regret this moment in time.

Aiden stands up. "Sweetheart, dance with me?"

He grabs my hands and pulls me up close to his body. His embrace is strong yet soft. Our bodies mold together. I wish we could stay like this forever. We sway to the music drifting through the breeze coming over the hill. Aiden hums the song. I listen to see what song is playing when he softly sings it in my ear. It's "Die a Happy Man" by Thomas Rhett.

I glance up into those piercing, emerald green eyes and it's just him and me. Everything else ceases to exist. We get lost in each other, and I'm not sure I want to find my way back. He slowly leans down and softly kisses the side of my lips.

His mouth takes mine in a heated embrace. I open for him and our tongues dance slowly. I can feel his growing hardness against my body. The heat spreads throughout my body down to my core. I sway my hips against him, my body taking over. My hands tangle in his hair, pulling him closer. One of his hands grabs my hair and yanks my head back, causing our kiss to end. I let out a silent moan at the loss of his lips. I feel him chuckle before his lips make their way down my neck and up to my ear. His other hand slides down my back as he tugs me closer to his hardness. Our bodies are still swaying. I'm not sure the music is still playing. The only thing I can hear is our heavy breathing and the beating of our hearts.

"Um… excuse me."

"Hello there."

I think someone is talking to us. I can't let Aiden go, and he's definitely not letting me go. Not right now. People, go away. Keep walking. Can't you see we're busy?

"Okay, you two are going to have to stop… *now*."

What the hell? Who in the world. I look over to where the voice is coming from.

"Oh. Hi, Officer Marks." I'm pretty sure I'm ten shades of red right now. I bury my face into Aiden's chest. Aiden's laughing but quickly adjusts himself. Seriously! I'm so embarrassed.

"Agent Roberts and Addison?" His eyes widen. "Oh, I'm sorry. I didn't recognize you while you were… Anyway… Um… You guys might want to take this to a not-so-public place," he says, lowering his voice, looking around. Now he's blushing. This is so awkward. I can't bring myself to lift my face and apologize. I've worked with Ryan on numerous occasions.

"Sorry, Ryan. We were enjoying the music and dancing. We'll behave." Aiden flashes a huge grin.

"No problem, guys. Just trying to keep things PG here in the park…" he laughs "…but hey, I guess I know what your answer was to Aiden asking you out, Addison." He is still laughing as he walks away.

"I can't believe that happened! How am I going to work with that man and not be embarrassed?" I'm shaking my head that's still buried in Aiden's chest.

CHAPTER THIRTY-FOUR
AIDEN

THANK GOD RYAN stopped us when he did. I'm not sure I would have had the willpower to stop on my own. Addison is going to ruin me. It's hard to explain the feeling I have when she's in my arms. I was truthful with her when I told her that I have never wanted something so badly in my life. Revenge has fueled most of my life's path, but I could forget everything that has ever happened just to be with Addison.

I lift her head from my chest. "Okay… so maybe we should sit and talk." I laugh out loud when she looks up, still blushing.

"Seriously. What were we thinking?" She's shaking her head.

"Well… I know what I was thinking," I say with a suggestive tone, waggling my eyebrows.

"Stop that!" She's trying to sound serious as she sits on the blanket but the sparkle in those beautiful blue eyes tells me she's not. I can tell exactly what she's thinking and her thoughts are probably right on par with mine.

I sit down next to her and grab her hand, lacing our fingers together. I can't be next to her without touching her. *When the fuck did that happen?* We talk for a couple hours. About her growing up in Texas, her aunt and best friend, Sydney, who is coming to town this week. Our conversation flows easy. It's perfect. She's perfect. I've never wanted to share my life with a woman before. My work has always been my priority in life. Addison is different though. My thoughts aren't immediately about *how* we're going to fuck tonight; I really want to get to know her. Don't get me wrong, I've already had a taste of Addison and it's addicting, so of course I've thought of all the ways I want her again.

I really need to ask her how she ended up at Travis's house last summer. I'm not sure if this is the right time, but I don't know if there will ever be a right time.

"How about you tell me how you ended up at Travis's?"

"Talk about a mood killer," quips Addison.

"It's something we need to talk about." I shrug. "Especially the part where you shot me." I wink.

"Ugh. Can we forget about that part? I had no idea you were FBI. And come to think of it, what the hell! You're FBI! I was being held against my will and you didn't seem to be doing anything to change that." She rolls to her side and playfully hits me.

I grab her fist and bring it to my mouth, kissing it softly. "Whoa. I made sure you were safe. I couldn't blow my cover, but when Travis told me that you were staying indefinitely, I *did* do something about it."

"*Really?* Did I miss something? I don't recall you helping me escape. I wouldn't have had to shoot you if you did!" She sits up and throws her hands up.

I laugh and shake my head, remembering the whole morning. "So the morning that you *shot me* and escaped, I actually had a plan in place for that night. A couple of FBI agents were going to come and help you escape. *If you would have been a little patient...*"

"What!" Her eyebrows furrow in frustration. "I needed to get out of there. How in the hell was I supposed to know that you were going to be my hero and get me out? You were one of the reasons I had to leave when I did." She looks down.

I understand that and couldn't have agreed more. Even if it stung like hell that she left, she didn't belong there. I lift up her chin so she's looking directly at me. "I get that, I do. I didn't want you to leave, but there was no way you were staying." I lean over and place a soft kiss on her lips. I have to force myself to back away or we're going to end up in the same predicament we were in a couple hours ago.

"I still have no idea why you were there in the first place though. Travis was very secretive about the whole thing. And when you left, he was furious. He had me search for every Emily in Texas. Although, I was almost positive your name wasn't Emily, so I knew it was a lost cause." I raise an eyebrow, hoping she'll explain.

"Aiden…" she pauses and starts to say something but stops again, sighing. Whatever she needs to say, it doesn't sound good. "I wish I could tell you, I do." She looks right at me. "But I can't. Some things are better left alone."

"Are you in trouble?" I'm worried about how this sounds. I would never let anything or anyone hurt Addison. Especially Travis. I wonder if she knows that he was extradited here. Or why? She's never asked me but if she's in danger, she might need to know. I just don't know if I can tell her that she's the reason Travis made a mistake. A mistake that allowed me to finally pin something on him. If Joe hadn't tried to attack Addison, then Travis would have never ordered a hit on Joe. I still can't believe on a drunken night that Bill sang like a canary, leading me straight to the body at the bottom of the Hudson. *Fuck*, if she doesn't ask, I'm not telling her.

"No. Nothing like that. It's hard to explain, but please don't push this. I know why you were there and it has nothing to do with your case," she explains as her eyes plead with me to stop.

"Addison, you know I'm FBI. It's hard for me to not question things. You of all people should get that. But I'll let it go." For now. "So why don't I tell you why I was there. You might think you know, but you really have no idea." She tilts her head but remains quiet waiting for me to continue.

"You know I'm from North Carolina. Well, my dad used to work out of town a lot. He was never home and when I was younger I really had no idea what he did. I didn't care. He was an asshole when he was in town. Drunk and always yelling. My mom was always there for Katie and me. Best. Mom. Ever. So involved with everything that it made it easier with my dad always gone. He wasn't a good man, at least the man who I knew. Life was easier, calmer when he was out of town. My mom would tell me how they met and fell in love and when she talked about him, it definitely wasn't the man I knew. Anyway, when I was fifteen my mom and dad were killed in a car accident." I hear Addison suck in a breath.

"I'm so sorry, Aiden." Her hand is on mine, and she rubs her thumb lightly across mine.

"The brakes had been cut and they went down a ravine and hit a tree. Died on impact. I guess I'm thankful that Katie wasn't in the car with them." I pause and see the compassion in Addison's eyes. "They never figured out who cut the brakes so it went unsolved. We stayed in our house. My grandparents from my mom's side came and lived with us. When I graduated high school they decided to move back to Florida where they had been living before the accident. Katie moved in with them. I got stuck with the job of packing up the house and selling it. While packing up the house, I found a journal of my dad's hidden in the bottom of a drawer. Looking through it, I found out my dad was embezzling money from his employer. Hundreds of thousands of dollars. I was surprised because we definitely didn't live like we had money—I'd actually say lower-middle class income. The dumbass actually had dates and amounts in the journal that he stole." I laugh, thinking when I found it I couldn't believe it. I shake my head and continue. "I did some digging around and found out that my dad was working for Travis Stein. I never found evidence that says he did it, but I'm pretty sure of it." Addison's whole body stiffens up, a look of fear flashes in her eyes. She recovers quickly, but I see it.

CHAPTER THIRTY-FIVE

THIS CAN'T BE happening.

I don't know why I thought maybe, just maybe, Aiden and I could work. That he wouldn't care that Travis was my father. Fate hates me. There is no way that bitch could let me be happy just once. *Just one fucking time!*

"One time what? Addison, are you okay?" Aiden looks at me concerned.

Shit! I didn't mean to say that out loud.

"S-sorry," I stutter. "I was thinking how fate took both our moms away from us too soon and I was yelling at her. She seems to hate me. I think I wronged the universe in my previous life." I look down at the blanket where our hands are intertwined, hoping my outburst is easily explained. It's hard to look into his eyes knowing what he just told me.

He pulls me into an embrace, holding me like our lives depend on it. He continues telling me that he went to school and then the academy for the exact same reasons I did: revenge. Our paths mirror each other's, leading us to the same person. Although, the end of our stories are so very different. He found his parents murderer and I found my father.

I have to leave. Everything begins to blur and move in slow motion. I tell him I have to go. I push away from him. He tries to stop me, but I can't. I tell him that I don't feel well. It's true. My heart is breaking. For him. For me. For us. He takes me home. Silence fills the air and it's suffocating. As soon as we're in front of my apartment, I jump out without saying goodbye. I rush into my apartment and close the door. How he got past the doorman so fast surprises me because he's already outside my door calling my name, pleading for me to open the door.

"Addison, I'm not leaving until you open this door!" He bangs loudly on the door. I can hear the frustration in his voice. "Please, Addison," he begs.

The pain I hear in his voice is killing me, so I open the door. My head is still in a fog. I'm holding back my tears but one escapes. He's standing in front of me, kicking the door closed behind him. He catches my one tear and caresses my face with his thumb. I lean into his touch. My head tells me to turn around and never look back, but my body betrays me. His lips crash on mine. Our kiss is frantic, hard, and passionate. Our hands are all over. The physical need that we crave from each other takes over. My shirt and bra are discarded quickly and his hands pinch, tug, and caress my breasts. Aiden picks me up as my legs automatically wrap around his body. He flicks his tongue over one nipple. I let out a moan of ecstasy. He turns us around and slams me to the wall. I can feel his hardness. My own arousal throbs, needing more friction. I reach down and unbutton his jeans, pull out his cock, and stroke it between us. The velvety hard length has my mouth watering.

"Woman, keep doing that and I'll finish before we start," he growls. He puts me down and quickly takes off both our pants, and we're back to the wall in seconds. He lifts one of my legs around his waist. His fingers making their way down to my sensitive nub. Demanding more friction, I grind my hips against his fingers. His lips are on my neck, nipping my ear. My head is tilted back and my body is on fire. It's definitely not going to take me long to explode.

"Aiden," I moan.

His spears two fingers into me.

"Damn, woman. You're dripping wet for me."

"Only you, Aiden," I say, not recognizing my own voice.

"Only me, sweetheart," he growls.

His fingers move rapidly while his thumb works its magic on my clit.

"Oh God, oh God, Aiden!" My orgasm rips through me as I contract around his fingers. He bites down on my nipple, prolonging my orgasm. Before I can come down from my high, he lifts me up and slams me down on his cock. I cry out. The immediate fullness that I feel is overwhelming. He pauses, looking into my eyes, silently asking me if I'm okay. I nod, biting my lip. His mouth comes down on mine, sucking my lip where I was biting it. He lifts me up, pulling his cock slowly out but before it comes out, he slams me back down.

"Addison, your pussy is so tight," he roars. He starts a punishing rhythm, fast and hard. I squeeze my legs around his waist, begging to feel more of him. *All of him.* My fingernails score his muscular back, grabbing hold for the ride. His face is buried into my neck. I can feel the heat of his heavy breaths. "Stop. Running. Addison," his raspy voice growls between each thrust. He grabs my hands and brings them over our heads. One of his large hands pins both of mine to the wall while his other reaches down to grab my ass. "If I have to handcuff you to a bed again to make you stop running from me, I fucking will," he grates out. I close my eyes to try and avoid the determination in his eyes. I can feel my body tensing, getting close, as he pounds into me harder. I moan as my body quivers with each thrust.

The hand cupping my ass moves farther down. He rubs in between my cheeks. A finger toys with the pucker of my ass. "Aiden." I suck in a breath at the foreign feeling, but he's just rubbing, pressing, teasing. The sensation has me grinding my ass against his finger. I can't believe I'm hoping he continues.

"Fuck, Addison. So responsive." Shivers course through me as I can feel my release building. I scream, my whole body convulsing in pleasure, pulsing against his cock. Aiden's control is shattered when he thrusts into me one more time. He roars through his orgasm. I can feel the heat of his release inside me. He leans up against me, resting his forehead against mine.

"Woman, you're going to be the death of me," he pants out. We're both still breathing heavily when he lifts up and pulls out of me. I whimper at the loss. My legs shake as he puts me down. I have to lean against the wall to keep from collapsing. He walks to my kitchen and returns with a wet towel. I hadn't even noticed that his release ran down my leg. My eyes go wide at the realization. "I'm so sorry, sweetheart," he whispers as he softly cleans me. "I've never done it without a condom. And I'm clean. I was just checked after I got back." His voice is rushed.

"It's okay. I'm on the pill," I quietly reply. I'm frustrated that I have no control over myself when I'm with Aiden. I didn't even *think* about him not putting a condom on. I throw my head against the wall a couple times, muttering a curse under my breath. I open my eyes to beautiful emerald green eyes assessing me. *Always assessing me.*

"Aiden." I blow out a long, shaky breath. "I think you need to go." I twist my lips, waiting for his reaction. He nods his head slowly as he begins to put his clothes back on. I put on my panties and shirt, never taking my eyes off him. I'm so confused. I don't know what the hell I want. One second I want him to get mad and leave, the next I'm scared to death that he'll leave and never want to see me again.

When he's dressed he walks over to where I'm leaning against the wall. He puts his hands on either side of me, leaning in. "Addison, I'm not a patient man. You need to figure your shit out so we can move on. *I want more.* I want more than just your sweet pussy," he growls as he rubs his hand against my sensitive clit. I inhale sharply. My whole body trembles. He slowly drags his hands up my stomach, over my nipple, stopping at my heart. "I want this, too," he whispers right before he places a soft kiss on my lips.

Aiden steps back, his intense eyes lingering on my body before he turns and walks out the door. I touch my lips, not ever wanting to forget how it feels when he kisses me.

"*Oh, Aiden*, you have my heart. Always have. I'm just afraid you'll shatter it when you find out the truth," I whisper to no one.

Only fate can bring two people together whose lives have been shaped by one determining factor, running parallel to each other the entire time. Paths paved by the same emotion, only to have them finally cross. Perfect for each other, but at the same time, they can never be together. Only fate knows the devastation that will come out of this union. Their paths are no longer parallel. No longer the same. *Now they're colliding. Crashing.*

CHAPTER THIRTY-SIX

I'M HOLDING A sign up that reads "Sydney's ride" as a joke while I wait for her at baggage claim. I think the joke was on me though because I had a few guys, yes, a few, actually tell me they were Sydney and ready for their ride.

I hear her before I see her. "Addie!" she screams, barreling toward me, throwing her arms around my neck. I give her a huge hug. I'm so excited to see her. Even though we talk quite a bit, it's not the same. I blink back my tears of joy. She's actually here.

"Syd, I'm so happy you're here." I hug her tighter. When we finally release, we walk over to the baggage claim to pick up her bag. We talk about her flight and how my aunt is doing. I can tell she's holding something back. She keeps looking at me like she's about to say something but stops.

"Sydney? Spit it out. Whatever you're wanting to say, say it."

"Who the heck is the gorgeous man singing to you on the YouTube video!" She huffs. "And why didn't I know about it!" She punches me as she pouts. I roll my eyes and sigh. That damn video. I still can't believe it's gone viral.

"It just happened on Tuesday!" I wrap my arm around her and guide her to my car after we grab her bag. "There is a much bigger story behind that video that you'll want to know. I'll tell you all about it at my place." I sigh.

"Please tell me you at least said yes! Because if not, you are one dumb woman," she says with a huge grin.

"I said yes," I answer, nodding my head.

*   *   *

Back at my apartment we're settled in the living room with a bottle of wine. Sydney is impatiently waiting for me to tell her the story. She's tapping her fingers on her wine glass and staring at me with expectant eyes.

"Have I told you, I love your hair?" I say, as I get comfortable on the couch. She's grown her hair out to an A-line bob and it looks classy and very chic on her. She shakes her head, but smiles wide.

"Addie! Stop stalling and start talking!" she screams and throws a pillow at me.

"Okay. Okay. I'm sorry I haven't talked to you about this before now. I've been confused and it's been a crazy situation. But I'm so glad you're here in person. I need help." I glance at her with a resigned look.

"Addie, you know I'll always be here for you," she says concerned. "But you've lost me. If I had a guy who serenades me and looks *like that*, there would be no confusion. Whatsoever. I'd skip the date and go right to dessert." She giggles.

"So... *that guy*, that's Jett." She immediately stops giggling and her mouth gapes open. "Yep. Meet my confusion."

"Now *I'm* really confused. Start from the beginning, girlfriend."

I tell her the story about the first time I saw him at his office and everything that has happened the last couple weeks up until last night. I sigh, getting ready to talk about last night.

"Okay. So, before you continue, let me make sure I have this straight. Jett is Aiden, an FBI agent who brought Travis down. He still wants you, obviously really bad. I know how you felt about him and you seem to still have feelings for him. I know you're hesitant because of the whole '*Travis is my father*' thing. You didn't choose him as your father. He's more like your sperm donor. But I know you, you haven't dated much since last summer. I have a feeling it was because you were comparing everyone to Jett... I mean Aiden. Ugh... that's confusing." She giggles. "He's hot as hell, he's the best sex you've ever had, and he seems like a guy who can put up with your stubborn ass, so I don't understand your confusion." She looks at me with a questioning expression.

"There's more." I sigh again. "Last night was our date. He took me to dinner and that's another story in itself." I roll my eyes, remembering Marco and the girls. I'll save that story for another time. "After dinner he takes me to Central Park, lays down a blanket, and we talk. We really didn't know anything about each other. He asked about my parents." I twist my lips and bite my cheek then continue. "I told him my mom died when I was ten and my dad when I was one." I wait for Syd's reaction. She knows that I hate lying, and I really need to hear what she thinks.

"Go on. I'm going to reserve my judgment till the end." She smirks.

"Funny, smartass," I reply, smiling, but I'm sure she'll see it my way when she hears it all. "Anyway... he brings up last summer. I knew that would come up eventually. Especially how I *left*. Come to find out, he had a plan with the FBI to get me out of the house that night." Syd's eyes fly open wide.

"So, you really didn't need to shoot him?" She giggles again. She understands why I did it, but she always joked about me being trigger happy.

"Well, I didn't know that!" I exclaim.

"It seems like you two think alike. Which is crazy because I've never met anyone like you." It's now that I throw the pillow back at her, both of us laughing.

"We're more alike than you think." I take a big drink of my wine and fill my glass up again. "He questions why I was there. Why Travis wanted me to stay. I tell him that I just can't tell him.

He then tells me that the real reason he was there was more personal." I take a deep breath and continue. "That it was more about revenge because Travis had his parents killed when Aiden was fifteen." Syd gasps in shock, her hand flying to her open mouth. "He also said that is why he became a cop and then went into the FBI. He wanted justice for his parents' murder."

"You are kidding me," she whispers.

"Fate. Fucking. Hates. Me," I say, emphasizing each word and then down my wine till it's empty again.

"How did the date end?" she asks.

"Oh... we fucked." I threw myself back on the couch. "And then I asked him to leave. Seriously, what the hell is wrong with me?" I close my eyes and shake my head.

"Was it as good as the first time?" I glance up to her and she's wearing a shit-eating grin.

"Really? Didn't you hear my whole story? *We won't work.* Aiden hates everything that is Travis. Whether I like it or not, I'm part of Travis!" I scream. "Syd, what am I going to do? I had started to think that he might not actually care about Travis being my father, that maybe we had a chance, until he dropped that bomb on me. My heart hurts, my brain hurts. What am I going to do?"

"Oh, girlfriend. I don't know. This is one messed-up situation."

"Thank you, wise one, for your insight," I say sarcastically.

"Well... I'll let you ponder on this one. We're going out and getting trashed tonight! My friend Harper will be here in an hour. We're going singing tonight! And she only knows that we met when he was undercover. So zip it around her." I cock my eyebrow up.

"Your secret is safe with me." She giggles and pretends to zip her lips. The wine is definitely making her feel good.

"Oh, guess what I brought with me?" she questions with a huge smile. I shrug with a questioning expression. "My boots and jersey! The Cowboys play the Giants on Sunday. We are finding a place to watch it. Even though we'll probably be the only ones with Cowboys jerseys on, we are representing!" she squeals. We love football, but we love our Cowboys more. The first game of the season is this Sunday, and I had already planned on watching it with her.

"Already planned on it." I wink.

Chapter Thirty-seven
AIDEN

"I NEVER THOUGHT I'd see the day that Aiden Roberts is pussy whipped." Damon chuckles, pulling a beer to his lips.

We're sitting in a bar, which is the last place I want to be right now, but Damon dragged my ass out for the night. I haven't talked to Addison since our date Tuesday night. That's three days ago. *Three fucking days*. I'm addicted to her already and having withdrawals. I think the main problem is that I *know* the effect I have on her. It's the same she has on me, but she's fighting it and I don't know why.

"Damon, what am I going to do?" I slam my beer down.

"Why are you asking me? You really don't want to know my answer. No woman should be this hard to get. I know Addison's beautiful and all, but she has your shit all tied up in knots. Not. Worth. It," Damon states matter-of-factly. "Look around. There are plenty of women to choose from. Like those girls right there..." He uses his beer to point toward a group of women who have made it known that they are interested. I glance in their direction but look away quickly before making eye contact with any of them.

I sigh. I can't stop thinking about Tuesday night. It's all I've thought about since I left Addison's apartment. I've slept like shit since that night, can't concentrate on work. And now I'm sitting in a bar fucking sulking.

Grow a pair, Roberts.

"I need another beer, and I don't want to wait for our waitress. Need anything?" I say, getting up to head to the bar. My need to drink is faster than our waitress is. Damon nods as I get up. A couple of the girls from that group make their way over. One smiles at me. She's pretty. Long dark hair, good body, blue eyes—but not the color of blue that I crave. I can't muster a hello. I give her a smile and nod then walk to the bar. I squeeze in at the bar and order a couple beers. There's a slight touch on my back, a woman's touch. I silently plead that it's Addison. I turn around and it's the girl who was at our table. I try to hide my disappointment. I don't want to act like an asshole.

"Hi there. Do you mind grabbing my drink since you're already up at the bar?" She hands me a ten-dollar bill. Well, at least she's not that type of girl to automatically expect that I pay for her drink, but there's no way I'll let her pay now.

"That's okay, it's on me. What's your poison?"

"Just a vodka sour." She smiles. She has a great smile. Normally she would be a woman I'd be interested in. Although, she might as well be my sister because I don't have any desire to talk to this girl. I hand her drink to her and head back to the table, beers in hand.

"Thanks for the drink." She walks right by me. Slightly brushing her arm against mine as we walk. Yep, nothing. No spark. "Are you going to sing?" she playfully asks.

"What?" I ask, confused. Oh, God, she's probably seen the video. I laugh, shaking my head. "Nope, no singing for me tonight. I'm trying to decompress after a long day." I'm trying to hint that I'm not interested. I really don't want to be an ass.

"Well, if you change your mind, you can always get on stage with me and sing." She must see my confusion because she points to a stage. "There's karaoke tonight." She smiles.

It all clicks as I watch them set up the stage. We get back to the table, and I sit down. The girl stands beside me, really close. Too close. We're at a high-top table, so we're about the same height now. She doesn't seem to get the hint that I'm not interested.

"Listen," I begin to tell her that it's not her, it's me, when the atmosphere in the room changes suddenly. I'm not sure if I hear her or I can feel her, but I glance to the front door and Addison walks in. I can't tear my eyes away from her. The girl standing too close to me is talking, but I don't hear a word she's saying. Addison is with Harper and another woman. I'm assuming it's Sydney. She's a beautiful woman. Much shorter than Addison though. Short blonde hair, good body, and a great smile, but standing next to Addison, she's average. Addison's wearing tight white jeans with a red halter top. Her lips match her shirt. Thoughts of those red lips wrapped around my cock has me readjusting in my seat. Well, at least I know my cock isn't broken. I just hope random girl standing too close doesn't think it's because of her. She really needs to leave. Now.

"Roberts, what are you staring at?" I hear Damon ask. I tip my beer in her direction. It's taking everything in me to not go to her, wrap those long legs around me, and kiss her into submission. She needs time to figure her shit out. But she better hurry the fuck up. I lean back in my chair, thinking what my next move should be.

"Who is that gorgeous woman with Addison?" Damon murmurs, slapping my back.

"I think that's her best friend from Texas," I reply.

"If women keep coming from Texas who look like those two, I'm moving." He laughs. I nod, taking a sip of my beer.

Chapter Thirty-eight

I CAN TELL I'm being watched. As soon as we're in the bar, I look around. My eyes land on emerald green eyes, and his stare pins me in place. He smiles his gorgeous smile, dimples on full blast, and winks. This small gesture makes my pulse quicken. I don't know how I'm going to be able to deny this man. He's made it clear that I will be his. But when he finds out the truth, he'll never be able to look at me without thinking about his parents. Even if he is able to see past that, will I be able to?

Syd notices that I've stopped walking and follows the direction of my stare. "You are in so much trouble." She laughs. "That gorgeous man looks like a tiger about to pounce on his prey."

"Well, that tiger looks busy," I say, nodding to the girl practically sitting in his lap. I pull Syd and Harper in the opposite direction searching for a table. Luckily we grab a table as a group gets up to leave. My phone vibrates in my purse. There's a text from Aiden.

Aiden: You look gorgeous

Me: You look busy

Aiden: Jealous ;)

Ugh. No... Yes. Syd looks at my text when I voice my frustrations. She laughs. Really? This situation sucks. I am jealous. Very jealous. I look over to him and with a knowing smirk, he raises his eyebrows, waiting for an answer. The girl is oblivious to our current banter. She's the only one though, because I see Damon staring in our direction. Although, his stare is pinned on Sydney. *Great!*

Me: Tell Damon to stop! Sydney's only here for a few days!

I hear Syd ask Harper if the guy standing next to Aiden is the other guy from the video. Upon confirmation, Syd replies "Yum!"

Me: And if that girl gets any closer to you, I might be inclined to remove her myself. ;)

I hear Aiden laugh out loud. His deep, sexy laugh has me smiling at him. Tingles spread all over my body. He whispers something to the girl, and she looks my direction with a sour face and walks away, grabbing her friend as she leaves.

Aiden: There's my feisty girl. As much as that sounds HOT, I've seen you fight... it wouldn't end well for her. ;)

"Addison stop texting your *boyfriend*. Are we joining them or staying here? Because we need to order drinks and get on the list to sing," Harper barks.

I look over to see Aiden sitting back in his chair, watching me. "We're going to stay right here. It's girls' night so let's show Sydney what us girls do." I hug Syd. I'm still so excited she's here. The waitress comes over and places three shots on the table.

"We haven't ordered yet," I say, looking at the shots the waitress delivered.

"Well, it seems you have admirers. These are from the table of insanely hot guys over there." She points to Aiden's table. We all look over to their table. A couple of other FBI agents have gathered around.

"Holy freaking hotness!" Syd says excitedly. "You did NOT tell me that you worked with the Chippendales of the FBI." All three of us laugh at her description of the guys. Picking up our shots, we "air" toast the table of guys.

Harper jumps up after we finish our shots. "Alright, girls, I'm going to go put us down for a song. Order more drinks!" She struts off to the karaoke sign-up sheet. I'm a little worried that she's picking a song by herself.

"So… is Damon single?" Syd wags her eyebrows.

"Syd! You're only here for a week." I pout.

"What if I told you that I might move here?"

"For Damon?" I ask, confused.

"No! For me. To be closer to you. I miss you so much, and I need a change. Jeff and I decided our relationship just sizzled out. He works too much anyway. We never saw each other, and when we did we argued. When I decided to come visit, I applied to a few places and have interviews lined up all week while you're at work." She's looking at me nervously, waiting for my approval.

"Oh, my God! That is amazing news!" I scream while I grab her for a hug. "Why is this the first time I'm hearing about this?"

"I was going to tell you when I first got here, but then we were a little busy talking about your *new man* and then we came out. I couldn't hold it in any longer." We're still embraced in a hug when Harper walks up.

We fill in Harper with the good news. She's excited, too. She and Syd get along great, which I knew they would. Our drinks arrive just in time for a toast. "Here's to Sydney getting a new job," I say as we all raise our glasses.

"And to me getting to have a taste of that gorgeous FBI man," Syd says right before she takes a drink. Harper laughs so hard she almost spits her drink out all over us. Thankfully I had swallowed my drink already because I'm dying laughing, too. My phone dings and I see it's from Aiden.

Aiden: What are we celebrating? I love hearing you laugh.

I look at Damon who is staring at Sydney and roll my eyes.

Me: Just girl stuff

After a few drinks our names are called for karaoke. When we get to the stage, we are all feeling pretty tipsy. Sydney has been a singer her entire life and has a beautiful voice, so I push her to the front.

When we see what song Harper has picked out we all giggle. We take our places on stage and the music starts. Adam Levine's "Moves Like Jagger" fills the room. Harper and I work the room with our dancing and back-up vocals while Syd works the room with her voice. I notice that she's zoned in on one person: Damon. The crowd is going crazy by the time we're done. Lots of clapping and screaming as we make our way back to our table. Enjoying our post-performance high, we're laughing and high-fiving everyone as we pass. Three drinks are already waiting for us when we get there. The waitress smiles at us as we take our seat. "You know who," she says before walking off.

I glance over to Aiden and mouth "*Thank you*" as I take a sip of my drink. I can see the heat in his eyes from where I'm sitting. I smile and wink at him. He picks up his phone and types. Next thing I know my phone dings.

Aiden: My cock and my hands are having a disagreement right now

I tilt my head to the side and twist my lips.

Me: ????

Aiden: My cock really wants to pound you, but my hands want to pound every asshole in here who is staring at you right now :(

Me: Awww. Jealous?

Aiden: Never...

I can tell he's texting again, so I wait before I respond with "*bullshit.*"

Aiden: Before you

As I'm about to press send with a reply, I look his way but he's not in his seat. I glance around to see where he went and then he's right in front of me. He wraps his hand behind my head and pulls me into a deep kiss. A kiss that is meant to show dominance, to show possession. I immediately submit, melting into the kiss. I grab his muscular arms to keep me up. When he moves back, there's a devilish glint in his eye.

"Mine," he leans down and whispers in my ear. The heat of his breath makes me clench my thighs and wiggle in my seat. He laughs as he turns around and walks back to his table.

I erase my original response and text

Me: Tarzan

"You guys are going to make beautiful babies," Syd says dreamily.

"That's what I said!" Harper jumps up and high-fives Syd. They're both giggling, talking about baby names, power couples, and nicknames. I shake my head and down my drink.

A few songs later we are out of our seats, dancing by our table. Drinks continue to appear as soon as we finish the current ones. I text Aiden asking if he is trying to get me drunk. He just laughs and winks.

I watch Damon stare at Sydney from across the room. I'm not sure if she even notices him. She hasn't said anything. When he notices that I'm watching him, he sports a huge grin. He grabs Aiden's phone. Not a second later, my phone is dinging.

Aiden: Introduce me to your friend :)

Aiden grabs his phone and texts me, too.

Aiden: Just so you know that was not from me!

I laugh out loud. Syd and Harper come look at what I'm laughing at. Syd smiles and dances. "I was wondering if he'd ever come meet me." She giggles. "He's been eye fucking me all night long."

I bust out laughing. "Sydney, when did you start cussing so much?" She shrugs and continues dancing.

Me: Come over and meet her yourself

I don't wait to see their response. I join the girls dancing.

Within a couple minutes, Aiden and Damon have made their way over to our table. They bring us more drinks since ours are empty. I look at Aiden, raising a curious eyebrow.

"What? I couldn't let him come all the way over by himself." He smirks. "And if she's your best friend, then I want to meet her, too…" he crosses his arms "…AND you didn't specify on *my* phone who you were telling to come over."

"Are you done?" I ask, walking up to him. He nods and smiles. "I wasn't questioning why you came over." I lean up and kiss him. Stepping back, I say, "I was wondering why you're trying to get me drunk." I tilt my head in the direction of all the drinks on our table they just brought over. "Are you trying to get lucky?" I hear Damon laughing. I look over to see what he's laughing at, and he's looking at me shaking his head.

"What?" I ask, poking him.

"Nothing bad," he replies with his hands up in the air. "You'll find out soon." What the hell does that mean? I look back to a grinning Aiden, so I narrow my eyes. He shrugs. I don't know what they are planning, but it's something. I should be scared.

Aiden laughs, pulling me to his hard, muscular chest. "You look beautiful tonight, sweetheart."

"Thanks," I say suspiciously. "Nice deflection."

Syd comes over, standing by my side. "Hi, I'm Sydney," she says in her sing-song voice introducing herself to Aiden. I smile at her then realize that I was supposed to be introducing her to these guys. Damn Aiden.

Always a distraction.

Aiden releases me. "Hey, Sydney, I'm Aiden. This here is Damon," he says, slapping Damon on the back after shaking her hand.

Damon takes Syd's hand and leans over and whispers something. She blushes as she giggles. I'm about to say something, but the DJ announces the next singers.

"Aiden, Dave, and Damon. Get your asses on stage," he orders.

"That's our cue," Aiden leans over and gives me a quick kiss and walks to the stage.

The crowd, especially the women, go wild when they see the three incredibly gorgeous guys on stage. I don't blame them. Someone yells, "Take it off!" Syd whips around, staring at me.

Oh, shit! Did I yell that? I laugh at my drunk self. I look back to the stage, and Aiden is shaking his head, mouthing "*You are cut off.*" Still laughing, I blow him a kiss.

Damon works the crowd with his sexy voice and banter. Catcalls and whistles sweep across the crowd. The music begins and Damon looks at us and says, "This one's for the ladies," and points to our table. The entire bar turns and looks at us. Instead of being mortified, our drunk selves scream and jump up and down, like Jon Bon Jovi just dedicated a song to us.

Aiden takes center stage and "Get Lucky" by Daft Punk fills the air. The crowd goes wild. Aiden's sexy, deep voice sings to me the entire length of the song. He has a devilish smile every time he sings about getting lucky. My body is on fire, watching him on stage. He's wearing dark jeans and a white, button-up shirt, rolled up, showing off his strong forearms.

When the song ends, the guys make their way back to our table. Women are throwing themselves at them left and right. Aiden's eyes never waver from mine. Instead of waiting for him to get to me, I run and jump into his arms, wrapping my legs around him. I bite his lower lip. "You are so fucking hot," I mumble into his mouth, devouring his lips. He wraps his arms around my waist, pulling me into him. Our kiss doesn't last long enough. He pulls away, walking over to my stool and placing me down. I pout, sticking out my lower lip.

"You, sweetheart, are drunk." He chuckles as he pokes me in the nose.

"Well, *that* is all your fault!" I reply, poking him in the chest.

One touch sends sparks through me. I twist his shirt in my fist, pulling him over to me. "I'm not done with you." I kiss him again. He doesn't pull away this time. Instead, he takes control of the kiss. His hands wrap in my hair, pulling it back, giving him easier access to my lips. I moan into his mouth.

"You two need to get a room." Harper interrupts our heated kiss. As we pull apart, Aiden squeezes my thighs.

"I will *never* be done with you," he growls in my ear then grabs his drink from the table behind me. When he drains his drink, he tells me he'll be right back. *Something about hitting the head.* When I lick my lips, a low growl erupts. "Woman," his raspy voice warns as he turns around to walk away.

"Golden vagina," Harper squeaks out. I look at her and we both giggle. I look around for Sydney but don't see her.

"Where's Sydney?" I ask Harper while she's wiping tears from her eyes.

"I think she's getting a *taste of the gorgeous FBI man*," she says, using air quotes.

What? "Holy shit, where did she go?" I look around. Harper just shrugs.

Aiden walks back up. "You're back awfully quick," I say, still looking around for Syd.

"Yeah, some asshole locked the bathroom so there's a line. Seriously, get a room," he barks. My eyes go wide. *Oh, my God!* Aiden furrows his brows then looks around. He must notice that Damon and Sydney are nowhere in sight. I roll my eyes, shaking my head. Aiden busts out laughing. "I guess I know who the asshole is."

Half an hour later we're all walking out of the bar. I didn't say anything to Syd when she made it back to the table. *But I will.* Since we're all drunk, the guys won't let us go home alone. Dave goes with Harper in a taxi, making sure she gets home. Syd and Damon go in one taxi, and Aiden and I go in another heading to my apartment. Our taxi arrives first. I've had a really hard time keeping my hands to myself in the car. Aiden gets out and pulls me into his chest, kissing me on the head.

"Aren't you coming in?" I ask suggestively.

Damon and Syd's taxi pulls up. Damon walks past us, carrying a passed-out Syd. "She sleeping in the guest room?" he asks. I nod my head.

Aiden narrows his eyes. "How the fuck does he know where your apartment is, let alone where the rooms are inside?"

I giggle. "I like jealous Aiden." I run my hand across his stubbled jawline. He raises a curious eyebrow when I don't answer. "I've had a few small parties here, and he's come over. I promise you, it's never been anything but friendship," I try to explain without slurring.

"Good," he replies, leaning me against a wall right outside the door to my building. "And no, I'm not coming in." I stick my lower lip out, and he bites it then sucks on it before kissing me. His tongue slowly caresses mine. The door beside us swings open forcefully, causing me to jump. We both look over to a brooding Damon. He walks down the street. His posture is stiff as he stalks away. My curious eyes meet Aiden's. He shrugs.

"I thought you wanted to get lucky?" I whisper, brushing up against him, taking my hand and rubbing the outline of his erection. He lets out an audible gasp. He grabs my hands and puts them behind my back, pinning me against the wall.

"You mean do I want to taste you? Sink my cock in your hot pussy so I can hear you scream my name?" he growls in my ear as he thrusts his hips forward. "Every fucking second of every day since I've met you, sweetheart." He bites my earlobe. I moan. My breathing is erratic. I can feel the heat between my legs as he rubs his thigh over my sensitive clit. "But I. Want. More," his raspy voice grates out between his teeth. I close my eyes momentarily as I exhale shakily.

"What if I can't give you more?" I say softly.

"Oh, you can. And I know you want to. I can see it in your eyes."

"It's complicated, Aiden." I sigh.

"Then un-complicate it." Freeing my hands, he cups my neck. Lightly brushing his thumb on my bottom lip. "Goodnight, sweetheart." He leans over and tenderly kisses me. Stepping back, he opens the door for me.

"I guess it's just me and my trusty bullet tonight," I mumble as I walk off. I don't know if he heard me, but at this point I don't care. Feeling the sting of his rejection, I'm comforted knowing that he has a serious case of blue balls right now. Serves him right for getting me drunk, singing to me about getting lucky, and then denying me.

Chapter Thirty-nine

IT'S SUNDAY MORNING and Syd and I feel good considering we spent most of our day yesterday with a major hangover. It's been a long time since I was that drunk. Now I know why. It sucks the next day. We both piece together our night like a puzzle because there are some fuzzy spots. I close my eyes in embarrassment over the alcohol controlling my actions and laying claim to Aiden in front of everyone.

I flop on the couch next to Sydney, laying my head on her shoulder. "Why did I fall in the love with the *one* guy I shouldn't have." I let out a soft sigh.

"Girl, I've seen that man look at you. I don't think he'll care." She leans her head on mine. "I think you should just tell him. Travis is only your sperm donor. You have nothing to do with him. Didn't even know about him until just a year ago," she explains, like it's something I don't know. Yeah, I know all right. It replays in my head like a broken record all day.

"How can he not care? My dad killed his parents!" I groan in frustration.

"And what does that have to do with *you*? Nothing!" She sits up and grabs my shoulders and shakes them. "All I know is that man is crazy for you. I can only hope a guy will look at me that way from across the room. I think I was flustered *for you* most of Friday night. At least the parts I remember." She giggles.

"Oh, you did have someone looking at you all night… *that's* why you were so flustered." I poke her in the stomach. She blushes as she laughs.

"Mmm… Damon is hot! He's not a long-term type of guy, though. Fun for a night or two, but that gorgeous man is too caught up on himself to think about anyone else," she says as she gets up off the couch.

"So, did you check off one of those nights of fun?" I ask. I hear in the kitchen snickering. "Don't think I didn't notice," I tease, looking back to see her raising an eyebrow.

"Detective Addison, I can neither confirm nor deny those accusations," she jokingly says as she walks into the guest bedroom.

I jump up after her. "Oh, no, you don't get off that easy." I say walking after her.

"Actually, I did." She winks, and we both hysterically laugh, falling on her bed.

"That is not what I meant." I throw a pillow at her. "But since you brought it up… what? Where?" I say, sitting up. "Oh, wait! I just remembered. The bathroom!"

She giggles. "We just messed around a bit. He was fun. End of story. You know he's not my type," she says, lying on her side, resting her head on her elbow.

"What… muscular, tall, gorgeous, and confident doesn't do it for you?" We both laugh, knowing that's exactly what she doesn't go for. Syd's a singer and a teacher. She usually goes for the artsy type.

"You know me, I go for safe. And Damon is definitely *not* safe." She shakes her head. "But he's got skills, I'll give him that." She lets out a long breath. "Anyway, I don't even live here."

"Yet," I quickly add.

* * *

A couple hours later we walk into my neighborhood bar to watch the noon football game. Syd and I are huge football fans. And not just for any team... but the Dallas Cowboys. Syd's parents had season passes when we were growing up, so it became one of our favorite things to do. Today is the first game of the season, and they're playing the New York Giants. We're both wearing our cowboy boots, which I haven't worn since my going away party, jean shorts, and our Dallas Cowboys jerseys.

When we walk in we're met with whistles and yee-haws. Ben, the bartender, is shaking his head as we approach. I've been coming to this bar since I've been in New York; it's a block away from my place, so Ben and I are good friends.

"Addison. You're breaking my heart!" he says as he grips his chest and groans. Syd and I laugh. "But holy hell, y'all look hot. Who's your friend?" He smirks, lifting his chin toward Sydney.

"Ben, this is my best friend, Sydney. Sydney, Ben. She's visiting me from Texas." I smile as I wrap my arm around her waist.

Ben sticks out his hand and they shake. "Nice to meet you, Sydney. What can I get *y'all* to drink?" We giggle at his over-the-top southern accent.

We grab our drinks and glide to a tall table. TVs are placed all over the bar so anywhere we sit we'll see the game. The atmosphere is loud and there are a lot of Giant fans. Not surprisingly, there are other Cowboys fans here, too. They stop by our table every so often to joke with other Giant fans. The bar goes crazy at every touchdown, no matter who gets it. Syd and I have always loved the competitive camaraderie at games. We love going to the other teams' tailgates and having fun.

It's half time and the teams are tied. Ben puts on music and we're out of our seats dancing. I feel my phone vibrate in my back pocket. Pulling it out, I see a text from Aiden.

Aiden: Hey, beautiful, what are you doing?

I show the text to Sydney and tell her to take a picture of just my legs and boots. I text back with only the picture. I can see him typing a response almost immediately.

Aiden: You are definitely wearing those next time we fuck

My pulse quickens at the thought of next time. I laugh as I tell Syd to take a picture of just my ass and legs. I send the picture to him.

Aiden: Are you trying to kill me? I'm hard as a rock seeing that ass of yours. Where are you?

I can't stop laughing, thinking about the picture I'm about to take. I know he's a Giants fan. We've never really talked about football before, other than when he mentioned being ready for football season to start and hoping the Giants have a good one. I grab a girl sitting at the next table and ask her to take a picture of Syd and me but to make sure to get our boots and everything. I text the picture but add text this time.

Me: Go Cowboys ;)

Aiden: That is just wrong! So. Fucking. Wrong.

We're laughing so hard we're wiping tears from our eyes. "Your man actually might have found something about you he doesn't like," Syd laughs out.

I text him back.

Me: What? Don't be a hater. Are you afraid of losing?

I figured he'd write back right away, but he doesn't. We get another beer before the game comes back on. Other people have gathered around us as we watch. Smack talk is going back and forth, but everyone's having a great time. I jump up out of my seat as Dallas has the ball and is running with it.

"Go, go, go!" I yell as they get closer to the end zone. He's almost there. I'm jumping up and down.

WHACK!

I whip around. "Who the hell just smacked my a—"

Lips crash over mine. *Aiden.* My mouth opens in automatic response, letting his tongue devour me. He demands control as his tongue does what it pleases: biting my lower lip then sucking it. I feel hands grabbing my ass, pulling me closer. I can feel his arousal on my thigh, the tingle between my legs growing into need. A low growl erupts as we break the seal. I look up into beautiful emerald green eyes laced with lust and it makes my breath catch.

"That was for teasing me with that ass shot," Aiden says as he takes a hand full of my ass and squeezes. I'm trapped in the aura of Aiden that I don't even remember there's a game happening. I have to take a step back to regain my own senses, to break his hold on me.

"What the— How the h—," I stutter, not being able to form a sentence. I hear laughing and look over at Damon, who's shaking his head at us. Looking away from Aiden brings me back to the present. I blow out a breath and look back to Aiden, who smirks a knowing smile. I grab my beer and chug the rest of it.

"Ben," Aiden's deep voice yells out without looking away, "Addison needs another beer."

"Aiden! How's it going, man?" Ben yells back. This has Aiden turning and walking his way. They shake hands as Ben hands him my beer. Aiden walks with such confidence and strength, I bite my bottom lip as I drink him in, appraising his body. A slow, smug smile appears on his face with a devilish glint in his eyes.

"So, you want to put your money where your mouth is?" Aiden asks as he gets to the table and sits down on my stool.

I arch my eyebrow. "What are you talking about?" I look over at Damon for help, but he is staring at Syd, who is talking to a group of people we met earlier. He doesn't look happy. A loud laugh has me looking back at Aiden. "Sucks, brother. Doesn't it?" he says as he slaps him on the back.

"Fuck you," Damon barks as he pushes off the chair and heads to the bar. I'm so confused. What did I miss?

"Inside joke?" I ask.

He smirks and nods. "Anyway, you asked if I'm afraid of losing. Do you want to bet that the Cowboys will win?" He smiles. I look at the score and it's almost the end of the third quarter. The Cowboys are up by seven points. I look back to Aiden and narrow my eyes.

"What's the bet?" I ask playfully as I take a drink. My tongue darts out to lick my bottom lip and catches a drop of beer.

"Woman, you constantly test my self-control," he growls as he adjusts himself. I giggle before taking another drink. "So, the bet... If I win, I get to take you on a date, anywhere, doing anything, no questions asked." He sports a sexy half grin, revealing one of his dimples.

I twist my lips. "And if I win?"

He shrugs. "You pick."

"Hmm... okay, if I win you take me to the next Giants vs. Cowboys game *and* you have to wear a Dallas Cowboys jersey." I see him swallow and glance up at the TV looking at the score. "*Are you scared?*" I tease.

What am I talking about? *I am.* Anywhere, doing anything, no questions asked? That makes my blood pressure rise just thinking about it.

"Nope, not at all. I know my boys are going to come through. So is it a bet?" He puts his hand out to shake on it. I hesitate. Do I really want to give him that much control over me for a night? I'm not usually one to just sit back and enjoy the ride.

Well, unless he's the ride.

Oh, what the hell! I reach out and grab his hand, and he pulls me to him. "May the best team win." He smirks. Instead of letting me go, he pulls me in between his legs. "By the way, you look hot and I am *not* kidding about you, me, and those boots." He rubs his hand where he slapped my ass.

Which reminds me... "By the way, you ever slap me again, you're going to lose a hand," I whisper in his ear.

"*Mmm...* there's my feisty girl."

CHAPTER FORTY

"OKAY! I'LL TAKE you to meet him," I say as I bring the straw to my lips, drinking the last few drops of my iced chai tea latte. All that is left is a full cup of ice. I sigh, shaking the cup.

I've been looking forward to spending today with Sydney this whole week. The change in weather seems to have brought all the crazies out. Every day we're inundated with new crime scenes, which meant late nights. Weeks like this make me question humanity. They also make me more aware of my surroundings. Like the man sitting on the bench across the street from us. He's reading a newspaper—at least that is what he wants us to think. Every time I glance in his direction, our gazes lock for a brief second before he looks down. He's tall and muscular and from what I can see of his face, he looks eerily familiar, especially his eyes. I can't seem to place where I've seen him before.

"I leave tomorrow. I need to meet the guy who named his restaurant after my best friend," Syd says, pulling me from my thoughts.

"We don't know that for sure. Maybe when he called me that, he liked how it rolled off the tongue." I shrug dismissively, still paying close attention to the stranger.

"Mmm-hmm." She narrows her eyes at me. "What or *who* has caught your attention, Detective Mason?" I laugh at the childhood nickname.

"You know me so well." Leaning forward, I say, "So there's a guy across the street, watching us. He's been there for about fifteen minutes." My voice is low and hushed. "I don't know why, but I feel I know him from somewhere, but for the life of me, I can't place him."

I peek over Sydney's head. I sit up straight, looking both ways down the street. "He's gone." Vendors are setting up shop for the day, city workers wash off the sidewalks, but no strange man.

"What did he look like?" Syd asks, turning around to look at the empty bench.

"Typical, nothing that really stuck out. Jeans, polo, baseball cap."

"You've had a rough week. Maybe you're reading too much into things," she says. "*Maybe* he was just checking out two beautiful women."

I sigh. "You're probably right."

"I am *always* right. Now get up and let's get our shopping on." She jumps out of her chair, picks up our trash then throws it away. The crisp morning breeze sends a shiver through me. The sun is peeking around the tall buildings, not yet spreading it's warmth in the shadows.

"Let's get in the sun. I'm cold," I say.

"If you'd... I don't know... *drink a hot drink*, you wouldn't be so cold."

"Okay, smartass. You know that'll never happen. Now let's go get lost in Macy's."

A few hours later and four armfuls of bags, we decide to make a pit stop at my apartment before continuing our shopping spree.

"After we drop these off, where to next?" I ask as we get off the elevator and head to my door.

"Let's go to Soho and shop around the little bou—"

"Shh." I stop her, holding up a finger to my lips as I grab my gun out of my purse. Syd stares at me with furrowed brows. "I went to unlock my door, but it was already unlocked. Stay here while I check things out."

"I am not staying out here when you're going in there with the gun," she whisper-yells. Dropping her bags, she stands right behind me.

We walk in slowly. Syd's touch is soft on my back, and I can hear both our hearts pounding. My gun is pointed and ready as I sweep the living room and kitchen. Sunlight floods the rooms; nobody could be hiding in either of them. Going from room to room, we don't find anything. Everything seems fine.

I lay my gun on the kitchen counter, recounting my steps this morning when we left. I've never left my apartment unlocked before, but maybe I was distracted. I look at Syd with twisted lips.

"Don't ask me. I left before you did to call home. I met you downstairs," she says. I nod, remembering that.

"I don't remember being distracted, but then I don't remember exactly locking the door either. I must have rushed out so I wouldn't keep you waiting." I shrug.

I don't tell Syd that I still have an uneasy feeling. I'm not sure if I'm overreacting because of the strange man this morning and now this, but nothing looks touched, out of place, or different.

"Would you feel better if you called Aiden?"

"Why in the world would I do that?" I ask.

She shrugs. "He's FBI."

"*Really?* I work for NYPD. Why would I call the FBI?" I look at her incredulously, my eyes wide. "I don't *need* Aiden to come running to my rescue." I sigh.

"Addie, you think you don't *need* anyone, but I know you want that man. You've never acted this way toward any guy. And you haven't seen him in almost a week. I thought maybe you'd want to talk to him," she says, smirking.

"We've texted this week," I say defensively. "And we've both been really busy with work. *And* that's not true about not needing anyone…" I jut out my lower lip "…I'll always need you," I say, wrapping my arms around her. She hugs me back.

"Well, yea. I'm your other half. The better one, of course." She snickers while I roll my eyes. "So now we know that nothing is wrong here, we have more shopping to do, girlfriend." Syd grabs her purse off the table.

I blow out a breath and shrug to myself. I guess I just left it unlocked. Before we leave I grab my gun and put it back in my purse, double-checking to make sure my door is locked.

* * *

"My feet are killing me," I whine. We've been shopping for almost eight hours straight, besides the short trip to my apartment earlier. "Can't we just order in?" I plop down on my couch and have no intentions of getting up.

"No." Syd walks over and stands over me with her hands on her hips. I internally laugh because she's about the same height as me sitting down. "I want to meet Marco. I know it's not too far from here so zip it. You're not getting out of it."

"Fine." I sigh. "Let's go get ready."

I'm really tempted to wear yoga pants and a T-shirt, but since it's a Friday night, and the last night that Syd will be here, I decide against it. Instead it's dark jeans, a black draped top that hangs over one shoulder, and chunky boots. The boots won't kill my already over-tired feet. I don't even feel like curling my hair, so tonight it's bone straight. When I'm satisfied with my modest makeup, I go find Sydney.

The music coming from Syd's room drowns the clumping noise my boots make on the hardwood floor. I hear our song start to play: "My Church" by Maren Morris. Syd's walking out of her bathroom as I'm walking in her bedroom. We both start belting out the song.

As the song ends, Syd turns the music off. I sigh. "You leaving sucks." I dread sending her back to Texas tomorrow. I sit on the bed while she finishes getting ready.

"I know." Her lips twist. "But hopefully some of my interviews went well this week and I'll be living here soon," she quickly says, sitting down beside me on the bed.

"Well, they'd be stupid not to hire you." I lean my head on her shoulder. We're silent for a few minutes.

"Come on, Addie. We can't stay here all night and wish something we have no control over." She grabs my hand and drags me out the door.

"Holy heavenly smell. It smells so good." Syd inhales deeply as we walk into the restaurant.

"I know. The food is to die for. And the garlic rolls... *Mmm*," I say, remembering the way they melted on my tongue. Garlic and olive oil. My stomach grumbles.

"Beautiful Addison," I hear Marco yell from across the room. Syd's eyes widen. I roll mine. I really wish he'd stop saying that.

He struts toward us and tells the hostess something in Italian. "Hi, Marco," I say. He grabs me in his typical hug, lifting me off the floor.

"Will Aiden be joining you tonight?" he asks. He tries to sound nonchalant, but there's a little sarcasm in his tone.

I ignore it. "No, not tonight. I'm here with my best friend, Sydney."

He takes Syd's hand and kisses it. "So very nice to meet Addison's best friend. I'm Marco." He smiles wide as he glances from Syd to me. Out of the corner of my eye, I see Syd tilt her head, watching Marco. I fiddle with my purse to break eye contact.

"So I have to ask. Did yo–" My head whips up as I grab Syd by the arm, my eyes wide, silently demanding her to shut up.

"Did I what?" Marco flashes a knowing smile at both of us.

Shit. I don't want to know if he named his restaurant after me. That'll make it way too awkward, and if Aiden ever found out... I shake my head just imagining what might happen.

Syd's mischievous smile stretches across her face. Shit, she's not going to let this go. She squeezes my arm. I'm not sure if she's telling me to brace myself or to calm down, but I'm nervous as hell.

"Did you…" she pauses as she licks her lips "…know that Italian is Addison's favorite food?" She cocks an eyebrow.

Marco laughs out loud. I purse my lips together, shaking my head. I'm going to kill Syd. I narrow my eyes at her.

"Ladies, your table is ready." Marco chuckles, leading us to our table on the terrace. It has the most magnificent view of the city skyline. We're only three stories high, but we have an amazing view of the Empire State Building.

"Wow," Syd says, spinning around.

"Only the best table for my Addison," Marco says, giving me a sexy grin.

I sigh. "Marco…" I look him in the eyes. I don't want to be a bitch, but I need him to understand that I'm definitely not *his*. And I don't want him to think that there's a chance. I need to figure out what's going on between Aiden and me first. I blow out a breath. "You know I'm dating Aiden." I'll just go with that; not sure it's true, but hopefully it'll work.

He holds his hands up. "You can't fault a guy for trying." He winks and smiles wide. "Your waitress will be here shortly. Enjoy the view, ladies." He turns and walks away. Both Syd and I watch. He is definitely easy on the eyes.

"Oh, my gosh, Addie. You now know, right?" Syd asks.

"What the hell was that earlier?" I whisper-yell. The traffic below is loud so no one can hear us.

"That was me trying to see what the heck is up with this guy. And he knew what I was going to ask." She stares at me.

I run my hands through my hair, glancing over to where Marco is standing. His eyes meet mine, and he smiles. I look away quickly. "So he liked the name he gave me. It's not like he knew I lived here." I shrug.

She twists her lips, tapping her finger on the table. "I don't know, Addie. He definitely has a thing for you though."

I try to forget about the Marco situation while we inhale our food. It's more amazing than the view. We enjoy a bottle of red wine, compliments of Marco, of course. Syd's phone starts to play "Bad Boy" by Inner Circle. My mouth gapes open as she answers and says hello to Damon.

I mouth, "*Really?*"

She giggles. She doesn't talk to him long. When she hangs up, I say, "You really gave him *that* ringtone?"

"Yep. It definitely fits." She wags her eyebrows.

We both laugh as we pick up our wine glasses. "To sisters, who'll hopefully be back together again soon," I say, holding out my wine glass.

"To sisters." We clink our glasses and take a drink.

A car horn pulls my attention toward the street. People crowd the sidewalks. That's one thing I love about New York City, it's always busy here. A red baseball cap catches my eye. I narrow my eyes to look at the person wearing it. He is sitting at the restaurant patio across the street from us, but his head is down so I can't see his face. A shiver runs through me as I notice the clothes. He's wearing the same clothes as the person from this morning.

"Syd," I say, putting my wine glass down, "there's that guy again."

Her head turns toward the guy. "Are you sure? There are millions of people in this city. What are the odds of you seeing the same person twice?"

"My thoughts exactly," I say. "Let's go."

"What? Go where?" She grabs my arm.

"I'm going to find out who the hell he is."

"Addie. Addison!" she yells as she catches up to me. "This is not a good idea. Maybe you should really call Aiden. Or… I don't know, the police? You know, all your *new* friends…"

When we pass Marco, I tell him we'll be right back. He looks at me with confusion, but I don't give him enough time to ask any questions. Taking the stairs two at a time, I'm outside in a couple minutes with Syd right behind me. She complains the whole time about this being a really bad idea. I put my hand in my purse and rest it on my gun as I cross the street.

The guy is still sitting there as I approach, but his head is still down as he continues reading. My heart beats fast and my hand grasps my gun.

I approach him. "Why are you following us?" I say in a tight voice.

The man looks up with a malicious grin. My spine stiffens. It's not the same guy. "I'm sorry, I don't know what you're talking about," he says snidely, but he's not surprised by my accusation. I narrow my eyes.

"We're sorry. We thought you were someone else," Syd says, yanking on my arm. He nods slowly.

As we walk away, I turn back and his smile makes my skin crawl. His eyes are cold and flat. As we walk up the stairs back to the restaurant, I look at Syd, who is watching me. "Someone is screwing with me," I spit out. "That guy has the exact same clothes and is the same build as the guy this morning. *And* he wasn't surprised to see us." Syd nods, her lips pressing together.

When we get home, I notice Syd hasn't said much. "I'm sorry. Tonight was supposed to be fun." My shoulders hunch over as I look down.

"Hey, I'm not mad at you, I'm worried. What if you're right?" She takes a water out of the fridge. "Maybe you should really tell Aiden."

I sigh. "I promise if anything else happens, I will."

CHAPTER FORTY-ONE

AIDEN

I'M REGRETTING MY stupid decision to not give in to Addison until she figures her shit out. What the hell was I thinking? I wasn't even the one who was drunk. Couldn't I have thought of something that wouldn't have left me with blue balls every night? On top of that, I miss her. And it's only been a week. She wanted to spend time with Syd, so I backed off. It's Monday morning and I'm supposed to be working, but nope, I'm sitting here thinking about Addison. I've picked up my phone at least five times to call her and ask her to lunch, but I'm afraid she'll reject me. *When the fuck have I ever been afraid of rejection? Oh, yeah, never, 'cause it's never happened!*

I don't understand what's in that head of hers. She's afraid of something. I throw my head back and groan in frustration.

Damon walks in and sits across from me. "What's wrong?" He's sporting a shit-eating grin. *Asshole.* He knows damn well what's wrong. He's been telling me all along that no woman is worth this much trouble. And before Addison those were my thoughts, too.

I say the only thing I can think of that'll piss him off. "Have a chance to talk to Sydney before she left?"

Sydney has had him fucked up all week, and I've loved the hell out it. "We talked real quick when she and Addison were at the new Italian restaurant. Mistero… something." He shrugs.

Marco. That reminds me, I need to look into him. I pull up our database and start typing.

While trying to find information, I ask, " Have you been to the new place?"

"A couple weeks ago. Why?" He narrows his eyes.

"Did you meet the owner?"

"He introduced himself."

"What did you think?"

"What's this about, Aiden?" Damon's tone turns serious as he leans forward with his elbows on my desk, glancing at my computer. I tell him about the other night and what Addison told me. And how the name of the restaurant is too much of a coincidence.

Damon nods. "He was a little too friendly, but really I didn't think twice about it when I met him." I continue typing while I listen.

"Bingo." I turn my computer and point to what I found.

"Hmm. Do we need to put him on a watch list?" he says, pulling a sticky note off my desk and writing his name down.

"I'm not sure yet. But I'll be watching out for him around Addison."

"You going to tell her?" he asks.

"Yeah, but not until after our date. She'll get pissed, thinking I'm just being jealous." I smirk.

"You are." He laughs, leaning back in his chair. "Did you decide where you're taking her yet?"

Giants beat the Cowboys by one point in the last five seconds of the game. I laugh, remembering how pissed Addison was.

"Yep. I'm taking her out with Max on Saturday. And then hopefully New Haven after."

"What? *Without me?* I want to go." He's dead serious as he furrows his eyebrows.

"Fuck no, you pansy. It's a date, and it doesn't include you."
I laugh.

"You think she'll be okay with it?" he asks, joking aside.

"You know Addison. You ever see her back away from a challenge?"

* * *

It's lunchtime and I'm done waiting. I need to see Addison. She's like a drug and I haven't had my fix. I call the front receptionist, and she tells me that Addison is still in her office. I grab Chinese food on my way over. I'm not even sure if she likes Chinese, so I bring a few choices. I'm riding up the elevator and starting to sweat. You'd think I was a teenager picking up a girl for a date. I sigh. Maybe I should've called her. The elevator doors open on floor three. Too late. People see me. I straighten my back, roll my shoulders, and walk in like I'm supposed to be here.

A few people say hello in passing. I'm so focused on getting to Addison's office, I don't even remember who it was. I walk up just as she's leaving her office. She looks up as she shuts her door, surprise on her face. "Aiden. What are you doing here?"

I hold up the bags. "I was hoping you'd have lunch with me." I flash a sexy-half grin.

"Oh."

"If you don't already have plans," I close my eyes and shake my head. "Sorry, I should have called first." Son of a bitch, this is not going the way I imagined it would.

"Aiden, it's okay." She places her hand on my arm. "I haven't eaten yet. I was just heading out with Harper, but I'll let her know that I'm eating here with you." She smiles as she turns to walk back into her office. I follow her in. She clears papers off her desk and calls Harper.

"So is this my no-questions asked date?" she teases as she shuts her door. I'm sitting in a chair when she leans over my shoulder from behind me and whispers, "Because I was kind of hoping it included you naked but that's not happening in here." She kisses my neck before standing back up and walking around to her desk. Holy shit, my pants just got tight!

"Oh, sweetheart, this is definitely not our date." I stand and lean over her desk so we're face to face. My tongue darts out to lick my lower lip, just barely missing hers, "Don't worry, there will be plenty of nakedness." I lightly brush my lips on hers before sitting back down. *Fuck my rule.* There's no way I'm going to be able to resist her for an entire weekend. I'm going to have to figure something else out.

She's flushed as she sits down, wiggling in her seat. I flash her a knowing smile.

"So when is our actual date?" She breathes out slowly, crossing her legs.

"Mmm… not soon enough," I growl.

To stop myself from jumping behind this desk and having her for lunch, I set the food out. I look up to her wide eyes, staring at all the food. "I didn't know what you wanted so there are a few options." I laugh, looking at how much food I actually brought.

"A few?" she says, gesturing with her hands. "That's like enough for seven people." "Just for future reference, I love Chinese food, almost all of it."

We talk a little about everything as we eat our food. Work, friends, mainly Damon and Sydney—and we're both not sure what happened there—football games, and then she asks about our date again.

"We leave Saturday morning. You'll need an overnight bag," I say wagging my eyes.

"That seems more than a date. That's more of a little vacation," she says.

"Ah-ah-ah… no questions. And I know you're free. I already asked Harper if you had plans, so I'll be at your place Saturday morning at nine." I smirk.

"I didn't actually ask a question," she says. "So are you going to tell me what we're doing so I know what to pack?" She cocks one eyebrow.

"Nope, it's a surprise. Pack casual and don't forget a swimsuit. Scratch that. You can forget the swimsuit." I wink.

Chapter Forty-two

PACKING AN OVERNIGHT bag for somewhere you have no idea where sucks. I'm going to be with Aiden for two days, and I have no idea what we're doing. I like being in control, and I'm having a slight panic attack right now.

Deep breaths, Addison.

I can do this. I have an hour before he gets here. It's still gorgeous outside, so I'm wearing denim cutoffs, my favorite blue tank top, and chucks on my feet. He said casual. I throw my swimsuit on the bed, staring at it, debating if I should actually *forget* it. I pick a similar outfit for tomorrow. I've made sure I'm wearing my favorite black panties and matching bra. Tomorrow, I'll have my pink set on. All that's left is what I'm wearing to bed. I know what Aiden's answer would be, but I don't even know where we are staying. What if we're with a bunch of people? What if we're going camping? Then I sure the hell am not sleeping naked. *Shit.* I throw a pair of cotton shorts and a T-shirt on the bed, just in case. After gathering all my toiletries, I throw everything in a bag. Falling back on my bed, I blow out my cheeks and let out a long sigh.

My thoughts flutter back to last weekend and the mystery man. I shake the memory from my head. Nothing strange has happened since. I'm still not sure what to think of it, but now is not the time to figure it out.

I hear a knock at the door. What the hell? Aiden must have become really good friends with my doorman because they are supposed to call me when I have visitors. I stop in the bathroom to make sure I still look okay and not a disheveled mess. My loose curls are free and I'm wearing minimal makeup: mascara and lip gloss. I take a deep breath, satisfied I don't look like a wreck and open the door.

Green eyes slowly rake over my body leaving a trail of heat in their wake. A low growl erupts from him as he steps forward. My pulse quickens as my desire and need awakens. The physical connection between us is undeniable. Unexplainable. Everything else ceases to exist. I've tried to back away. Tried to tell myself we weren't meant to be together, but the second we're together, my body succumbs and defies what I know to be true. I'm too weak to stop it. The pull is too powerful.

"Hi," I say softly.

He wraps his arms around me, pulling me into his solid chest, tucking his head in my neck. "Damn, woman." He inhales deeply. "What are you doing to me? You own me the second you lay your gorgeous blue eyes on me."

I run my hands through his hair, grabbing hold of it. When he lifts his head, I slowly press my lips to his, running my tongue along his lips. He opens for me, his tongue caressing mine. The kiss isn't rushed; it's a slow, intoxicating kiss filled with passion.

Aiden groans in frustration when he breaks the kiss, leaning his forehead on mine. We're both breathing heavy. "Addison, we need to be somewhere by noon." He mutters a curse. "Let's go before I change my mind." He grabs my hand and takes my bag as we rush out the door.

He opens his car door, and I slide into the sleek, black leather seat as he places my bag in the trunk. When he gets in, he reaches for my hand and brings it to his lips. Glancing at me, he growls and shakes his head before darting into traffic.

"So, are you going to tell me where we have to be by noon?" I smile at him, leaning my head back on the seat. He raises an eyebrow as he flashes a huge smile. I wait for him to say something, but he keeps quiet, staring straight ahead. I take this time to study him. He's such a gorgeous man. He's wearing khaki shorts with a white polo shirt that makes him look youthful, innocent. The polo shirt sleeves are snug against his muscular arms. His jaw twitches as his lips curl into a mischievous smile, revealing his dimples. A tingle between my legs has me crossing my legs in my seat.

"See something you want?" he asks in a suggestive tone, noticing my slow perusal of him. Instantly, I figure out how I'm going to get him to tell me where we're going. Thankfully the highway isn't busy.

I take off my shoes and put one foot on the dashboard. He quickly peeks at my leg before looking straight again. I pull some lotion out of my purse and slowly and sensually drag my hands from my foot up my leg, up my inner thigh. I get to my center aching to be touched by him. As I drag my finger over my shorts, across my swollen nub, a shiver shoots through me.

"Addison," he growls as he puts his hand over mine, cupping my sex. He adds pressure as his fingers press into my slit through my shorts as his palm adds delicious pressure to my clit. I arch my back, grinding into his hand. His touch ignites me. "Take off your shorts," he commands. I immediately unbutton my shorts and pull them down. "Is this what you want, sweetheart?" His fingers push my panties to the side. I reach down the side of the seat and adjust it so I'm lying back.

"Yes. I want—" I cry out as he slips a finger in me. He circles his finger as his palm rubs my sensitive clit. My hips move to the motion of his finger. He stills, removing his finger. I whimper at the loss. "Why—" I can't even finish my sentence I'm so shocked that he stopped.

"Shh. I have a surprise for you." Opening his console he pulls out a small decorative bag. I look at him confused while amusement fills his face. "Put out your hand," he commands as he continues to watch the road, glancing quickly at me. I open my hand and he turns the bag upside down and a small, silver, wireless bullet falls into my hand. I gasp in surprise.

"Um..." I'm speechless. My face flushes from embarrassment but also desire.

"Turn it on, sweetheart." I hesitate. I've never used a toy with a man before. I roll the small bullet in my hand. "Now, Addison," he growls. I press the button, bringing the bullet to life. It buzzes, tickling my hand. I inhale sharply and moan when he buries two fingers in me. I grind my hips down on his fingers and my eyes roll back. "I know you know what to do with that," he says with a salacious grin as I glance at him. I'm about to ask him how when he starts thrusting both fingers in and out, curling them, stroking my g-spot. I cry out. "Addison, show me how you pleasure yourself," his raspy voice commands. The need for *more* has me rubbing the bullet on my clit.

"Aiden!" I scream out as pleasure explodes through my body. I lose control, my whole body trembling while I ride out the sensations. He slowly removes his fingers and brings them to his mouth, licking them clean.

"Fuck, Addison. I've missed your sweet taste," he growls. His dirty words have my sensitive pussy clenching. "You are so perfect." He pulls a towel out of a bag in the backseat. I clean myself up and put the bullet back in its bag. Aiden glances at me with a sexy half grin. That smile can make me do things that I'd never dream of. I reach over and run my hand through his hair. "Mmm... I like your hands on me," he murmurs as he moves his head against my hand.

I notice him adjust himself, so I reach over and grab the hard outline of his cock through his shorts. "Like this?" I ask playfully.

I heavily rub it against my hand. The car jerks forward and Aiden's hand is quickly on mine.

"Fucking hell, Addison. If I don't wreck before we get there, it'll be a miracle," he murmurs.

I unbutton his pants and slowly unzip them. "Aiden, *you're FBI.* You should be able to handle two things at once," I tease, pulling out his hard, glorious cock.

"Oh, baby. I think I already proved that I am *definitely* capable of handling two things at once." A megawatt smile spreads across his face, and he winks, flashing his dimples. A wave of heat spreads through my body.

I unbuckle my seat belt and bend over the console. I tease the crown of his cock with my tongue. Licking up and down his shaft before taking him all in. He groans as he pushes his hips forward. Feeling him at the back of my throat, I swallow, squeezing the tip with my throat before sucking it all the way out.

"Jesus Christ!" he roars. I feel the car come to a stop. Aiden slams the car in park. I don't stop devouring his cock to see where we are. He wraps my hair around his hands and groans as his body tenses. He takes control, driving the pace of my mouth. His groans fuel my need to make him explode. "*Fuuuuck!*" he exhales sharply as he thrusts one last time. Warm, salty liquid runs down my throat as I swallow all of it.

Aiden gasps as I swirl my tongue over the head of his cock. "Sweetheart..." he says panting, not able to finish his thought. He tugs my hair, bringing my face up. I lick my lips and smile. He pulls me into his chest, our faces inches apart. His beautiful green eyes move from my lips to my eyes. The way his eyes blaze makes my skin tingle. I can feel his heavy breaths as his chest moves against mine. I'm about to break the silence, but he crushes his lips to mine in a heated, sensual kiss. I moan into his mouth. I rub my hands on his broad, muscular chest up to his hair, threading my fingers through it. He bites my bottom lip before pulling back. "Addison, why can't I get enough of you? *It's never enough,*" he murmurs. He sneaks a quick kiss before pushing me over onto my seat. "You need to stay over there or we'll never get to where we are going."

I laugh. Then I remember. "Damn it," I say, throwing my head back. Aiden looks over, raising a curious eyebrow. "I was trying to seduce you into telling me where we are going but the second you touch me, I forget my own name." I sigh. He flashes me a smile and winks before facing forward and putting the car in drive.

Looking at him, I wonder why I'm even trying to deny *this*. He has control of my body. And he definitely has my heart. The only thing stopping us are my thoughts. And at this moment, those are insignificant. I drift off to sleep thinking… *maybe.*

* * *

We cross the state border to Connecticut, and I wonder how far we are actually going. I think back to this morning when Aiden mentioned we had to be somewhere by noon. It's now eleven, so we must be close. After some of the sexual tension was released, the drive has been very relaxing. This time of year is beautiful; it's been a gorgeous, scenic drive. Aiden holds my hand like it's an extension of his. He squeezes it, and I look up. He winks as he brings my hand to his lips and lightly kisses my knuckles. I smile over at him.

"I'm so glad you came," he says. I try to stifle my laugh because I know he's being sincere. He narrows his eyes until he figures it out and flashes a wicked smile. "I'm also glad you have a dirty, dirty mind, baby." I can't help but laugh out loud this time.

"I'm glad I'm with you." I squeeze his hand back. "But since I have no idea what we're doing, I'll reserve the right to say 'I'm glad I came' until tomorrow," I say with an amused smirk.

We get off the highway and drive for a little while longer

before turning toward an airplane hangar. I look over at Aiden and he's beaming. He looks like he's a kid in a candy store.

I giggle. "Are you a little excited?"

He pulls into a parking space and reaches his hand over to massage my head. "I am fucking ecstatic." He steals another quick kiss before jumping out of the car. His excitement causes my heart to flutter. He opens my door, pulls me out, and immediately lifts me up. My legs wrap around his waist, my back leaning against the car. I stare into his sparkling green eyes that are full of mischief. "Are you ready to have some fun?"

I look over his shoulder and see a few airplanes. My eyes widen in wonder. I look back at his face, his eyebrow cocked waiting for a response. "Do you fly?" He's never mentioned being a pilot, but I wouldn't be surprised.

"I do know how to fly, but I'm not flying to—"

"No fucking on my tarmac, Roberts." A booming laugh comes from behind Aiden, making me jump. I look around him and see a *very* sexy, very large man walking up with a megawatt smile. He's wearing black cargo shorts and a black polo. I can see tats running past the sleeves of his polo on his right side, but I can't tell what they are. He's a little shorter than Aiden but makes up for it in muscle. This guy is a machine. He has an amusing smirk as he shakes his head. Aiden puts me down and whips around to give the guy a manly hug with a pat on the back.

"Max, you're not usually a cock blocker," he says, hitting him in the stomach. They step side by side, both sets of eyes trained on me.

"So this is her, huh?" Max asks with an assessing smile. They both stand with their feet shoulder's width apart, arms crossed, and stare at me like I'm on display. My body heats up having two beautiful men stare at me.

"I feel like I should be putting on a show," I say seductively to

Aiden. I tilt my head and smirk, remembering the show I put on for him at Travis's when all he did was sit there and stare at me.

Realization crosses Aiden's features as he steps closer to me and growls, "Don't think about it."

Max throws his head back laughing. "Holy shit, never thought I'd see the day, man," he says as he walks around Aiden, shaking his head again. "Max Shaw." He holds out his hand.

"Addison Mason," I smile, gripping his hand. His grip is powerful, just like the man. He holds it for a few too many seconds because Aiden growls again.

"Max," Aiden warns. Max turns and walks away, still laughing.

"I like him," I playfully say, knowing it'll get Aiden more revved up.

He walks up to me, cupping my head. He lowers his mouth to my ear and whispers, "Mine" before slowly kissing my neck. His other hand wraps around my lower back and pulls me into him. His assault on my neck has my nerve endings tingling all over my body, which causes me to shiver. My hands grab onto his arms, holding myself up before I melt from his touch. He brings his lips to mine and bites my bottom lip before attacking my mouth. It's a possessive, dominant kiss. I moan into his mouth. It's over as soon as it started. My breathing is heavy, needy. "Don't. Forget. It," he rasps before grabbing my hand and pulling me toward the plane.

Mmm... jealous Aiden is hot!

CHAPTER FORTY-THREE

BY THE TIME we make it to the hangar, jealous Aiden is gone. His excitement is back. I look over and see Max messing with a plane, holding what looks to be a checklist.

"Are we going up in that plane?" I ask, wondering where he might be taking me.

"Yep," Aiden responds, guiding me toward the hangar.

"Is Max flying us?"

"Yep." He flashes an amused smirk.

I'm about to ask another question when we walk into a room. Jumpsuits hang on the wall. Aiden walks up to one and grabs it, handing it to me. "Put this on." My eyes go wide, looking from the plane to Aiden and back as it dawns on me what we're about to do. He's standing still, holding onto the jumpsuit, assessing my reaction and waiting for a response.

"You want me to jump out of *that* plane?" My voice comes out high pitched as I motion to the plane. My heart is beating so loudly, I'm sure he can hear it. I'm not sure if I'm nervous or excited.

"Yes. With me," he says confidently. My eyes dart around the room, back out to the plane. "Addison, look at me," he commands softly. I gaze up at him, concern now in his eyes. He cups my face with one hand, stroking my cheek with his thumb. His touch helps settle my nerves. I lean into his hand and close my eyes momentarily. When I open them, I let out a long, slow breath. "That's it, breathe. Sorry, I should've prepared you instead of surprising you. I just thought—"

"*Shh,*" I say as I put my finger to his lips. "It's okay. I can do this." I softly smile. He pulls me into his chest. The heat of his body relaxes me. It always surprises me how fast my body willingly submits to Aiden. Nobody has ever had this effect on me before.

I step back out of Aiden's arms and take the jumpsuit from his hands. I stand there and watch him put his on, leaving the top hanging off his waist. He pulls out a bag and grabs a T-shirt. When he pulls off his polo, I can't help but purr. My eyes follow his taut chest down to his perfect six-pack abs, moving to his delectable, chiseled V. I bite my bottom lip as I drink him in.

Damn, he's gorgeous.

He starts to put his shirt on but I interrupt. "Wait." I walk up to him and run my hands along his stomach up to his chest. He grabs my hands and holds them in place.

"Addison," he warns.

"Sorry, you're just too *distracting*. Don't get naked in front of me if you don't want me to attack you." I smirk as I nip his nipple and step back out of his reach. I turn away to regain my control.

I put on my jumpsuit before I turn back around; thankfully, Aiden's put a shirt on. He smiles and winks when I sigh. Pull your shit together, Addison, you're going to be jumping out of a perfectly good airplane and need to know what the hell you're doing.

Aiden puts on my harness and shit just got real. I'm really doing this. Inside, my stomach is doing summersaults. He tells me what I'm supposed to do when we jump. Cross arms, lift legs, head back against his shoulder. Sounds easy enough. He goes over hand signals and what's going to happen the whole time. He wants me to repeat what I'm supposed to do to make sure I wasn't *distracted*.

Ha ha, funny man.

I look out the window watching Max mess with the plane while Aiden checks his gear. "So, how many times have you done this?" I ask.

"Thousands, baby. Don't worry. I've got you," he says confidently. I'm surprised to hear how many jumps he's done. I turn around and lean against the window, tilting my head, studying him. I can tell he's going over a checklist in his head. His strong hands work efficiently, checking all the lines, attachments, and everything else I have no idea about. When he finishes, he looks up at me, catching me study him. He smiles and walks over, pulling me in a hug. "I've jumped too many times to count, but I've never been more excited than I am to jump with you right now. I'm so glad you didn't say no," he says, squeezing me tighter. My heart swells.

"I'm so happy that you brought me. I'm excited. Nervous as hell, but excited." I smile against his chest. He chuckles as he kisses the top of my head.

We're walking out to the plane hand in hand wearing really uncomfortable harnesses and jumpsuits. I hum "Danger Zone" by Kenny Loggins from *Top Gun*. Aiden throws his head back, laughing.

"What?" I say, smiling a wide grin.

"You're so awesome." He laughs, shaking his head. "And you look fucking hot in that jumpsuit." He slaps my ass.

I elbow him. "I told you what would happen with that hand," I warn. Max has been watching us walk up and hears my last statement, causing him to laugh out loud.

"I like her already." Max smirks. "If you both are ready, let's head up."

The trip up is exciting. Looking out the windows I can see the ocean. The sun reflecting off the water momentarily relaxes me. The landing strip is getting smaller and smaller. Aiden tells me that when we hit twelve thousand feet, it's our time to go. I'm surprisingly not nervous. Max tells us we've got a couple minutes.

We stand up and Aiden attaches himself to me and makes sure my goggles are on tight.

"Remember, cross arms, legs up, head back on my shoulder as we jump," he says in my ear. I give him the thumbs up. Then he says, "It's just me and you on the way down. Leave everything else up here. Clear your mind." I don't have time to think about that as the door opens and a gust of wind shoots into the plane. The nerves I didn't have a few minutes ago just amassed into a ball in my stomach. "It's okay, baby. Just breathe." Aiden wraps his arms around me. I nod my head, letting him know I'm ready.

We get to the door and Aiden holds on while I take position. Arms crossed, legs up, head back. I quickly pray that now is not the time for fate to show me how much she hates me. The next thing I know we jump.

The initial drop takes my breath away. Literally. I have to take deep breaths through my nose to steady my breathing. After a few seconds of shock, I feel like I'm flying, not falling. It's surreal. Looking out and seeing the world below brings a sense of calm from deep down. I soak it all in, trying to bottle up this feeling inside for later. I never want it to end.

Our free fall, which lasts around a minute, ends as Aiden pulls our chute. A gentle tug pulls us up before we glide back down to Earth. I take in a deep breath and exhale.

"What'd you think?" asks Aiden.

"Indescribable," I breathe out.

"Take hold of the handles for a few seconds," he says.

I tense. What? No one mentioned me having to fly this thing.

Aiden must feel my hesitation because he quickly adds, "Addison, it's okay. Just keep the handles even while I adjust a few things." I slowly put my hands through the slots as his come out. He loosens a few belts around my waist and my goggles so they aren't so tight.

I gasp. "Holy shit, I'm flying!"

I wonder what would happen if I pull one a little more than another. Immediately we're spinning. "Oh, shit!" I scream as Aiden's hands wrap around mine and set us straight.

"That was fun," I say, giggling. All of a sudden we're doing a tight spiral dive as I feel one of his hands pull one side down quickly. I scream.

Evening us out, he weaves his fingers with mine. "Addison, thank you," he whispers in my ear.

"Thank you, Aiden. For *everything*."

I love you. It's on the tip of my tongue. I've never felt a love like this. It completely fills me, but it also will completely destroy me. Once our feet touch the ground, our world will consume us again. I understand now why Aiden has jumped so many times.

When our feet hit the ground and Aiden unhooks us, I jump in his arms. The adrenaline running through me fuels my desire and need. I fuse our lips together in a frantic exchange. Our tongues collide. Explore. Savor. He sets me down but doesn't break our connection. We both discard our clothes in urgency. I crave to feel him as I hastily move my hands in exploration of his body. My hands contour every muscle as I sensually touch him. A low growl erupts as I wrap my hand around his cock. I stroke it, rubbing it against my oversensitive clit. He moves his hand to my drenched and throbbing sex. I grind against his hand, begging for relief. It's never crossed my mind where we are, only how fast I can get Aiden inside of me. He inserts two fingers, and I moan out in pleasure. He rubs his thumb against my clit as he plunges his fingers wildly. I wrap my hands around his neck to hold myself up. The onslaught of kisses and nips down my neck has me throwing my head back, moaning. I whimper as the heat builds inside me. Pleasure explodes through my body. My knees go weak as I ride my orgasm out.

Aiden picks me up, wrapping my legs around his waist. He carefully lays me down on something. I look to my sides and we're lying on top of the parachute. I can feel his cock at my entrance. "Sweetheart, I want to feel you. Only you, nothing between us, no barriers." He hesitates, waiting for me. I nod, smiling up to him. He enters me slowly and groans as he fills me to the hilt. I inhale sharply at the feeling of fullness, the feeling of being stretched. He slowly pulls out. I bring my legs up higher on his back, wanting to feel more of him. He thrusts back in causing me to scream. Arching my back, I moan as he continues the same tempo. He leans down and flicks his tongue over my nipple. I can feel the ache building inside me already. He braces his arms beside my head, his eyes on mine as he continues his torturous sensual pace. Slow and hard. This isn't anything like our first two times having sex. It's unlike anything else I've ever felt. Aiden's eyes are dark and full of need.

"I love you." The words easily fall out of my mouth. The corners of his mouth curl up into a sexy half grin. He tongue darts out to lick his lower lip. I bite my lip in response. He slides his mouth over mine as he groans into my mouth. His thrusts increase in pace as he grinds his hips. He moves faster and harder. The ache grows inside me, spreading heat through my body. It's a delicious burn. Reaching one hand between us, he circles my clit. All my nerve endings explode. I scream his name as I succumb to my orgasm and dig my fingers into his back as it crashes over me.

Aiden digs his head into my shoulder as he slides his cock in and out, his control slipping. "Addison, I love you, too," he growls, kissing and nipping at my neck. He sits up on his knees, grabbing my hips as he pounds into me. His beautiful, muscular chest is slick with sweat. I fist the parachute, trying to hold on to something. I can see his muscles tense right before he collapses on top of me. He thrusts one final time. "*Fuck*, Addison!" he roars as his pleasure rips through him. We're both panting heavily.

"*God*, you're so perfect," he breathes out as he brushes the hair out of my face. His eyes soften, gazing into mine. I've never experienced this level of intimacy. My stomach flutters as the emotional feelings I'm having erupt. *I want more.* I cup his face, running my hands along his jawline. "Addison, I've never felt like this. You are so intoxicating. I can't get enough of you."

Pulling him down to me, we savor each other in a slow, sensual kiss. I can feel his cock starting to fill me again. "I can't even begin to explain what it does to me knowing that part of me is inside you," he says in a low growl.

"Oh, I think I can feel what it does." I smirk, wiggling my hips. He thrusts his hips up causing me to moan.

"Well, that, too. But the feeling I get. It's primal, almost animalistic. I just want to roar that you're mine now." His possessive tone sends heat shooting through my body. I never imagined a man claiming me would cause this visceral need within me.

"*Mmm...* Tarzan. Get down here and claim my mouth," I breathe out.

Aiden flips us over so I'm sitting on top. I moan out in pleasure as this new position has him deep inside me. "You feel so good. You're tight pussy is dripping. Ride me, Addison," he growls. My breath catches as his dirty words send an electric current straight to my inner core.

Grabbing his hands for support, I grind my hips, pulling him out slowly then plunging back down. He sharply inhales. My body tingles from the sensations of him filling me. I cry out. I continue riding him, quivering every time I slide back down his cock.

"Sweetheart, I'm not going to last long," he grinds outs. He lets go of one of my hands and deliciously assaults my clit. "Tell me that you're mine, Addison."

"Aiden! Yes, I'm yours. Only yours," I scream, throwing my head back. My sex clenches down hard on his cock. He grabs my hips tight as he rides out his release in quick pulses. I fall into his chest, exhaustion consuming my body. He softly rakes his fingers across my back.

The warmth of the sun reminds me we're in the middle of who knows where and I'm naked. I sit up and look around. I giggle when I see our clothes haphazardly spread out everywhere. Aiden sits up, still inside of me, causing me to shiver. "I love how responsive you are," he whispers. Seeing our clothes everywhere, he laughs. "We were in a bit of a hurry." When he pulls out of me, the feeling of loss surprises me.

"I need to text Max before he sends his team out to find us." He chuckles, throwing me a towel he grabbed out of his backpack. *Max has a team?*

As he texts Max, I look around. We are in the middle of a pasture, maybe, surrounded by trees. "Where are we?"

"This is Max's land. He inherited it when his dad died years ago," he replies, pulling up his shorts. Hmm... so he has land, a plane, and a team. What the hell does Max do?

* * *

"It's about damn time. You know, I almost sent my team out," Max says as we load into his Jeep. Aiden laughs out loud from the front seat.

I lie back in the backseat, closing my eyes, soaking in the sun coming from the topless vehicle. The vibration from the ride on the dirt road and the sun's warmth soothes me to sleep. I wake to Aiden carrying me. I inhale his scent of man and sex. I'm in a blissful state of euphoria as I snuggle into his neck. He gently places me in the front seat of his car.

I fist his shirt before he can stand back up, bringing his lips to mine and stealing a kiss. "I love you, Aiden," I say against his lips.

"I love hearing you say that," he whispers into my ear, nibbling on my earlobe. "I need to move or I'm going to throw this seat back and have you for lunch," he murmurs.

"I'm good with that." I giggle as he stands up. He growls, stepping away, shaking his head.

"Max would kill me. We're going to lunch with Max before we head out," he calls over his shoulder. *Hmm...* I wonder where we are going after lunch. I don't think anything could beat what we've done so far. All my anxiety about relinquishing my control to Aiden is gone. I can't deny my feelings anymore, so how do I move on with this relationship without destroying it? I jump when Aiden gets into the car. He looks over at me, cocks an eyebrow, and twists his lips.

"Whatever you're thinking... *stop*," he softly commands, grabbing my hand. "Whatever it is that you think will make me run, you need to let it go. I'm not going anywhere, unless it's something like you're my long-lost sister. *In that case, I should know.*" He chuckles as he pulls my hand to his lips.

"I'm definitely not your sister." I laugh.

"Then that settles it. There's nothing that'll keep me away. So stop thinking there is." He bites my hand.

"*Ouch!*" I pull my hand away and slap his leg.

"What was that for?" I say, inspecting my hand for any puncture wounds.

"For thinking too damn much. Now let's go have lunch with Max." He smiles and winks. I stick out my tongue. Juvenile, I know, but so is biting!

Chapter Forty-four

THERE ARE VERY few people I've met in my life that I instantly like. Max is one of those people. When he talks, I can tell that he works hard and plays even harder. I've learned that he used to be an FBI agent but went solo about three years ago. He now owns a private security firm that does the kinds of things people never hear about for the government. I'm so caught up listening to his stories, I don't even notice that we've been sitting at lunch for three hours.

"I can't believe your team is up to six now," Aiden says. I glance to Aiden and my heart skips a beat. He's relaxed, leaning back in his seat with his hands behind his head. He flexes his arms as I'm admiring them. My eyes dart up to his, and he sports a wicked grin. I laugh and roll my eyes.

"Don't let the word get out that the way to Aiden's heart is to shoot him," Max barks out, followed by a booming laugh.

My head whips toward Max. "You know?"

"Addison, I know everything," he boasts. "What I'm surprised as hell about is this thing between you two. I never would have believed it if I hadn't seen it with my own eyes." He leans over and grasps Aiden's shoulder, squeezing it. I can tell they're close by the way he looks at Aiden. Just like Syd is to me, so it shouldn't surprise me that Aiden told him about me. It makes me like Max even more. Aiden grins and winks at me.

I look around and spot the bathroom. "I'll be back in a few. I need to use the restroom," I say, standing up. I yelp as Aiden snags me, pulling me down to his lap. His lips brush mine for a quick kiss. I can hear Max chuckling behind me.

When he helps me back on my feet, he slaps my ass. "You're asking for it," I warn.

"Always, sweetheart… *always*." He flashes his megawatt smile, showing off his dimples.

On the way to the bathroom, I look for my phone in my pocket. I want to call Sydney and tell her about my skydiving experience. I pause when I remember I left it on the table so I spin around to go back and get it.

"Are you going to tell her about Jessie?" I overhear Max ask as I approach the table from behind them. *Who the hell is Jessie?*

"No. Why would I? I haven't seen her in over two years." Aiden shrugs. *Crap.* I don't know what to do. Do I turn around and go to the bathroom and come back after they're done talking? What if they notice me on my way to the bathroom? *That won't look obvious.*

Max clears his throat as soon as he sees me. "That was probably the quickest I've ever seen a woman go to the bathroom," he jokes.

I want to ask who Jessie is, but I don't want it to sound like I was eavesdropping. But holy shit, I'm curious now. Obviously she meant something to Aiden or Max would've never mentioned her. Instead, I just smile and grab my phone. "I want to call Syd and tell her about my day." I look at Aiden, holding up my phone. He cocks an eyebrow. It's an awkward couple seconds because I know he's trying to figure out if I heard anything. I decide if it's something he wants to tell me he will. I lean down and kiss him, silently reassuring him everything is okay.

After my call, I make my way back to the table, making sure they hear me approaching so I don't overhear anything else.

"About damn time, woman. I was about to call a search party to look for you." Max grins.

"Hell, I figured I wouldn't see you again for at least an hour with you talking to Sydney," Aiden sarcastically says.

"Well aren't you two a bundle of jokes," I say, laughing. "Syd says she going next time we jump."

"Next time, huh?" Aiden teases. He pulls me into his lap again.

"Um, yes. You can't give me a taste and then expect me to never want it again."

Aiden mumbles under his breath something about *he knows* and *last summer.* I shake my head, knowing exactly what he's thinking. I cock my eyebrow.

He grins. "Of course I'll take you again."

"Oh, who will jump with Sydney?"

"Is she hot?" Max chimes in.

"Does it matter?" I say, looking over to him. I see Aiden nodding his head out of the corner of my eyes. I turn toward him, narrowing my gaze, and playfully hit him. He laughs, holding his hands in the air.

"She is, but you might have to fight Damon over her," Aiden says. I get up to sit in my own chair.

"Well, we know who would win that match." Max chuckles as he brings his beer to his lips. My eyebrows rise as I look at Max. This is a story I want to hear. "I kicked his ass while we were at Quantico. Of course, his version is a little skewed when you ask him about it." Max holds up his thumb and index finger while they both laugh out loud.

"But y'all are friends, right?" I'm sure that Aiden had mentioned Damon jumping with him.

"Oh, yeah. He's like a brother, too. Joking aside, I'd never try and take a girl Damon is with. Not my style," he says.

"Well, Syd and Damon aren't together so this isn't even an issue." I shrug. "She doesn't even live here."

"Well, whenever Sydney comes into town, bring her and we'll jump." He smiles and winks at me.

Max looks over to Aiden. "So, you ready to come work with me?"

Aiden's smile widens. "You had to ask, didn't you?" He chuckles.

"You know, one day I'm going to get you to change your mind." Max gives him a pointed look. At first I don't know if he's kidding, but now I know he's not. Would he seriously think about moving? My gaze switches from Max to Aiden, my eyes widening. Worry starts to build in my chest. Dammit, I just admitted that I loved him and now he might leave. *What that hell?*

"Calm down, Annie Oakley." Both guys laugh. My mouth gapes open. I can't believe he called me that. I can't believe they even know who that is. "He can work from anywhere."

Blush creeps into my cheeks. Aiden reaches over, grabs my chair, and pulls it closer to him. He leans over and whispers in my ear, "I'm not going anywhere. But I love that you were worried." Closing my eyes, I inhale his scent. I have to grip my chair so I don't melt into him. When I open my eyes, I catch a glimpse of Max observing our interaction. He warmly smiles at me and nods. I pull back out of Aiden's grasp, sitting back in my chair, relieved. He takes my hand, intertwining our fingers before he relaxes back in his chair.

I narrow my eyes at Max, tilting my head and say, "So, how do you know who Annie Oakley is?" Max grins but doesn't answer. "I remember doing a paper on her when I was in high school. She was my hero," I murmur.

"I am not surprised," Max says. "Next time you come out, let's go shoot. I want to see if you're really as good as Aiden says."

"Definitely." My face beams. Yep, Max is my new best friend.

"Well, we need to get going so we can get there before dark," Aiden says, standing up and pulling me with him. Before I can even ask where *there* is, Max stands up and gives Aiden a hug then tugs me into a tight embrace.

He leans down and whispers in my ear, "You're good for him." He gives me a peck on the cheek.

Aiden's arm wraps around my waist and pulls me into his hard chest. "Stop whispering sweet nothings and kissing my girlfriend," he rasps out. Max's laugh booms loudly.

"I was just telling her that I'm best man at the wedding." His smile spreads across his face as my eyes bulge out. Where the hell did that come from? I turn to look at Aiden, and he's smiling, wagging his eyebrows at me. Okay... we need to leave. It just got warm in here. A little too warm and uncomfortable for me.

"So, we need to leave, right?" I say quickly, grabbing my purse. Both guys are now laughing. I don't even wait for them to compose themselves, I walk quickly toward the exit. When I get to the car, the boys have caught up to me. Aiden opens my door. As I'm stepping in, Max yells out from his car, "And the first son's name is Maximus."

Oh, my God. I'm rethinking Max's best friend status. I shake my head, closing the door. My heart is beating so fast that I think I might be having an anxiety attack. I lean back in the seat and breathe in and out slowly, trying to calm myself. Aiden gets in and I can feel his eyes on me, but I can't look at him yet.

I feel his hand grab mine. "Sweetheart, you okay over there?" I hear humor in his voice. I blow out one last heavy breath before I look over to him.

I narrow my eyes. "Why aren't you more freaked out? It's not like we've been together very long? And coming from someone who has always run away from relationships, I would think even mentioning marriage and babies would make you sweat." Hell, it's making me sweat.

He shrugs. "Addison, I can't explain how you make me feel because *this* is all foreign to me. Since I met you, I don't know which fucking way is up or down. My life has always been pointed in one direction: straight ahead. But now I feel... *lost.*" He squeezes my hand. "But I want to get lost *with you.*" If he knew that Travis Stein would be his father-in-law, he might feel a little differently. I start to panic and try to pull my hand from his, but he holds it tighter. "We don't need to rush this. We'll let it play out however it does." He brings my hand to his lips.

I nod. I look away and watch the scenery pass by in a blur as we drive again. Reality sets in. What the heck am I doing? *I do want more.* Which scares the hell out of me. I've never felt this way about someone else, and I do love Aiden. I just don't know if it's realistic for him to accept Travis as my father. *Sperm donor.* Syd's words echo in my head. I want to believe he'll be okay with it, but every time I start to bring it up, I chicken out. I run my hand through my hair and let out a sigh. *I'm a chicken shit.*

"I'm sorry, Addison." I turn toward Aiden, who peers at me with a look of uneasiness.

I shake my head. "It's okay. I'm okay. It just caught me off guard," I say softly.

"I'll kick Max's ass next time I see him." His lips curl.

"So, where are you taking me?" I need a change of subject.

He offers a knowing smile. "Well… I'm taking you to my house."

My eyebrows rise and I turn my body to face Aiden, putting one leg under the other. "What?" I say. "Your house?"

He drums his fingers against the steering wheel and glances over at me. His beautiful green eyes gleam. My heart melts at his excitement about this house. It's must really be important to him.

"I bought a house in New Haven when I was in college. A fixer-upper. A few guys from college and I would go there one weekend every month and fix something in it." He smiles wide. "It was like our getaway from school. We'd work on it during the day and party all night."

"Wow. It was like your own little fraternity," I joke.

He laughs loudly. "Something like that."

"Well, it sounds amazing. I can't wait to see it."

CHAPTER FORTY-FIVE

THE HOUSE IS beautiful. It's a one-story, craftsman-style home, painted gray with white trim. When I get out of the car, the smell of salt water and humidity hits my senses. When we walk into the house, it's obvious that the entire house has been updated. I'm impressed. The guys did an amazing job. The entire house has tile that looks like dark wood. There are area rugs, which kind of shocks me. The farther we walk into the house; I'm met with the most spectacular view. With the kitchen on my left and the living room on my right, floor-to-ceiling windows overlook a pool with the Atlantic Ocean in the background.

"That's breathtaking," I whisper, looking out the windows. Aiden comes up behind me and wraps his arms around me.

"Almost as breathtaking as you," he whispers back into my ear.

"Shut up," I say, blushing, as I turn in his arms. Stepping out of his hold, I look around the rooms. They're beautifully decorated. The kitchen has dark cabinets with white granite. Very clean lines. The living room has pillows, rugs, and artwork. A pang of jealousy shoots through me. A man definitely didn't decorate this house. I look at Aiden with a curious lifted brow. "Um... I've seen your apartment, so I know you didn't decorate this place," I say, trying to sound nonchalant.

He laughs. "Sweetheart, you can't hide your jealousy from

me." He smirks as he grabs my hand. "I hired an interior designer. This is actually the first I've seen it set up," he says, looking around the room.

"It's stunning. They did an amazing job." I walk around, taking it all in. Aiden takes me on the grand tour, showing me all three bedrooms. Whoever decorated it, I would love for them to decorate my next house.

"Pizza and beer by the pool tonight?" he asks as we make it back to the kitchen. I nod as I pull out a barstool from under the island to sit. I think about the day I've had with this perfect man. Thoughts about Travis slowly creep up, but I push them back down. I don't want to think about that right now. I will give Aiden all of me, *even if it's just for this weekend.*

* * *

We're relaxing by the pool on a doublewide lounger listening to the ocean waves crash against the shore. Can't we just stay here forever? Aiden's holding my hand, mindlessly rubbing his thumb against my knuckles. His phone starts playing "We Are Family" by Sister Sledge. I bust out laughing as he lunges for the phone quickly.

"Hey, Katie." I'm assuming by the ringtone, it's his sister. While he listens to her, he watches me. "No, you weren't interrupting anything." He smiles and winks.

I mouth, *"Nice ringtone."* He rolls his eyes and mouths back, *"It's her fault."*

"Yes, she's right here. Remind me to kick Max's ass next time I see him." He laughs at her response. Watching him talk to her, I can see how much his sister means to him; his eyes lit up as soon as he answered. "I promise you'll meet her soon." My eyebrows shoot up and he nods at me. "Sounds good. I'll talk to you soon. Love you, too." He presses end and turns to me.

"So, I guess I'm meeting your sister soon?" I question.

"Yes. She doesn't believe you're real. I guess Max called her and told her all about you. She thinks he's lying. She has to see it to believe it because she doesn't believe in *mythical creatures*." He chuckles using air quotes.

"Wow. So I caught the uncatchable, huh?" I tease, poking him in the chest.

"No, I'm pretty sure I caught you." He lets out a booming laugh. He grabs me and lifts me up like I weigh nothing. I don't even have time to question what he's doing before he jumps in the pool with me in his arms. I scream as I'm pulled under water.

After Aiden shows me how much fun pool sex can be, we go back to lying on the lounge chair. "I'm running inside to go to the bathroom. Do you want me to grab you a beer on the way out?" I roll over on my side, gliding my finger down his ripped stomach. He grabs my finger and sticks it in his mouth, sucking on it. This man is insatiable.

"What did I do before I had you?" He smirks as I pull my finger out.

"Oh, I'm sure you had someone to help you out," I tease, getting up off the lounger. He swats my ass before I can get out of his reach.

"I don't remember anyone but you, sweetheart," I hear him say as I'm walking away. I laugh at his corny statement. A few minutes later, I'm grabbing the beers out of the kitchen refrigerator and I hear the front door open.

"Aiden, babe! Where are you?" a woman's voice calls out. I round the corner to see who the hell just walked into Aiden's house. "Who the fuck are you?" she barks out with her hand on her hip as soon as she sees me.

Really? Who am I?

"I think that should be my question, *not yours,* seeing as you just walked into a house that you don't belong in," I reply, trying to stay calm since I'm not sure who she is yet. She's a beautiful woman with dark hair, maybe a little shorter than me, but skinny with fake boobs. I can tell she's older than me.

"Bitch, this is my boyfriend's house. So, I'll ask again, who are you?" she screeches while she looks me up and down. Wait... *What?* So much for calm.

"If you call me a bitch again, I'm going to–"

"Addison, what's taking so long?" We both whip our heads toward Aiden as he walks through the back door. He looks at the girl and then quickly to me. I tilt my head, twisting my lips, waiting for an explanation.

He walks and stands by my side. His lack of surprise by this woman inside his house has me darting my gaze between the two. My mouth goes dry thinking maybe what she said was true. "Aiden!" the girl happily screams as she rushes to him. He stops her right before she jumps into his arms.

"Jessie," he hesitates, looking at me before turning back to her. "What are you doing here?" So this is the Jessie who Max was talking about. I'm waiting for him to explain who she is before I decide what to do next. Kick her ass or his.

"Aiden, who is she?" Jessie snidely asks, pointing to me.

"Jessie, this is Addison. She's my girlfriend." My heart flutters momentarily until Jessie decides to spew some words again.

"Excuse me?" she seethes, her tone deepening. She now has both her hands on her hips. "What the hell did you just say? You brought a whore to our house?"

"Whoa! Jessie, what the hell?" Aiden's brows furrow.

Yep. *That's it.* "Aiden, can you please hold these beers for me?" I ask calmly.

"Nope," he replies. "Uh-uh, that is *definitely* not a good idea," he says with amusement lighting his voice. I whip my head in his direction, wondering what the hell he thinks is so funny. I'm squeezing the bottles so hard, I'm surprised they aren't breaking. "*Sweetheart,* I'll take care of this." He tries to hide his smile, placing his hand on my arm. He gently rubs his thumb on me. I let out an exasperated sigh.

"I've been nice up to this point. She calls me another name, I'm going to do something about it." I glare at him so he knows that I am not kidding. He nods.

"Jessie." He looks toward her, taking a step between us.

Like that'll stop me. I roll my eyes.

"I'm not sure what you're talking about, but this is my house," he says in a matter-of-fact tone.

"Your house!" she shrills. "Look around, Aiden, I've made this a home for us. I told you that I'd wait for you, take care of our house while you were gone." She throws her hands out. "Did you already forget whose name you were calling out the night you left?" She looks at me with a cocked eyebrow, her voice taunting. Aiden looks to me with a pained look, shaking his head.

Bitch, it's on. I walk to the counter and place the beers down. When I spin around, Aiden is already behind me. "Addison," he begs, grabbing my waist with his hands. I clench my jaw and reluctantly nod my head. I want to walk outside, but I need to hear this story. I need to know who she is to Aiden. He's told me he's never been in love, but this woman was either lied to or she's short a few screws. I'm leaning toward the latter right now.

He turns slowly. He crosses his arms, planting his feet wide. "Jessie, you are an interior designer that I *hired* to decorate this house. I have *always* been upfront about what we were doing. Never have I given you any reason to think that we were together." Aiden's restraint is slipping. "It's been two-and-a-half fucking years, Jessie!" he roars, aggressively running his hands through his hair.

"Aiden, baby, I'm sorry," she says, walking up to him. "*I forgive you.* I love you. We'll get through this. Just take her back to wherever she came from." She reaches out to put her hands on his chest. I gasp. My eyes go wide in shock. He grabs her hands.

Definitely a few screws lose.

"Jessie, you need to leave." His words come out harsh. He turns her around and guides her to the door.

I've heard enough, so I grab the beers and walk out to the pool. I recline on the lounger. I don't have any doubt that Aiden is telling the truth. I watch him walk out the back door. He's still running his hands through his hair, his expression serious. I feel bad for him, but I'm still too upset to comfort him. He comes over and lies down beside me, rolling onto his side, resting his head on his hand.

"I'm sorry, Addison." His voice sounds strangled. I roll over so we're facing each other. He takes his other hand and brushes loose pieces of hair behind my ear. "Are you mad?" he asks, looking down.

I take a deep breath, exhaling quickly. "I'm upset you didn't warn me about a psycho ex-girlfriend," I say sarcastically.

He shakes his head. "She is *not* an ex-girlfriend," he says in a thick voice.

"An ex-fuck then. So exactly how long was this *arrangement?*" He winces.

He rolls onto his back, bringing his arms behind his head, staring up to the sky. "I met Jessie the second year I moved in, so eight or nine years ago. She's from here. I already told you about how the guys and myself would come here to fix up the house and have parties. The local girls would all come over and party with us. Jessie and I would hook up whenever I was here," he explains. He rolls back over, facing me. "But I always told her that I didn't want anything serious. She agreed. I mean, hell, I don't even live here. I don't know when her expectations changed, but when I left, I definitely didn't promise her anything." He cups my neck. "Addison, please say you believe me."

I sigh. "I believe you." He pulls me in for a kiss, but I pull back, "What the hell did you think was so funny when I was about to kick her ass?"

He chuckles. "Mmm... I *love* when you get feisty. When you get mad, it's seriously sexy." He wags his eyebrows. I laugh, shaking my head. Forcing me down to his lips, he kisses me softly, "I love you. *Only you.*" His low, sexy voice causes my body to tremble. He rolls me on top of him. I can feel his arousal on my stomach.

"Good. But if she shows up with a baby claiming it's yours, I'm going to kick her ass." I smirk as I thread my fingers through his hair.

"Don't fucking say that," he says, his voice turning serious. "That isn't even funny."

"*I'm just saying,* I wouldn't put it past her. She's seems a little unhinged," I explain. If he thinks she's just going to go back into the hole she crawled out of, he doesn't understand women. I just hope we're gone by the time she thinks of her next move. Now that I know about her, I'll be keeping my eyes open and my gun close by.

"I'm done talking about her." He slides his fingers down my ass, under my swimsuit. As his fingers slip between my folds, thoughts of anything other than what those glorious fingers are about to do to me leave my head.

Aiden is done talking. He lets his body tell me everything he needs to say. We fall asleep sated and naked in each other's arms back in his bedroom. I definitely didn't need my pajamas.

Chapter Forty-six
AIDEN

I'M WOKEN UP with Addison's beautiful mouth on my cock. "Oh, *sweetheart*. That feels fucking awesome," I growl. I can see her head bobbing up and down under the sheet. She moans.

What the fuck?

I bolt up, hearing my dick pop out of her mouth as I lift the sheets. Jessie sits up smiling at me, wiping her mouth. "Where the hell is—" The bedroom door opening interrupts me. Addison walks in. My chest tightens at the look on her face. She shuffles back a couple steps as she gasps. I grab the sheet, covering myself, jumping out of bed in a panic.

"Addison, it's not what you think," my voice shaking as I plead. I grab her hands, but she flinches from my touch. She shakes her head, holding up a finger. This can't be happening. She has to understand that this isn't my fault. She goes to say something, but stops. Her lips twist. My eyes plead with hers for understanding.

"Baby, you don't need to explain to her what we're doing in our own room. She's the one walking in on us!" Jessie exclaims, her voice reminding me that she's still in the room. My jaw clenches as I grind my teeth. Addison turns to walk over to her bag. She can't leave. I look around the floor for a pair of shorts. Finding them, I put them on quickly. I need to stop her from leaving. She has to let me explain first.

Jessie screams. I whip around to see why the she's screaming.

Fuck! "Addison, put the gun down," I command.

"Aiden! She's going to shoot me!" Jessie screams, running behind me. A fleeting thought that I should just leave and let her shoot Jessie runs through my mind. Shaking that thought from my head, I look at Addison. Her eyes narrow as the gun is pointed at me now. I'm having a déjà vu moment. At least this time I'm not worried she's going to hurt herself. Now, Jessie, I'm a little concerned for.

"Addison, she's not worth it," I say quietly, taking a step toward her. She's standing stock-still as I inch my way to her. I can hear Jessie's whimpers behind me. "Sweetheart, please don't do this." She looks to Jessie and then to me. I move in front of the gun, pressing it to my chest. Moving my hands slowly to the gun, never breaking eye contact, I wrap my hand around hers. "Please." I beg her. She loosens her grasp on the gun, allowing me to take it from her. I pull her into my chest, pressing my lips to her hair repeating, "*I'm so sorry.*" She stands with her arms straight down, not touching me. There's a feeling of emptiness inside me, fearing I've lost her. I hold her tighter willing her to touch me.

"Oh, thank God you got the gun, Aiden." Jessie exhales quickly. "Keep a hold of her and I'll the call the police." I hear her fumbling for something behind me. Her voice sends a stabbing pain through me.

I spin around finding Jessie with her phone in her hand. The heat of pure hatred runs through my body. I stick the gun in my waistband so I don't accidently use it. "Get the fuck out of my house, Jessie," I grind the words out through gritted teeth. Her eyes widen as they gloss over.

"If you ever come into my house again, I'll have you arrested. If you come near Addison or me, I'll file a restraining order. Get.

Out. Now," I roar as my control slips. She jumps at the sound of my voice. She stumbles around, grabbing her clothes before running out of the room. I hear the front door slam closed. I turn back to Addison reaching for her.

"Don't," she says in a strangled voice as she puts her hand up. She walks out of the room. I follow her into the living room.

"Addison, please, let me explain," I demand. "I didn't even hear her come into the bedroom. For fuck's sake, I thought it was you!"

She freezes and stares at me with wide eyes. Shit! *Obviously that was the wrong thing to say.* "Come on, Addison! She was already under the covers when I woke up. It didn't take me long to figure it out!" I grab my hair in frustration.

"Fuuuuck!" I roar, balling my hand into a fist and slamming it into a wall. I hear a crunching noise. I'm not sure if it's from the hole I put in the drywall or the bones in my hand.

"Aiden!" Addison runs to me as I pull my hand out from the wall. She softly holds my hand in hers, inspecting it. The simple touch of her hand has my heart beating fast. Emotions overtake me as my eyes well up with tears.

I look down, pinching the bridge of my nose, ashamed of the whole situation. "I'm so sorry, Addison," I choke out. I hear her take a deep breath, exhaling slowly. I lift my gaze to hers meeting those beautiful blue eyes. I blink back the unshed tears, "I love you."

A tear falls from her eye. I cup her face, wiping it away with my thumb. "Aiden, I know it wasn't your fault. I get it, I do." She looks away momentarily, pulling her face out of my hand. Blowing out another breath, she continues. "But walking in on a girl who's just had her mouth on your dick is making me want to do things that I shouldn't want to do. I just need a little space." She looks down at her hand cradling mine. "I'll get you some ice," she says, turning toward the kitchen. My brows furrow.

"Can you define *space*?" Concern fills my voice as I follow her.

"If you need to be alone for a little bit, that I can do, but if you need to take a break from *us*, I'll take two steps forward," I warn. I've worked hard to get her to finally admit her feelings, I will not back off now.

She comes back and places the bag of ice on my hand. "Go take a shower, I'll make us some breakfast." The resignation in her voice worries me. I narrow my eyes, assessing her. "I promise I'll be here when you get out," she responds. I reach down to kiss her but she backs away. She shakes her head. "Not yet."

CHAPTER FORTY-SEVEN

I KNEW THE bitch wasn't finished with Aiden. I can't stop thinking about what I saw. Walking in on Aiden having his dick sucked by Jessie makes me want to scream and kill someone. My body trembles with anger. How do I move past this? Rationally I know that Aiden was tricked, but irrationally it's destroying me that he might have enjoyed it for the couple minutes she had her mouth on him.

I take deep breaths in and out. I need to calm down. Grabbing a water, I head out to the patio. I'll deal with breakfast later. I lie down on the lounger facing the ocean trying to focus on something else. The sounds of the waves calm me. My hand brushes over the spot where Aiden lay yesterday, where we made love. The warmth from the sun helps me relax. I'm still in my sports bra and running shorts. Aiden looked so peaceful sleeping this morning, I didn't want to wake him up so I decided to go for a run without him. I should've woken him up.

"Excuse me, are you Addison?" I jump at the sound of a male voice.

"Holy shit, you scared me," I say with my hand over my chest. I look at the man standing in front of me. The police. *No she didn't.* Anger builds in my chest as I stand up. My body tenses as I bring my hands to my hips.

I should've shot her when I had a chance.

"What was that?" The officer asks with a raised eyebrow.

My eyes go wide. Oh, shit! Did I say that out loud?

"Nothing." I wave my hands around. I need to pull my shit together or I'm going to end up in jail. "Officer, what can I help you with?" I say flatly. His eyes move all over my body. It catches me off guard. I clear my throat. "Eyes up here, buddy." I don't care who he is, he's being unprofessional.

"Yes, Officer Gates, eyes fucking up there," Aiden growls as he comes outside. The officer turns toward him with a wide grin. Aiden laughs and shakes his head walking in the direction of the officer. They embrace in a hug, smacking each other on their backs. "Good to see you, brother." My body relaxes, realizing this is a friend of Aiden's.

"Don't you know how to pick up a phone and call? How long have you been back?" the officer asks.

Aiden chuckles. "A few months. I've been busy," he says, looking over at me, smiling.

"So I've heard." He turns his gaze onto me. Again, I feel like I'm on display. What is it about Aiden's friends' assessing eyes? Not in the mood to entertain today, I roll my eyes and recline on the lounger.

"Ryan, this is Addison. Addison, Ryan." Ryan walks over and shakes my hand. Aiden sits next to me as the officer grabs a chair, straddling it backward while he rests his arms on the back. "Why do I have a feeling you're not here for personal reasons?" Aiden leans forward with his elbows on his knees.

Ryan looks at me, twisting his lips. "So, Addison, I hear you work for NYPD's forensic department." He doesn't really ask, it's more of a statement. So I just nod wondering where he's going with this. "Do you have a department-issued firearm?" Ah, there it is. That bitch *did* go to the police. I open my mouth to answer, but Aiden speaks first.

"What the hell, Ryan? Stop beating around the bush. What did Jessie say?" he says, raising his voice as he stands up.

"Aiden, what the hell am I supposed to do? Jessie comes in and reports being held at gunpoint from someone in your house. I didn't even know you were in town, let alone have a *serious girlfriend*. I had to call Max and ask who the hell she was before coming here." He pushes off the chair and paces. "I don't want to arrest her, but fuck my hands are tied." At those words, I jump off the lounger.

"*Arrest me*? How about you arrest that psycho who broke into Aiden's house and sexually assaulted him!" I yell, throwing my hands up. "She wouldn't leave and I felt like I was in danger because she's psychotic." The last part was a bit of an exaggeration, but hell if I'm going to jail for that woman.

His brows furrow, and he glances to Aiden. Aiden nods his head in agreement. He tells him what happened last night and this morning. I stare out to the ocean, trying to block out the details. It's not working. I close my eyes and cringe when he begins to tell him about this morning. I can't do it. I can't listen to it. I turn around to walk into the house.

"Addison," Aiden calls out. His voice is thick with emotion.

I stop but stay facing away from them. "I can't listen anymore, Aiden, but continue. He needs to hear it. I'll be inside if you have any questions, Ryan," I say over my shoulder before walking away.

I decide to take a quick shower. Walking into Aiden's room, I notice the entire bedding has been ripped off. I look around, but don't see it anywhere. Hopefully he burned it. I'm a little relieved that we're not staying here tonight.

The guys have made it inside by the time I'm done getting ready. The shower did very little to help me relax. I need to leave this place. Get as far away from Jessie as possible. My bags are packed and ready to go. I hear laughing coming from the kitchen as I walk out of the hallway. I lean against the wall, watching the two guys joke with each other. Aiden's telling Ryan the story of how he got me to go on this weekend date. He catches me watching him and flashes a sexy half grin. I softly smile back.

"Hi," he says in his low, sexy voice.

"Hey," I respond quietly.

Ryan turns around looking in my direction. "Cowboys, huh?" he says with amusement on his face.

I walk over to where they are sitting at the island and lean against it, crossing my arms. "So you're a hater, too, then?" I ask playfully.

We start talking about football and then they move on to telling stories about when they were younger. Aiden, Max, Ryan, and two other guys I've yet to meet were all best friends in college. Ryan fell in love with a local girl so he stayed here, became a cop, and married her.

"Yeah, she's best friends with Je—" he stops midsentence. But I already know what he's going to say. I just nod. "Sorry. Anyway, I talked to Jessie and told her to stay away from you both and if she comes back on the property that she'll be charged with trespassing. I'm sorry, Addison," he says somberly.

"Well, that settles that. Can we never talk about her again?" I quickly ask, wanting to move on. The guys both nod. Ryan changes the subject, asking me what I thought about skydiving.

"I loved it. I can see why people can get addicted to it," I say.

"When Max told me you went up without me, I was pissed!" He punches Aiden in the arm. "But then when Max explained who you went up with, I about fell out of my chair. And *then* he tells me to watch this video, and I was sure you must have hit your head at some point in the last two years." He laughs.

"Why is it so hard for all your friends to imagine you in a relationship?" I say, lifting a curious brow at Aiden. He shrugs with a smug smile. Ryan laughs again.

"We thought Aiden would be a bachelor his whole life. He's

always been focused on work; he didn't make time for women. Well... he made time, he just didn't want one around constantly," Ryan jokingly says.

"I hadn't found the right one yet," Aiden says matter-of-factly, winking at me. His words send a jolt through my body. All my nerve endings tingle as heat spreads through me. I glance away, needing a distraction. I open the refrigerator, welcoming the cool air as I pretend to look for something.

"How did y'all meet? Through work?" Ryan questions. I close the door and glance at Aiden to answer. I know that Damon and Max know, but I'm not sure who else he told.

"Something like that," he answers, pinning me with his intense stare. He tilts his head, cocking his eyebrow. Those beautiful emerald eyes are trying to find the answer to something, I just don't know what it is. "Are you hungry?" he asks.

I really hadn't thought about food, but since we skipped breakfast, I could eat. "A little." I shrug.

"Hey, let's go have lunch at the barn." Ryan stands up, slapping Aiden on the back.

"The barn? *Sounds fancy*," I say. They both throw their heads back, laughing.

Aiden stands up, sliding to stand by me. "It's just a local restaurant, not really a barn. We used to go there to eat every time we came into town. They have the best chicken fried steak." He brushes my hair behind my ears.

I bite my lip as I hesitate to answer. "I'm not sure, Aiden. I don't know if I can handle any more surprise visits from more of your *friends*." I gesture with air quotes. "And I'm not talking about that type of friend," I say, pointing at Ryan.

"Ryan, give us a few seconds," he says, nodding his head toward the front door. As soon as Ryan leaves, Aiden traps me with his arms on both sides of me. I can feel the cold granite at my back. The intimate space between us has my pulse quickening.

"We can leave if you want," he whispers as he lays his forehead on mine. I'm having a hard time thinking about anything but him and how close he is. I grab the granite at either side of us.

"Addison, touch me," he pleads. "I need to feel your touch like I need air to breathe. It's killing me inside that you're hurt. I would do anything to take away that pain. For you to look at me the way you did yesterday. *Please, Addison.*"

The pain in his voice breaks me, causing all my restraint to crumple. I run my hands up his shirt, feeling his muscular chest. I close my eyes, breathing him in.

"Let me kiss you," he whispers into my ear. I shiver from the heat of his breath and the slight touch of his lips on my ear. I nod, parting my lips. He lightly sweeps his lips across mine. "I love you," he whispers before pressing his mouth to mine. I bring my hands up to his hair, threading my fingers through it. He moves his hands behind my back, pulling me into him. Our bodies sway to the music of our hearts. It's a slow, sensual song, with a lot of beat.

"So are you guys going to lunch? I don't have all day. Some of us have to work." Ryan's voice pulls us out of our trance.

Aiden rolls his eyes. "What is it with people always interrupting us?" He chuckles. "Should we go to lunch or do you want to eat on the way back home?"

"The barn is fine." I smirk.

Lunch ends up being delicious. Ryan's an awesome guy. His face lights up when he talks about his wife. The guys reminisce about fixing up the house and trashing it at night. A few locals stop by to say hi, excited to see Aiden is back in town. I can only imagine the trouble those boys brought to this little beach town. Although, it seems everyone has grown to love them. *Some, a little bit too much.*

"It was good seeing you, brother." Aiden pulls Ryan into a hug. "You and Macie should come see us."

"We will. Maybe we'll come down for New Year's." He looks

over at me. "Keep him out of trouble. *And don't go shooting anyone,*" he says sarcastically. Aiden's and my eyes go wide. I bring my hand to my mouth to stifle my laugh. "Am I missing something?" Ryan asks, narrowing his eyes at us both.

Aiden slaps him on the back. "Some things are better left unsaid." He laughs.

We say our goodbyes and head back to the beach house to pack. On our way we make a quick stop at a hardware store. When I glance at Aiden, he says, "Seems I need to change my locks before we leave." I sigh, nodding my head.

A few hours later with two locks changed and new security codes, we are on our way home. Our drive home isn't as exciting as our drive here. So much has happened in these two days it feels like it's been a week since we left. It's a little overwhelming to even think about. My mind drifts off to the free fall from the plane. I let out a long sigh. I want that feeling back.

"What are you thinking about?" Aiden says, grabbing my hand.

"Free falling," I whisper, looking in his direction. He squeezes my hand and nods but doesn't say anything.

Syd's ringtone goes off from my purse. The song immediately lightens my mood. I pull out my phone and answer.

When I press the end button, I'm grinning from ear to ear, trying not to scream. I wiggle in my seat and clap. Aiden squeezes my thigh. "I hope I can make you that excited someday?"

"Oh, you definitely know how to get me excited," I purr.

He growls, "Addison."

I laugh and grab his hand as it starts to inch up my leg. "Syd got a couple of callbacks from her job interviews. They want her to come back for a second interview," I say, trying to contain my excitement. "She's going to come back next week."

"That's great news, sweetheart. I know one guy, in particular, who might be just as excited as you." He smiles, shaking his head.

CHAPTER FORTY-EIGHT

AIDEN

"AGENT ROBERTS," I answer my phone.

"Hey, Aiden." It's Trent, the Assistant District Attorney. "I wanted to give you a heads up. I'm not sure why, but Travis Stein is requesting to see Addison Mason." He pauses. "I know that you know Addison." He chuckles. Of course, the infamous video. "I'm a little concerned about Travis requesting to see her. You might want to keep an eye out in case he is trying to seek revenge."

Of course the ADA doesn't have any idea about Addison's short-lived stay at Travis's and I'd like to keep it that way. What game is Travis playing?

"Thanks, Trent, for letting me know. Do you think I can talk to Addison about this before you guys do?" I need to make sure she doesn't decide to accept.

"Sure, but you better hurry. I'll bet he has his attorney trying to find her and pass on his message. We need to make sure she isn't in any kind of danger."

"I'm on it today. Thanks again, Trent." I press the end button. I blow out a long breath. Addison and I are getting closer every day, even after the disaster with Jessie. I still can't believe that shit.

This week, even though work has been extremely busy trying to find the killer taking out entire families, we've been able to see each other a couple times. As much as we've been through already, I feel like I'm about to poke a sleeping bear.

God, I hope I'm wrong.

* * *

I walk into the crime lab and make my way over to Addison's office.

"Hey, Aiden. Addison's on the phone," Becca, the front receptionist, tells me. I keep walking and wave my hand at her. I chuckle to myself, thinking I've been in this office hundreds of times since our departments work together and no one has ever questioned or assumed why I'm here other than work; now when I come in, everyone automatically thinks I'm here for Addison.

I can see Addison hanging up her phone as I walk over to her office. *"Knock, knock,"* I say as I peek through her door. She's wearing her lab coat and her hair is in a ponytail. Fuck, she's beautiful. When she glances up, her eyes sparkle and she smiles wide. *For now.* It kills me to bring up Travis. She's finally ready to let go of whatever it is she's holding in, and I'm afraid I'm about to open it right back up.

She's tilts her head. "Well, it doesn't look like you're here to sing me a song." She nervously laughs. She's good at reading people, reading me.

I walk in and close her door. "We've got to talk," I sigh. Her eyes widen in surprise but quickly turn questioning. "Travis Stein has requested to see you."

Her face turns to stone. Any emotion she's feeling, she's hiding. The silence is deafening. I need her to act surprised or appalled that he wants to see her. I need her to talk to me.

Something.

I break the silence. "Addison, please tell me why he wants to see you." She remains silent. "Talk to me, dammit!" She jumps as I slam my hands down on her desk in frustration.

"Aiden, can you please leave?" Her voice is hollow. She's shutting down. Shutting me out. Fuck that.

"No." I lean forward, pinning her with my stare. She doesn't get to shut me out this time. I want answers. Now.

She gets up, takes off her lab coat, and grabs her purse. "Then I'll leave." She walks around me and it takes every piece of willpower that I have not to grab her and stop her, but she'll hate me if I cause a scene at work. She calls CJ, her boss, and tells her that something came up and that she needs to leave.

I follow her out of the building and as soon as we're outside, I grab her and spin her around. "Addison," I bark, "your place or mine?" Our intense stare down causes onlookers to stop and watch us. "Don't make me handcuff you and carry you away, because I *fucking will.* Don't tempt me, sweetheart." My words come out harsh and low as I increase my hold on her arm. I am done playing games.

"Mine," is all she says as she twists her arm out of my grasp. I follow her a couple blocks to her apartment. Once inside, she goes straight to her room and slams the door. *Really?* Can this woman be more difficult? Of course when I try and open it, it's locked.

With my forehead against the door, I slam my hand down on it. "You really think this lock is going to keep me out of there, Addison?" I seethe. "Open the damn door or I'm going to break it down." I'm literally counting the seconds in my head. I'm giving her sixty seconds. She opens on forty-eight.

She sits on the edge of the bed, looking down with a pained expression that brings me to my knees as I walk over to the bed where she is sitting. Pushing her knees apart so I can get closer, I wrap my arms around her. "Addison, please talk to me. I'm begging you," I whisper as I cup her face. "Nobody knows you were held hostage there. I'm assuming he knows about us, so I need to make sure you aren't in danger." She stays still as tears run down her face. I catch her tears with my thumbs, caressing her cheeks. "Please, baby. You're killing me." I rest my forehead against hers.

After a few minutes, though it feels like hours, she murmurs so quietly I almost miss that she is talking.

"I thought Travis had my mom killed." I lift my forehead off of hers and her eyes are locked on mine. I immediately want to ask her a million questions, but I stay quiet. I nod my head so she'll continue. "My mom was murdered when I was ten. I saw the guy who did it. I had the license plate number and found out that the car belonged to Travis. I knew they had never caught the guy, so I decided I'd go check out Travis." Pained blue eyes no longer look at me but past me, lost in thought. With a poignant stare, she says, "Obviously, you know what happened after that."

"I do." I wink, giving her a half smile. She offers a small smile in return but she doesn't continue talking. What the hell am I missing? There must be something else that is causing this beautiful woman to break down in front of me. "Addison, nothing I'm hearing is any surprise."

She lets go of my hands and stands up and walks to the window. Crossing her arms, she takes in a deep breath and breathes out slowly. "Aiden." Still facing away from me, she says, "Travis is my dad."

What?

My silence has her turning around to look at me. "That's why we can't be together, Aiden." Her words spear through my heart. She misinterprets my silence. I'm trying to piece together everything in my head. It all makes sense now: the DNA test, Travis wanting to keep her around, the eyes. The Caribbean blue eyes. Why didn't I see that before? *Fuck, I'm an FBI agent.* I took notice of the similar color, but that is all that they share in physical appearance. I thought it was a mere coincidence.

I notice Addison shrink into the chair next to her window. Tears fall freely as she stares at me. "Aiden, don't make this harder than it is. Walk away. I don't blame you." She sniffles. That's it?

She thinks that I'm leaving because of this?

"What the hell, Addison!"

Chapter Forty-nine

HIS HARSH WORDS have me looking up at him, his eyes searching for answers. Answers that I don't have. My heart is shattered in a million pieces. This day was inevitable. I just should have told him sooner. His silence cuts through me. What do you say to the woman whose dad killed your parents? I push myself out of the chair, desperate to put distance between us. I walk into the living room.

"No. You don't get to decide the fate of our relationship by yourself!" Aiden jumps up after me. Running his hands through his hair, he paces the room.

"I'm not deciding it! Fate fucking did that on her own when she brought us together! Our path was meant for devastation before we even got started. I should have worked harder to stay away from you. I tried, I just couldn't. How can you ever look at me again and not think of Travis? Not associate me with that bastard who killed your parents?" I'm shaking uncontrollably. He pulls me into his hard chest. My tears soak his shirt.

"Addison. *Sweetheart*. I don't blame you for what your... Travis did. You might share DNA with the guy, but you are not part of him." The strength of his hold keeps me from falling to the floor. "I could never blame you for what Travis did. *Ever*. You need to believe me," he says, desperation thick in his voice. "I can't lose you, Addison." He lifts my chin so we're looking into each other's eyes. His lips brush mine, and he whispers, "Please don't push me away again." His voice cracks and his eyes gloss over.

"You haven't had time to think this through." I look down so I don't see the pain I'm causing.

"I'll go. But only so next time I come back here you know that I've thought about it and I haven't changed my mind. You. Are. Mine. Addison. Nothing will change that. Nothing." He tangles his hands in my hair and pulls back, forcing me to look up. He softly kisses my lips and murmurs that he loves me before he walks out the door. Not being able to hold myself up anymore, I slide down the door in a heap of heartbreak.

* * *

A knock at the door wakes me. I must have fallen asleep on the couch after Aiden left. I look at the time and notice it's only been an hour. I run my hands through my hair as I catch a glimpse of my reflection in the mirror. I look like shit.

Looking through the peephole I see Aiden on the other side. I open the door slowly, not sure why he is back. I lean against the door for support, crossing my arms. Tears start welling up in my eyes at the sight of this man who I can't have.

"Hi," he says quietly. I take a deep breath, sniffling.

"Hi."

We stand there motionless, staring into each other's eyes. No longer able to stand the silence, I ask, "Aiden, what are you doing here?" My voice cracks as I look down.

He steps closer to me, lifting my head so we're peering into each other's eyes again. "I thought about it. Nothing has changed, Addison. I love you."

He brushes his lips against mine softly as mine quiver from emotion. My lips part and grant him access. He pulls me against his chest as our tongues explore each other. Before I know it, I've been pushed into my living room. Aiden kicks the door closed and carries me to my room.

"I told you, sweetheart. You. Are. Mine."

* * *

A couple hours later, we lie in bed naked. He absentmindedly rubs his fingers up and down my arm. I close my eyes, realizing that there is nothing left to keep us apart. No secrets, no barriers, nothing. I can love this man with all my heart and soul.

Finally.

A tear runs down my cheek onto Aiden's chest. "What's wrong?"

"Absolutely nothing," I say, looking up to his beautiful green eyes. "I love you, Aiden." I stretch to kiss him on the lips. We stay wrapped in each other's arms until we fall asleep.

The next morning, Aiden brings up the small issue of Travis requesting to see me. Which probably isn't *so* small. I had totally forgotten about that until now. He asked if I knew why Travis was being held in New York. I knew he had been arrested for having a man killed, but I didn't want the details. The less I know about Travis, the better.

"Well, that must explain it," I say.

"Explain what?"

I sigh. "Someone was following me one day when Sydney was here. And they might have come into my apartment."

He darts up in bed. "And I'm only hearing about this now?"

"Nothing was out of place. I just brushed it all off as a coincidence. But now hearing that Travis wants to see me, maybe it wasn't." I shrug.

Aiden swings his legs off the bed. He goes to stand up, but I grab his arm. "Where are y—"

He brings his finger to my lips quieting me. "Aiden, nobody is—"

He leans over and whispers in my ear, "Woman, would you be quiet."

I stick my tongue out at him while he pulls out his phone and plays music loudly. He moves to different places in my bedroom, touching things, rubbing his hands under furniture. My stomach turns when I realize what he's doing.

Oh, my God! What if someone has been watching or listening to me this whole time? I fumble out of bed and grab a shirt. When Aiden doesn't find anything in my room, I blow out the breath I'd been holding in. I follow him into the living room and silently watch as he works his way around the room.

When he finds nothing, I feel my whole body relax.

"Well, I didn't find anything," he says after turning off the blaring music. "I still have a bad feeling about this. I'm going to have someone come and set up a security alarm, but you need to tell me if you notice anything out of the ordinary." His voice is serious as he walks toward me.

"I will, but don't you think you're overreacting? You know I'm all about being safe, but he's my father. He won't hurt me. And anyway, Sydney is coming back tomorrow so I won't be here alone," I say.

"No, I don't think he would hurt you. But if anyone finds out you're his daughter, you could be in danger." He grabs my hand, intertwining our fingers. "And I won't lose you again," he growls.

CHAPTER FIFTY

AIDEN

"I NEED TO see Travis," I say as soon as Trent, the ADA, answers the phone.

"Not sure that's a good idea, Aiden."

"I need to know what his game is with Addison, Trent."

"You think he's going to talk to you?" He laughs. "He hasn't given up anything to us. Except that he wants to talk to Addison."

"But if he thinks I can bring her to him, maybe he'll talk. I need to try."

"Okay. But if he doesn't want to see you, we can't make him. You know this might complicate things." Trent ends the call. He's not happy since I'm not supposed to have any contact with him since I was undercover, but I don't care. Addison is my number one priority and I need to see what he wants from her.

* * *

Travis is currently at the local prison awaiting his Grand Jury date. I walk into a room and Travis is already sitting at a table, hand-cuffed to it.

I had to pull some strings to make sure we weren't in an inter-rogation room. I don't want anyone hearing our conversation.

I'm definitely walking a line that I normally wouldn't. I spent two years of my life trying to take down this guy. I shouldn't be risking it, but I would do anything to keep Addison safe.

I sit down and face Travis. I haven't seen him since the night we were arrested. "Why do you want to see Addison?" I don't have time to bullshit.

"Jett…" Travis nods "…or should I call you Aiden?"

"I don't fucking care what you call me, Travis. Answer my question."

"Well, it really isn't any of your business, but nice video of you serenading her." He sits back and smiles. I fist my hands under the table.

"Travis. My report didn't include Addison. You know that if anyone finds out about her, she could be in danger so cut the bullshit and tell me why you want to see her. What good can come from it?" My voice is low and serious. He tilts his head and narrows his eyes.

Yes, asshole, I know.

Minutes tick by before he talks. "You don't know the whole story, Aiden."

"Story?" I ask. "What story? The one where you get a little girl's mom killed right in front of her? That story?" I seethe. His eyes turn cold and his jawline goes rigid. I hit a nerve.

He leans forward on the table. "I know who you are, Aiden."

I stay silent and shrug.

"This is off the record," Travis says, sitting back.

"Travis, I'm FBI. I know you've heard the *'You have the right to remain silent, anything you say can and will be used against you'* line so please tell me how this is off the record?" I say.

He drops his head. "She wasn't supposed to be in the car." *Fuuuuck.* I should have expected that he would find out who I really was. This shouldn't be a surprise, but hearing him talk about my mom pisses me off.

"Again..." my voice is cold and harsh "...why do you want to talk to Addison, Travis?"

Travis ignores my question and continues. "She was supposed to be at work. But something happened and she had to go back home. I didn't know. She wasn't supposed to be in the car, Aiden." He sounds remorseful, almost.

I can't hold it in any longer. "What the fuck do you want me to say? I forgive you for killing my parents because it wasn't supposed to happen? Fuck. You." I slam my hands down on the metal table.

Travis looks up at me, our eyes in a heated battle. He shakes his head, his voice cold. "No, you misunderstand. Your dad was a dead man walking. He signed his own death warrant."

I drop my head to the table. The cold metal feels good against my overheated body. It's taking every fiber in my body not to get up and kill Travis right now. I straighten my back, look him square in the eyes.

"Okay, I know the story now, Travis. *Thanks.*" I blow out a breath. "Can we get to why you need to see Addison?" My patience is running out.

"You only know the end of the story," Travis says in a stern voice, shaking his head.

"Stop playing games," I yell.

"Your dad stole my most valuable treasure from me."

"What the hell, Travis? A couple hundred grand is your most valued treasure?" I say.

"If someone took Addison away from you, tell me... what would you do?" Travis deadpans, his face set in stone.

"Is that a fucking threat?" Chills run down my spine as I jump up and get in Travis's face. I will kill any motherfucker who touches Addison. I don't care if it's her father or not.

"I can see in your eyes that you'd have the exact same response I had. Unfortunately, I should have taken care of your dad before it came to that." Travis stares, waiting for me to connect the dots. My mind pieces the puzzle together. A puzzle so convoluted it seems unbelievable.

"NO! " I scream as I jump back and throw the chair across the room.

The door opens and a security guard looks at me. Concern on his face. "Agent Roberts, is everything okay?" he asks while looking at Travis, his hand on his gun.

"Yes." No. It's so far from okay it might not ever be okay again. I'm about to lose the love of my life. Addison was right, our path always led to devastation. He seems to accept my response and backs out of the room. I pace the room with my hands on my head.

"How do I know you're not lying?" I know he's right though. Our mothers were murdered the same year: hers first then mine. I knew this, but never in a million years would I have connected the two.

"If you need proof, you can always show Addison a picture of your dad. But you know I'm right, Aiden." I continue pacing. That won't happen. Ever.

The room closes in on me. I need to get out of here. I stare at Travis. "If you have any shred of love for your daughter, you'll leave her alone. Forget you ever found out she was alive. For her own safety." I slam the door open. I hear him saying something else, but I'm not listening. I'm not doing anything other than getting the fuck out of here.

Chapter Fifty-one

IT'S BEEN THREE days since I've talked to Aiden. When he left my house Tuesday morning, he told me he loved me. I believed him. Now he won't return my calls. I've tried texting him but no response. I went to his office and Damon told me he had taken off for a few days. Each day that goes by, it gets harder to breathe. Hope slowly dwindles to barely hanging on. He doesn't want me. I remind him too much of Travis. Time has changed his mind.

Travis's attorney made a visit to my apartment yesterday. He still wants to see me. My life is in a tailspin, going round and round with no stop in sight. It's going to throw me off if I don't start putting my foot down and make it stop myself. I need to find out if Travis is the one having me followed.

I force myself to get out of bed. It's Friday morning and the thought of seeing Travis today has me wanting to go right back to bed. Syd barges into my room right as I'm about to lie back down.

"No, Addie," she says as she grabs me and pulls me to the living room. Too bad this *living* room can't breathe any life back into me. She pushes me down on the couch and brings me over breakfast. "You need to eat, girlfriend. Enough is enough. The situation you are in sucks. But you've never been a quitter. Don't start now."

"Why? My *life* sucks. My entire life has been nothing but a roller coaster and I want off." I throw my head back and stare up to the ceiling. "I'd rather be on the *It's A Small World* ride. Smooth and slow." I sigh.

Syd laughs. "Oh, *pleeease*. You hate that ride. You complained the whole time about it being the most boring ride you'd ever been on." I look over at her. Really? Does she think that I really enjoy my roller-coaster life? "I'm not saying that your life has always had desirable outcomes," she says as she looks at me with a raised eyebrow. "You've had some pretty shitty lows, more than anyone should in one's lifetime, but you've always come out on top. You've got some great people in your life..." she smiles as she wags her eyebrows "...and Aiden loves you. You can see it every time he looks at you." She leans her head on my shoulder. "I don't think Travis being your dad is going to change that. Maybe he just needs some time to think things over."

"Maybe." Something is wrong, though. I tried to push him away, but he was so sure that it didn't matter. I'm tired of trying to figure it out. It's all I have thought about since he won't talk to me. Syd is right. I have to keep living. I've been through heartbreak before. My heart has so many damn breaks, I'm surprised it's still beating. But it is. The hurt reminds me everyday.

A couple hours later I walk into the jail to see Travis. They have me wait in the visitor's room. I'm at a table with two chairs. I glance around and there are a couple of other tables filled with inmates and their visitors. Voices are quiet and soft; crying can be heard. The longer I have to wait, the more I fidget. This will be a quick meeting, I keep telling myself. Have my say and then leave.

They bring Travis in, hands in handcuffs, and he sits down in the chair facing me.

"Hi, Addison." He softly smiles. He's a good-looking man and being in jail hasn't been too hard on him, yet. I can see how my mom would have been attracted to him.

I stare at him. It feels weird having him call me by my real name.

"I still can't get over how much you look like her. I'm glad to see you. Glad you came," he says quickly.

"I didn't come to talk about my mom or us. I came to find out what you want. Then tell you that I'm never coming back." My voice is void of any emotion.

He nods as he twists his lips. "I never meant to hurt you." His voice is low. "I hate seeing you in pain. I should have never told him the truth."

My eyes jump to his and I tilt my head to the side. "What are you talking about? Who are you talking about?"

"Aiden," he says slowly with a questioning look.

"When did you see Aiden? He already knows about you... and me," I say.

"He came and saw me on Tuesday." He looks at me assessing my reaction. "Did he not tell you?" I slowly shake my head. Still confused. "It's... you look heartbroken, I figured he—" Travis stops talking, shakes his head. "Sorry, I never should have said anything," he says, looking down quickly. "I've done nothing right for you. I'm so sorry, Addison." He lowers his head and runs his handcuffed hands through his hair. The powerful and confident man I met last summer is not the man in front of me. For a slight moment I feel bad for him.

Aiden came and saw him on Tuesday. I glance around the room, like I'll find the answers hidden somewhere on the walls. It can't be a coincidence that Aiden was willing to accept that Travis was my father before he visited him. What changed? What could he have possibly said that would make Aiden run away from me? I look back to Travis and his head is still lowered.

"What did you say to Aiden?" My voice cracks. Travis looks up. I can see the pain etched in his eyes. They probably match mine.

"Addison..." he sighs and pauses.

"Tell me!" I yell, slapping the table. "I haven't heard from him since Tuesday morning. He knew about us and said it didn't matter. What could you have told him that changed his mind?" I plead.

His voice is quiet. "I told him why his dad died."

"You mean his mom and dad?" I force through gritted teeth. He will not discount the murder of his parents to me. He can't give me a good enough reason for killing Aiden's parents.

"I know this will mean nothing to you, but his mom was a mistake. She was not supposed to be in that car." He's looking straight into my eyes, his voice apologetic. He's right. It means nothing to me. "But his dad took something of mine. Something irreplaceable."

I can't believe he's admitting to killing Aiden's parents. He then says, "and something irreplaceable to you." My brows furrow.

"What do you mean?" I have a fleeting thought that Aiden was right in this same situation a few days ago. He won't talk to me now. What does his dad have to do with my mom?

My eyes widen when confusion turns to realization. I let out an audible gasp. "No, please tell me it wasn't him." I'm pleading, begging, hoping. The resignation on his face tells me everything. Tears that I didn't think I had any more of break free. I'm shaking my head, in shock, repeating, "No… no… no." If I thought mine and Aiden's strained relationship couldn't get any worse, it just did. There is no way back from this.

A hand softly touches my hands on the table. It makes me jump. "Don't touch me!" I seethe with a chilly voice. "Do you realize that you are the root of my fucked up life? You're the part that keeps me from having a normal life. You are the poison in me, seeping its way through at every turn. Because of you, I can't be happy!"

I jerk to my feet, the chair sliding back on the floor making an awful screeching noise, and run out of the visitor's area. I find the closest bathroom and empty my stomach. After I can't dry heave anymore, I sit on the toilet and cry. I force myself to get up and glance at myself in the mirror but don't recognize the person looking back. My face and eyes are puffy and red. My hair is pulled back in a ponytail, with pieces falling out everywhere. Grabbing my sunglasses, I put them on to cover my bloodshot eyes.

Walking out of the jail, I pull out my phone to call Sydney. She's already called me five times. I know she's going to be worried. She's always worried about me. Why does my life have to be so messed up? I can't even fall in love right.

When I look up from my phone to walk down the few steps to the sidewalk, I notice Aiden leaning against the building at the bottom of the stairs. I stop walking and we stare at each other. He looks horrible. Like he hasn't slept in days. I know the feeling. His broad chest takes in deep breaths. His hands are in his pockets and his eyes are pinned on mine. Panic flickers in his eyes. I'm thankful mine are behind my sunglasses. We stand there, neither of us taking the first step toward the other. He breaks our connection and looks down.

I want to run to him and tell him it doesn't matter. It doesn't matter what his dad did. He's not his dad, the same thing he told me, but something keeps me frozen in my spot. Tears run down my face. Reality is I'm not sure that it doesn't matter. He looks up and sees me brush away my tears. He pushes off the wall rushing to me.

"I'm so sorry, Addison." He grabs me into his muscular embrace and holds me. I can't believe just days ago our roles were changed, ironically the same story, just *slightly* different.

Fucking fate!

CHAPTER FIFTY-TWO
AIDEN

I PULL ADDISON to my chest. Her arms wrap around my waist. We stand there with not a slice of air between us. I can't pull her close enough to release this feeling of emptiness. I knew Travis would tell her. I'm not sure if it was his way of paying me back, but the asshole hurt more than me. He destroyed his own daughter.

After leaving Travis on Tuesday, I needed to get away for a few days. I drove to the beach house to try and clear my head. The only thing I cleared was a couple bottles of Jack. I should've talked to Addison, but I couldn't. How was I supposed to tell her that my dad killed her mom? That the coldhearted killer she saw is part of me. I squeeze my eyes shut. I told her that I didn't care about Travis, that it didn't affect the way I felt about her. And I meant every word. I love her and I sure as fuck don't want to lose her. But how can I ask the same thing from her? Will she ever be able to look at me and not think of my dad? Losing my parents was traumatic, but at least I didn't watch them die at the hands of Travis.

I came back into town last night. Barely sleeping these past couple of nights, I crashed on my couch last night. I woke up to a call from Trent that Addison was visiting Travis. He's starting to question things. I told him to back off. I don't care what happens now to Travis. Ironic, huh? I spent most of my life wanting revenge for the man who took my parents away, and now I'd let him go just to be with his daughter. Life's a bitch sometimes. I'm starting to agree with Addison about fate. She's got a sadistic sense of humor.

"Addison, I don't know what to say," I finally break the silence. I'm still holding her, afraid if I let her go that she'll walk away. There's a stabbing pain in my chest with just the thought. I hate that I can't fix this, that I have to live with what she decides. I've never felt so powerless, hopeless, and broken before. This feeling sucks.

Please say you don't care.

When she doesn't say anything, I squeeze her tighter. She's slipping away from me. "I want you to tell me how I can fix this. I can't lose you," I say, my voice choking on my words. She digs her head into my chest and shakes it. The feel of her chest quivering as she silently cries has me wanting to kill someone. I loosen my hold on her, taking my hand under her chin and lifting it so she can face me. I push her sunglasses to the top of her head. With my hands on her face, I brush away her tears with my thumbs. I lean down, putting my forehead against hers. I momentarily close my eyes and a tear escapes. I open my eyes as I feel her hand on my cheek, wiping away my lone tear.

When I look into her eyes, her eyes frantically dart away. "Addison, look at me," I command softly. She lets out a shaky breath and looks up. "I love you, Addison." I can feel her pulse quicken under the palm of my hands. She places her hands on top of mine, locking our fingers, pulling them down to our sides.

She looks down at our hands, but quickly looks back up. "Oh, Aiden..." her breath catches "...I love you, too." My heart races hearing her say that. "But is that enough? How do we move past this? How do we build a life together with this as our foundation?" She hiccups through her tears. Her head falls back, looking to the sky. She lets go of our hands and takes the couple steps to the ground, pacing. She lets out a loud sigh in frustration. "Why can't anything in my life be fucking easy?" she yells.

I take the few steps to meet her, each one feels like my shoes are full of cement. Even though I understand her hesitation, it stings. I stand frozen in place as she walks back and forth in front of me, my eyes never leaving her. I stuff my hands in my pockets to avoid reaching out and grabbing her. I mutter a curse and she slowly turns around to face me, tilting her head.

"I get it, Addison. I understand this situation sucks. But don't let our paths be determined by the actions of our fathers. I love you. You are the air that brings life into me." I take a step closer. "I had one goal in life: revenge. Until I met you. You, Addison. After you left last summer, my desire for revenge was gone. You were always invading my thoughts. And that's when I thought I'd never see you again." I take another step forward. "Call it fate, destiny, written in the stars, what the fuck ever… we were given a second chance." Another step, and I'm standing right in front of her.

She shakes her head and a bitter laugh escapes her lips. "A second chance for what, Aiden? Heartbreak? Closure on our parents' deaths? We were meant to meet, yes. Were we meant to fall in love? If I hadn't been kept there for those five days and we met on the street, at a club, wherever, would we still have fallen in love?"

"Fuck, Addison," I growl and run my hands through my hair, "It didn't take me five days to fall in love with you! It took me five seconds. When I walked into that room and saw you, I immediately felt my heart surge back to life. I might not have known it that second, but I felt it when you left." My chest heaves. I turn around. Now it's my turn to pace as I try to control my anger. I'm angry that she questions my love for her. I'm angrier that I'm questioning her love for me now.

"Aiden," she hiccups. I turn around to face her. Tears cascade down her face. She wipes them as fast as they fall. She takes a couple deep breaths. "Please don't doubt my love for you. You weren't the only one who felt it immediately. But the entire time we've been together, I haven't been able to give you a hundred percent of me. I've always had to hold back because of what I knew. What I was hiding."

"Everything's out now, Addison." I throw my hands into the air. "It's all in your hands now. I don't know what else to do," I say in resignation.

"Just give me some time."

I take a couple steps to her. My hands cup her face. I swipe my thumb against her lower lip. "I'll give you time. But if you wait too long, I'll come find you." I brush my lips against hers and whisper, "I love you" before I smash down on her lips. She opens for me, letting my tongue assault her mouth with frantic need. I feel her hands on my chest, knotting my shirt in a fist. I wrap my hand in her hair, pulling her into me.

As we break the kiss, we're both breathing heavy. She takes a step back. Those gorgeous eyes that hypnotized me the first time I saw them pin me in place.

"I love you, Aiden." She softly smiles as she walks around me. I turn in place and watch her walk away. I'll give her fucking two weeks max. Then I'm going to take what is mine.

Or so I thought. Fate has other plans.

* * *

Two seconds.

Two seconds was all it took.

The whole thing happened in slow motion. Addison walking away from me. A black van door slides open as she's about to cross the street. A black van that I should've seen. A black van that I normally would have taken notice of but didn't.

Not fucking today.

In a second, a man grabs Addison, and I see him stab a needle in her neck. She tries to fight. I grab my gun and run after her. The next second, they throw her in the van. I scream for them to stop. A man in the front seat wearing a hat, points a gun at me. *I know him.* He shoots and pain reverberates through my body. I fall back not being able to catch my breath. Screams surround me as I shout and call for Addison. I don't even recognize my own voice. The tires from the van squeal away. I hear more screams that aren't mine, then sirens. Then blackness.

Two seconds was all it took for my world to go dark.

To be continued...

ACKNOWLEDGEMENTS

This is the easiest part of the book! First, thank you to all the readers who took a chance on this new author. I hope I was able to fill your beautiful minds with a story worth continuing to the end.

To Tiffany, I couldn't have done this without you. I can't thank you enough. When I first started writing and bouncing ideas off of you, your support and encouragement is what kept me going. Thank you for reading my book more than once to make sure it was the best it could be and letting me spoil everything before you read it (because I'm sure that was fun).

Traci and Michelle, my beta readers, thank you both for not thinking I was crazy when I told you I wrote a book. Your excitement and praise for me are what true friendships are made of.

To Lori, the best sister ever, thank you for helping me edit. Your strength is definitely my weakness.

To my husband, thank you for being my biggest cheerleader when you found out about my dream and encouraging me to keep going without any hesitation.

Max, thank you for helping make my words come alive and shine *and* helping me understand that deep down should always lead to *somewhere*.

Thank you, Elaine, for giving my books' words the finishing touch.

Now on to book two!

ABOUT THE AUTHOR

Tina Saxon lives in Dallas, Texas, with her husband and two kids. She's not afraid to try new things because it's outside the box of *typical housewife*. CEO of her home is by far the most rewarding job she has ever had. Her jobs include, but are not limited to, seamstress, carpenter, craft extraordinaire, PTA President, chauffeur, dance mom, mediator—*of mentioned kids*—and author. Once upon a time she was a Financial Analyst but traded budgets and forecasts in for diapers and bottles. The former was definitely easier but the latter more fulfilling.

Tina's love for reading surged into her passion for writing. Wanting to bring the reader an intriguing story that's hard to put down with steamy love scenes that heat you up, she's always thinking of the perfect way to take you down that path.

Fate Hates is book one of the Twist of Fate series. Continue on Addison's journey to prove that Fate isn't always a bitch. *Fate Heals* is book two coming out in June 2017, following *Fate Loves* coming out in July 2017.

www.tinasaxon.com

Made in the USA
Middletown, DE
01 September 2017